MONSTERSONA

Chloe Spencer

Tiny Ghost Press

*actual size

ISBN:
E-book 978-1-7399834-9-9
Paperback 978-1-915585-00-4
Hardcover 978-1-915585-01-1

Cover artwork by: Alex Moore
Additional graphics supplied by: Freepik

To find out more about our books visit www.tinyghostpress.com and sign up for our newsletter.

For any girl who ever felt like her trauma made her a monster.
Keep surviving. Keep thriving. And never let them win.

Content Warning

Monstersona is a sci-fi horror story which centers on giant monsters and trauma. Included within this story are depictions of gore, death (including parental death), strong language, kidnapping, as well as physical violence and gun violence. Much of the story also focuses on the onset of PTSD and those symptoms, thoughts, and experiences. There are also brief discussions of biphobia and sexual assault.

Day 10 - Early Morning

THE IRON CHAIN SLIPS through my bloody hands. Carefully, I tighten my grip around the cleanest edge and slowly begin to wrap the metal strands around Aspen's sleeping body. I don't know how long these are going to hold her—or if they're going to hold her at all. Time is of the essence here, and I don't have much of it.

I take a step back to examine my handiwork. All I've done is wrap the chain around her torso and wrists. I don't even have a lock to secure it with. My only option is to tie a knot. I crouch down to try again, but the ends are too short; I won't be able to tie them unless I unravel some of the chain.

I look at Aspen, still sleeping in the chair. Blood is splattered across her face like sun-kissed freckles. Her blond hair is sticky and stained crimson, yet she isn't as soaked as I am—from my head to my toes, I am covered in the reeking iron stench of the two men that were slaughtered. Waves of nausea overcome me, and I gag, clapping my hand over my mouth to stop the bile from escaping. My head is reeling and my vision blurs with tears as I struggle to regain control.

Outside, Tigger paws at the door and barks urgently, demanding to be let inside. But I can't let him in—it's far too dangerous. I stare at Aspen for a few moments before finally turning my back to her. Laying on the table in front of me is a small syringe, filled with a strange neon-orange liquid. It glows in the darkness of the shed. The syringe itself is surprisingly unthreatening; short and stubby, like the ones they use for the flu vaccines. But that liquid... I've never seen anything that screams "DANGER!" louder than this.

Yet, I have no choice.

It's either her or me.

With the syringe in hand, I turn back to Aspen, and I jump back. She's awake, staring at me with those unsettling forest-green eyes. She grimaces and tugs at her restraints. Huh. I was worried these chains I found in the shed would be too brittle and break, but it looks like I need to have more confidence in my knot-tying skills. Aspen's body shakes with fear, yet her voice remains firm as she speaks.

"Riley. You need to put that down."

"I…" My voice trails off. Tears roll down my cheeks, and my panicked heart flutters in my chest. I'm dizzy and breathless and terrified all at once, and I'm so tired of feeling this way.

"Riley," she says again, her voice coarse, her tone terse. "You have no idea what that thing does."

"It's supposed to fix you."

"You have *no* idea what it does. You're just repeating what they said." She grunts and tugs at her restraints again. The betrayal in her voice is reflected so clearly in her gaze. It kills me. "You're trusting them over me? Really?"

"Do you have any idea what you've done?"

The terror on her face dissipates for a moment. It's replaced with an icy-cold expression.

She says, in a low whisper, "I did what I had to do."

I shake my head over and over again. Images flash through my mind: their faces caved in, their skulls a soup of blood and flesh and teeth. We had to protect each other, but not like that. Anything but that.

"They *begged* for mercy, Aspen."

"They didn't want mercy. They wanted an opportunity. I can't believe you would even *say* that to me. Like I'm the bad guy." She wriggles against her restraints. "You think I'm the bad guy now?"

"N-no. I-I don't know. I don't know anymore."

"I'm gonna give you one last chance." Her eyes burn into me. "Put it *down*, Riley."

I shake my head. Tighten my grip on the syringe. "I can't."

Tigger's barking grows louder and louder outside, shaking the walls. I take a step toward Aspen, and she shrinks, her eyes wide. She stares at me, her mouth gaping open, and then her expression darkens. By now, I'm all too familiar with that expression, and I can't help but edge backward. She smirks. When I do muster up the strength to creep forward again, she kicks at me, her foot striking me in my shin. My weight buckles underneath me and the syringe flies from my hands. The force of her kick causes her chair to rock back and forth before she finally tumbles onto her knees. Motionless, we lay there, staring at the glittering orange vial in front of us.

Still tied to the chair, Aspen wriggles forward on her knees. I crawl after her, my shin still throbbing; unable to stand. As I inch closer, she shoulder-checks me, but I grab onto her, forcing her to pull us both closer to our goal. Wordlessly, we scream at each other, a writhing mess of bloody limbs and tangled hair, as we both edge toward the syringe…

Day 0 - Morning

I WAIT ANXIOUSLY FOR my Pop-Tart to finish its time in the toaster and pour myself a third cup of coffee that morning. I've been up since five a.m., and before you ask, no, I'm not a morning person. My overactive fluffboi, Tigger, needs to go for a walk before I go to school. So, every day—except for weekends, when Mom can do it—I take Tigger out on the paths behind our house. It sucks because, y'know, it's freezing in the morning now that it's fall. Snow isn't even on the ground yet, but I think we're going to have an early winter. I have to pile on a sweatshirt, coat, and mittens before I even head out the door.

I sip my coffee, and frown. Something smells odd... and it's not the instant coffee grounds. There's a small trail of smoke sifting up from the toaster slot. The toaster is just one of the many appliances in our old-ass house that never works right, but for whatever reason, Mom won't replace it.

With a grimace, I set down my mug, rush over, and unplug the toaster, turning it upside down and shaking out the contents. My smoldering Pop Tart falls onto the plate, along with some unfortunate crumbs and blackened bits of toast. The pastry is charred around the edges, but it'll have to do, considering there's nothing else to eat. Lately, Mom's been struggling to find time to go grocery shopping. I've begged her to pass over the credit card so that I can do it for us—I mean, I can drive to the store, after all. I have my truck and everything. But the thing about my mother is that she always insists on making life difficult for others around her.

One of the ways in which she has made my life difficult? By choosing to move from Oregon to Maine. Divorcing my father last year wasn't enough of a dramatic life change for her, she also had to add uproot my daughter from her friends and family in the middle of her high school career to have an adventure in the backwoods of the Northeast to that list.

If you couldn't tell already, I'm just a *little* bitter.

I grab my plate and coffee and migrate to the living room, where Tigger is sitting on his doggy-bed, contentedly tearing at his old reindeer tug-toy. He's so absorbed in this that he doesn't bother to look up when I sit on the couch. Good for me though, because now I get to eat breakfast without his incessant begging. Tigger is a Great Dane Golden Retriever mix— not nearly as big as a full-blooded Great Dane, but still pretty big. His paws are almost the exact same size as my hands. We named him Tigger on account of his brindle-colored fur, which makes him look like he has tiger stripes. He's about five years old now, but somehow still rambunctious. My grandparents got him for me after I made the Honor Roll in middle school, which may seem like an unjustifiably huge reward, but if you saw how bad my grades were back then, I mean, you'd get it. Trust me.

I tear off a charred chunk of pop tart and dip it in my mug, which normally I would find quite nasty, but it helps to soften it. Besides, between studying for chemistry until eleven last night and waking up at this ungodly early hour, I feel nothing but nasty. My dark circles are so deep and black, I look like a raccoon. Might as well dumpster dive for a better breakfast. I'd fit in with the other critters, plus I'd probably find something that tastes better.

I can hear the faint *twuk-twuk* sound of kitten heels on the carpet from my mom's bedroom. She exits and walks past me into the kitchen. Today, she's dressed in her wide-legged black pantsuit: an overly elegant outfit for a job in the middle of the boonies. For a while I didn't get why she was overdressing for work, but then I realized Mom has the hots for her boss. She repeatedly says that he looks like Tom Selleck, as if that's supposed to mean something to me. Only my mother would get excited over some dude with an 80s porn 'stache. I'd never say it to her face, but she has no taste in men. Then again, neither do I. The women I'm into tend to be conventionally attractive, but the guys, not so much.

Maybe it's genetic? Oh God, I hope not.

Mom pours herself a to-go cup of coffee in the kitchen and hovers in the doorway. She takes a tiny sip, then swipes her tongue over her front teeth, trying to remove faint traces of lipstick. Today's shade is *Va-Va-Voom* red, and I resist the urge to cringe. She always wears that when she's going out on a date. I told my mother that's a bit obsessive-compulsive. She insists she's being "meticulous."

Suddenly, her nose scrunches up in disgust.

"What smells like smoke?"

I smirk, holding up my Pop-Tart. "My breakfast."

"Riley, I told you not to use the toaster."

"Toasters are meant for toasting things that need to be toasted. Like Pop-Tarts."

She rolls her eyes. "Can't you just use the microwave?"

"That's blasphemy."

"Blasphemy, or burning down our house? Which do you prefer?"

She reaches into the fridge and removes a single cheese stick, jamming it in the corner of her mouth before turning her attention to our messy kitchen table. Her phone often gets lost in her purse, so she frequently panics and just dumps her stuff out on the table. Mom gnaws on her cheese stick as she packs up her various pieces of makeup, post-it notes, and assortment of ballpoint pens.

"You know that we could just *buy* a new toaster, right?"

She finishes putting her lipstick case in her purse, and glares at me. One of her eyes is bugging out, and the other is pinched closed, and super squinty. When I was a little kid, I called this her Wicked Witch face. Now that I'm older I call it something else.

"I'm not going to drop fifty dollars on a new toaster right now."

"A toaster does *not* cost fifty dollars, Mom."

"Sure. If we want to buy a toaster *exactly* as shitty as the one we have now, we can buy a new toaster for under fifty dollars," she whines as she applies more powder to her face. "I don't have time for this conversation, Riley. I'm going to be late to work."

She walks into the living room to give Tigger a brief pat on the head, then goes back into the kitchen and exits through the side door. I don't bother to watch her car leave the driveway; I just sit and stew in angry silence.

Every teenager argues with their parents about money at some point, but usually it's the kid asking their parents for something expensive and unnecessary, like concert tickets or a new phone, not basic kitchen appliances. I'm sixteen years old, and instead of her telling me *I'm* irresponsible, it's the other way around. Who knows how much she spent moving out here and renting this house? I'm getting more than a little tired of her complaining about how we don't have money. We were comfortable when we were living in Portland, we had people we could rely on, like my grandparents, or Aunt Cheryl. Yeah, she left my father, but was the divorce so bad we had to run away from everything?

It's been three months since we moved, and I still don't know why she came here. Worse, I don't know why she dragged me with her. I mean, okay, I do know. She's the one who got primary custody. And she claims that she moved out here because an old friend from college offered her a job when she heard about the divorce. While she was boxing up my things, Mom kept insisting it was a fresh start. Maybe it's a fresh start for her, but for me, this move meant the end of my social life. Goodbye, vibrant and bustling Portland. Hello, backward and boring Little Brook. The most exciting thing that happens here on a Friday night is some college kid getting too drunk at the alehouse and falling off the mechanical bull. Which, yes, is a thing that they actually have here, and it is just as stupid and tacky as it sounds. Even worse, most of the town's nightlife— if I can even *call* it that— revolves around that dang thing.

After finishing breakfast, I shower, get dressed, and bike to school. I would drive my truck, but my mom prefers for me not to drive so much. Even though I got my license before we left for Maine in August, she insists since I'm a new driver in a new town, that it's too dangerous for me to go out by myself—especially in such an old truck (which she bought, by the way.) She prefers that I bike around in the near-dark during a thunderstorm because somehow that's supposed to be safer. Mom logic.

Little Brook is small, so there aren't many routes to take to school. Normally I just head south on our street, hang a right at the end of the road, and keep pedaling until I reach the hill the high school sits on. Some mornings, if I'm running late, I'll cut over to main street so I can grab a coffee and a breakfast sandwich from Cuppa Joe's. Or, if I've got a little extra time, I'll get some lunch from Ciao Cat Pub House. For as small and dumb as this town is, I have to admit, they have good food here. The first time I tried a lobster roll I almost cried. That much buttery goodness almost makes me believe in God.

Today, I'm neither late nor early, but I don't stop because it seems like the restaurants are already packed. Men and women in lab coats and mud boots waddle in and out of places, carrying steaming cups of coffee and to-go bags of food. These people all work for Titan Technologies, which is pretty much the whole reason Little Brook exists. Even Mom works there doing data entry or something. It's kind of hard to believe such a small town would be the headquarters of a major science conglomerate, but stranger things have happened. Like, Walmart is headquartered in Bentonville, Alabama. Pretty fricking random, right?

The road that leads to school heads up a steep incline, surrounded by lush, green trees and bushes. Although it's annoying to bike every day, the ride gives me some of my favorite views of this town. There's a small creek that branches off the Allagash, and cuts through the wilderness that surrounds the town. At this height, you can just see it shimmering through the trees, softly reflecting the sunlight. My classmates have mentioned going swimming there a couple of times. I haven't been yet, but it's on my to-do list. Just got to work up the courage to actually put on a swimsuit, I guess. And I'll only be able to work up that courage when I decide to stop being lazy and finally shave—and I'm not talking about my legs, if you catch my drift.

TMI, Riley. TMI.

A couple of buses are dropping off some of my classmates, who congregate outside on the school's front lawn. It's kinda weird to see people taking the bus—most people live right in the town, but then I remember that there are kids who live on farms, or between this town and the next. I lock my bike to the rack outside the front doors and my phone buzzes. I fumble inside my backpack and check my phone to find a text message from Mom.

> **Sorry for being a PITA this morning.**

PITA is Mom's abbreviated way of saying "Pain in the ass." I smirk, but don't text her back. Three little dots dance across the screen—she's the world's slowest texter. Which is funny because all she does is type all day. Isn't that what data entry is, basically?

Another ping.

> **I'll be out late tonight. Gotta work on something with Miles. Frozen dinners in freezer. Love you. Have a gr8 day.**

Miles is Mom's boss. I think back to the lipstick I saw her wearing this morning. *Ahh.* So, I was right. Except she's still lying and trying to pass it off like it's about work. I roll my eyes and stare at the screen, trying to think what to message back.

When the bell rings, I pocket my phone and leave her on read.

I'VE BEEN TOLD THAT the junior class has about 150 students. Apparently, we're going to be the largest senior class the school has had since the 1970s. I don't know why they tout this fact like it's some badge of honor. When I wander through the hallways of this near-dilapidated school, with its outdated rusty water fountains, leaky ceilings, and linoleum-lined floors, it only reminds me that there are more kids suffering in this place than ever before.

The hallways are almost always jammed at Little Brook, so after briefly stopping at my locker, I worm my way through the crowd of people to get to my first class. Mrs. Breitenwald is my English teacher, and she's a polite, albeit milquetoast, woman who doesn't so much as teach as she does spend her time playing Solitaire on the computer. When she does manage to teach, the only things she ever seems to talk about are *The Iliad, Lord of the Flies,* and *To Kill a Mockingbird*— which is her personal favorite book. In a nearly all-white school that seems (structurally) stuck in the 1960s, I guess a book about racism through the eyes of a four-year-old white girl with a stupid name is still considered groundbreaking literature.

Because Mrs. Breitenwald is useless and there's little-to-no work ninety percent of the time, most of the students just socialize. Except for me, since I have no friends. Typically, I use this period to catch up on sleep or homework—mostly sleep. I always pick a seat at the back of the classroom and carry an extra sweatshirt with me to class to use as a pillow.

But when I try to lay my head down to sleep today, I'm interrupted by bubbly giggling—the kind that pierces your ears and keeps you from your peaceful slumber. Through bleary eyes, I stare across the room at the offenders. Of course, it's the band kids. There's five of them that sit over by the back window, wearing their band shirts with the school's bobcat mascot emblazoned across the front. Two of the girls, Helena and Bennie, are laughing about some TikTok playing on their phones. Helena blows a quick bubble, snaps her gum, and then sticks it underneath her desk, adding to the colorful collection already festering there. The boys, Nathan and Jared, are chatting about some party while doodling in their notebooks. One, two, three, four…wait. One of the girls is missing.

As if on cue, the door opens, and a girl with a waifish build skittishly tiptoes inside. This is Aspen Montehugh. She has stringy platinum blond hair that trails past her shoulders, and the prettiest green eyes I've ever seen. They're like little jades with flecks of gold in them. She looks like a porcelain doll, with her hair and perfect, alabaster complexion. When I first saw her at the beginning of the year, I did a double take, because I couldn't believe someone this pretty wasn't like, the daughter of a supermodel. But oddly enough, she's not nearly as popular as I expected her to be. She's the quietest out of all of the band kids, and generally, the one that's always late to class.

She bites her lip and anxiously looks toward her friends. She hesitates; as some sort of emotion surfaces in her eyes—fear? Frustration? I can't tell exactly. Her fingers fumble with the ends of her knit sweater and she quietly makes her way over to them. The girls welcome her with smiles as she sits, but the boys glare at her. Jared, in particular, is staring at her with contempt. He grinds his teeth and glares so ferociously you'd think he's trying to laser a hole through the back of her head. Nathan glances at Aspen, then turns back to Jared, and whispers something urgently underneath his breath. Jared shakes his head and grumbles a response, but I can't make it out. The girls keep trying to talk amongst themselves, but his mumbling becomes too loud for them to ignore. Bennie's eyes flash and she whips her head around to Jared.

"What?"

Jared shrinks backward. "Nothing."

"I thought it was nothing." Bennie's eyes bug out for a second, and then she turns her attention back to her friends. She puts a gentle hand on Aspen's shoulder and squeezes it.

I knew that Aspen was dating Jared at the start of the school year, but I guess they finally broke up. I figured it was an inevitability. I never spoke more than two words to the guy, but he comes across as a super arrogant douchebag. He's got one of those endlessly smug smiles that gives you the impression he loves to start arguments on the Internet. He always made Aspen sit by him in English, and the entire hour, he'd have his arm wrapped around her shoulder. Possessing her like an object, and she just put up with it. Day after day, I'd watch her desperately try to scribble down notes under the weight of his arm.

Even though I don't know her very well, I really like Aspen. If she catches me looking in her direction, she'll offer me a friendly smile. She always lends me mechanical pencil lead when I ask her for it, and that stuff is like currency in high school.

Speaking of mechanical pencils… I pull one out of my bag, along with my tattered Algebra II textbook. Even though I finished my homework for today and yearn for the sweet release of slumber, it would be nice to get a head start on the next assignment. If I get done with all my homework today, then I can free up my weekend to do something fun. I've been playing *Hades* on the Switch and although I suck at it, I really think I'll be able to beat the second boss soon. Hopefully.

Mrs. Breitenwald gets up to turn on the morning announcements and I start reading through the problems. The grainy television set clicks on, and on its fuzzy screen two students stare blankly into the camera, monotonically giving today's sad-ass cafeteria menu. Salmon nuggets, flatbread pepperoni pizza, and bean sprout salad? Gross. I don't know why the healthy-choices people try so hard.

After the meal announcements, a girl wearing a glittering crown and a flowing cape steps in front of the camera with a sign. The camera operator struggles to zoom in and focus on it. The glittery blocky letters read "HOMECOMING GAME AND DANCE! TONIGHT! 7PM!" along with some ticket prices underneath.

"Come to the homecoming game and dance!" the girl says cheerily. "This year's theme is Roaring Royalty! Show your pride and strut your stride, bobcats!"

Damn. I gotta hand it to her on the slogan. It almost convinces me that spending fifteen bucks on a ticket is worth it. Unfortunately, high school dance music sucks ass. Surprisingly, there's only so many times you can listen to Aerosmith's *I Don't Want to Miss a Thing* during slow dances—and I have no one to go with anyways. Plus, I wouldn't want to leave my dog at home alone for all that time when Mom's not going to be there.

My classmates whisper amongst themselves about their homecoming plans. They turn to talk to each other and giggle about their own inside jokes. They look so excited. Bright eyes. Big smiles. Bodies jittering in their seats, like they can't wait for the end of the day already. For a moment, I get this empty feeling in my chest, and my heart flutters to fill up the uncomfortable space. During moments like this, I suddenly remember how much I miss having people to talk to and make plans with. Yeah, school dances are awful, but I'd be lying if I said I didn't miss dancing to the Cupid Shuffle with my friends.

The ruckus gets a bit too loud for Mrs. Breitenwald, and she hisses at people to chill out before returning to another rousing game of cards. Helena and Bennie remain the loudest people in the room, eagerly conspiring about their plans for after the dance. Jared glares intensely at Aspen's back. Aspen pulls her hoodie over her face and lays her head against her desk. She remains like that for about fifteen minutes while I work on my homework, before suddenly pushing her chair back.

She wraps her arms around her body in a tight hug, the way you do when you're about to cry or throw up. Judging by how ashy-green her face is, it's the latter. Suddenly, she launches to her feet and rushes out of the room, gagging. Helena and Bennie's eyes widen, and they stare at each other, but Mrs. Breitenwald seems relatively unphased. She pushes her glasses up her nose again and rolls her eyes, turning her attention back to her computer screen.

Helena raises her hand impatiently. "Mrs. Breitenwald? Can we go check on Aspen?"

"Take the hall passes with you." Mrs. Breitenwald doesn't look away from her screen.

Slowly, the girls rise to their feet and move toward the door. They grab two laminated hall passes off the hook under the American flag and exit the room. Jared snorts and rolls his eyes, bouncing his leg on the floor, agitated.

"Gimme a break," he mutters to Nathan, who smirks in response.

"What was that, dude? Barfing up her breakfast this early…?"

His voice is teasing, and from his tone, I know what he's insinuating. An involuntary shiver courses down my spine. The idea of being pregnant at any point in my life repulses me but imagining myself as a pregnant teen both repulses *and* terrifies me. Poor Aspen.

Jared scoffs and rolls his eyes. "As if. She doesn't put out. Her legs are closed tighter than a friggin' bank vault. Least they were for me."

Nathan laughs uproariously at Jared's joke, but Jared doesn't smile. Some of the other kids smirk in their direction, their cheeks darkening. They clearly find it funny. I don't. If I were a braver person, I'd call him out on his bullshit, but I'm not about to make myself Jared's enemy.

I'm just trying to get through the day.

Day 0 - Afternoon

ASPEN RETURNED TO ENGLISH class that morning in tears. Helena and Benny helped her back to her seat and she laid on her desk and cried. Mrs. Breitenwald asked if she wanted to go to the nurse, but she shook her head over and over again. I didn't see Aspen again until our algebra class, and she still looked just as miserable as she was that morning. I feel awful for her. She's not going to get a break from Jared anytime soon—after all, the homecoming game is tonight, and the marching band plays at all the football games.

The rest of the day passes in a forgettable blur. Before I know it, I'm back on my bike, heading toward home. School buses chug past, coughing out black exhaust. I have to tuck my head against my shoulder to keep the smog out of my eyes. A couple of kids make dumb faces at me and flick me off as the bus smolders by, but I don't pay them any attention.

Seems like the whole town is out celebrating the big game. Restaurants along Main Street are as busy as they were this morning. The streets are so packed that I have to be especially careful with the cars, who seem reluctant to stop for me when I try to cross the street.

When I arrive home, Tigger is already at the door, whining and demanding to be let outside. He launches himself into the front yard then promptly squats. We go for a walk, and when we come home, I feed Tigger, and get started on dinner. When I open the fridge, there's little to nothing to eat. We killed off the leftover spaghetti on Wednesday night, and I think Mom took the rest of Thursday's casserole with her for lunch. Which is pretty rude, considering that she has like eight different Lean Cuisines in the freezer. If she doesn't want to eat her bitter orange chicken with stale-ass rice, what makes her think that I would want to?

Luckily, in the pantry, there's a can of tomato soup, and there's still some leftover bread and cheese slices. A grilled cheese sounds perfect for a chilly fall evening like this, and I'm pretty damn good at making grilled cheese, if I do say so myself. When I was little, my dad used to make me all different kinds of fancy grilled cheese. My favorite thing to do was to go to the grocery store with him and pick out what kind of cheeses we'd want to try. Havarti, gouda, the unfortunate Stilton…we tried whichever ones we could pick out. My personal favorite was white cheddar mixed with a little Mimolette, and a thin layer of apricot jam. But tonight, all I have is a couple limp slices of American cheese—a far cry from the intricate artisan delicacies that I'm really craving right now.

When I finish my creation, I send a picture of it to Dad.

A Kraft singles masterpiece.

Dad never takes more than a minute to respond to one of my messages. He sends back a string of laugh-cry emojis—my dad uses more emojis than a tween girl—along with this message:

Not my daughter eating Kraft singles! Nooo X'D

Mom won't let me go grocery shopping for some reason

Why? :<

Doesn't want me out driving around without her I guess?

But you have your license...?

Yea idk

Hmmm I might talk to her about it. Can you talk rn?

Yea

Within seconds Dad calls.

"Hey, Dad."

In the background, I can hear him shuffling papers on his desk and the din of the city. He must be near an open window.

"Hey kiddo. Sorry I haven't talked to you in a couple of days. I've had this huge project at work, and every time I get a chance to call you, y'know, you're already in bed asleep."

I smirk. "I'm up until like, midnight every night, Dad. I'm always around."

"You should be getting sleep. Nine to ten hours."

"You're one to talk."

Dad is a software engineer, so when he has updates and developments to make, he enters crunch time. He's always super busy, but things got better for him when he landed a new job in Seattle. When I was a little kid, the only time I'd ever see him was on the weekends.

Dad laughs. "So, what're you up to tonight?"

"Not much. Kicking back and watching TV with Tigger."

I'm not going to tell him about homecoming. If I mention that I don't want to go, he'll launch into this lecture about how I need to put myself out there more and try to make friends, and that learning to be friends with strangers is what college is about and this is good practice, and yadda yadda yadda. I know it's good advice, sure, but I don't want the lecture. He doesn't know what it's like here. All of these kids have known each other since they were in diapers—*maybe* even in utero—and I'm the weirdo with the hippie Portland-born Mom who just rolled into town on a whim. You can't exactly break into a new social scene if you don't have an "in." And we're teenagers, so the novelty of being "the new kid" doesn't really exist anymore; not like it did in elementary school, when meeting a new classmate was exciting.

"On a Friday night?"

"I just kinda want to chill at home for a bit. It's been a long week…was up late last night studying." I slice my grilled cheese in half and pull it apart. An intricate web of gooey yellow cheese extends from the two pieces. Beautiful. "Besides, there's like eight thousand things I want to binge on Netflix."

"Like what? *Stranger Things?*"

"That, but also the '98 version of *Godzilla* just dropped—"

My dad audibly shudders. "Ugh. Terrible movie."

"Yeah, but that's why it's fun to watch. It's cringe."

"Don't you and your mom have anything better to watch?"

"No worries about that. Mom's uh, busy tonight. Working late."

There's an uncomfortable silence. Dad lets out a little sigh.

"Kinda sucks to be at home by yourself on a Friday night."

From his tone I can tell he's frustrated, but he never talks shit about Mom. Which I guess I should appreciate—he doesn't want to badmouth her or make me think less of her—but sometimes I just wish he would be mad when he's mad. It's not that I don't think he cares, he obviously does. It's annoying that he's such a stereotypically passive aggressive Oregonian. Sometimes I wonder if my parents just divorced because they were such terrible communicators. No one ever really says what they feel in this family. And now that they're divorced, I guess we never will.

"It's fine. I'm probably going to Facetime Khalil and Caia later on tonight." They're my friends from back home. "Maybe we'll watch something together."

"Alright…how's school been going?"

"I mean, it's only been what, like a month since it started? It's been fine. School is school." I glance down at Tigger, who has finished his dinner and is now whining for a bit of mine. "Uh, Dad, sorry, I gotta go. Don't want my food getting cold."

"Alright. We'll talk later. Love you."

"Love you too, Dad."

I pocket my phone, then pick up my mug of tomato soup and my sandwich, and head over to the couch. I flick on the TV and immediately switch over to Netflix. Tigger hops up on the couch beside me, and I shake my head.

"No. *Down.*" I snap my fingers and point to the ground.

He sheepishly obeys, flopping down on the ground at my feet. He glances up at me as I take the first bite of my mediocre sandwich.

"You're not getting anything." I don't even bother looking at him. I just flip through the queue to find my show and press play.

SOMEWHERE IN BETWEEN EPISODES four and six of *Stranger Things,* I fall asleep. I wake up to discover that I'm already on the final episode. My dinner plate is sitting on the side table, and I can see from the faint traces of drool from where Tigger has licked it clean. But he's nowhere to be seen. His reindeer toy is on the floor where he normally sits.

I sit up, yawn, and rub the crust from my eyes. Outside the window, the sky kinda looks…blood-orange? It's gorgeous; a vibrant gradient of reds and pinks and peach. I pick up my phone to take a photo, and my eyes widen when I see the time. Eight p.m.? Sunset was hours ago. So why is it so bright outside now? A chill runs down my spine, and I creep closer to the window. There's no sun, and there's no moon, only bright, bright colors, like being trapped inside a kaleidoscope. Black clouds of smoke drift overhead, their billowing forms like twisting dragons in the sky. As I stare in shock, more sounds come into focus: the distant whine of emergency sirens and screaming.

Something is very, very wrong.

In the kitchen, Tigger is whining. I throw back my blanket and rush over to him. He's pawing desperately at the door. I push him back, pull on my shoes, and step outside, following the sirens. Tigger whines and barks from the house, mournfully calling out for me, but I ignore him.

When I get to the end of the driveway, I turn and look in the direction of Main Street. Over the crest of the hill, the town rises in all its glory.

All its fiery glory.

Orange-yellow flames engulf the entirety of main street; black smoke circles from crumbling buildings and rises into the sky. A ton of cars are rushing around in all directions, honking, desperately trying to escape the city. The tumultuous sound of the chaos fills my ears—

screaming, honking, tires screeching, emergency sirens droning on and on—nearly piercing my ear drums.

In the farthest distance, I can see the Titan Technologies building. My heart hits my stomach and I feel a wave of nausea overcome my body. It, too, is completely on fire. The dome has collapsed in from the flames, and there's smoke escaping in billowing clouds. I immediately pull out my phone and try to call Mom. The line rings and rings before finally—

"We're sorry, but the person you are calling cannot be reached right now. Please try your call again later."

Tears fill my eyes almost immediately. When I hear the dial tone, I begin to ramble into the phone.

"Mom? Mom, where are you? Call me back, *now*."

I hang up and dial again. A firetruck, its lights and alarm blazing, rushes by my house at an impossible speed. It races toward Main Street before disappearing behind a building. Then the most ungodly, horrific sound rips through the air: an almighty, thunderous roar—

—and I watch as that same fire truck launches into the sky, lights flashing, before crashing to the ground.

For the next few moments, my head is fog. I can't hear the sirens or the screams, or the dial tones from my phone. My legs quake, and my tears blur my vision.

What the hell just happened?

Something…*launched* a fire truck into the air. Right? There was no explosion—if there was, the fire truck would have been a smoldering mass of twisted metal. It was *perfectly* intact, like a toddler's toy that had been carelessly tossed away mid-tantrum.

But I don't have any time to process. Flames are rippling along the streets, engulfing trees, mailboxes, and fences. They hungrily lap at the puddles of gasoline and motor oil left behind by cars on the street. Surrounding homes are swallowed in seconds. Oh shit. It's not going to take much longer before it reaches here. I need to find Mom, but I'd have to cut across the downtown area to get to Titan Tech, and there's no way in hell that I can do that right now.

Mom. Did she escape already? Is she safe? If she's safe, why won't she answer her phone?

Tigger's sharp bark snaps me back to reality, and I rush into the house, trying to fight the nausea bubbling in my stomach. I have no choice. I have to hope that Mom makes it out okay if she hasn't already, or I'm not going to make it out alive. The first thing I sprint for is my backpack. I flip it upside down and dump out the contents. I save my wallet, pencil pouch, and a notebook, but leave my textbooks behind. Then I rush into the kitchen and try to grab food from the fridge. I take our wilted apples, all the cheese slices, and the remaining pieces of bread. *Tigger*. Tigger needs food. I run into the laundry room and grab the container, then set it on the kitchen counter.

Smoke floats past our windows, but I no longer hear the fire trucks' sirens. I don't have much time left. Quickly, quickly. I grab the keys to my truck— they're my only way out. I grab Tigger's reindeer toy, the flashlight from the kitchen drawer, my phone charger, and spare pair of glasses from my bedroom. Clothes. *Shit.* I need clothes. I grab a duffel bag from my closet and unceremoniously throw shirts, sweaters, pants, socks, underwear, all into the bag. What else am I missing? What else do you need in an emergency? First aid kit. Cabinet underneath the bathroom sink. *Money.* I sprint into my mom's bedroom. I know she keeps an emergency credit card in her nightstand drawer. When I open it, I also find a checkbook, and her Oregon driver's license. I take everything I see, and scramble back into the kitchen.

I fill my backpack to the brim. All the while Tigger barks impatiently, running around in circles. There's urgency in his voice; panic in his brown eyes. With shaking hands, I pull my backpack onto my shoulders and leash him up, then sprint outside.

The flames are about a quarter of the way down my road now— until today, I had no idea that fire could move so fast. I put Tigger in the passenger seat and the key in the ignition. The engine coughs and sputters. I slam my hand on the steering wheel, screaming for it to go. Tigger keeps barking as he stares out the window.

If Mom let me drive more often, this wouldn't be happening. No, stop, *focus.* What did Dad teach me? Press firmly down on the brake pedal. I put all my weight on it. Then turn the key. The engine sputters to life. But there's no time for me to breathe a sigh of relief. I buckle up, flip the car into reverse, and spin out of the driveway.

Main Street leads to the highway, but it's engulfed in flames, so I can't leave through there. *Think, think, think, Riley.* Where else did Mom say that you could get on the highway? I spin through the backroads and accelerate past the other houses, looking for a connecting road. All the stoplights are down, and everything around here is deadly silent. Front doors and garages have been left open. Most people must've escaped already. Or was everyone downtown tonight? So many questions, and I don't have any time to find the answers with the fire so close in my rearview mirror. I don't even bother to stop at the stop signs, I just push through. I flick on my headlights, and they barely slice through the hazy red fog. I flick on my hazards. And my high beams. There's no one around to stop me.

Finally, I reach it—the connecting road that leads to the highway. Some of the highway signs point to the freeway entrance. But as I make a beeline in that direction, something catches my attention: a lopsided figure limping across the steaming asphalt road. Tigger barks ferociously, his lips pulled back in a snarl. And I slam on my brakes; nearly throwing myself through the windshield. My tires squeal and I scream as I screech to a halt.

The figure turns to face me, and I recognize her immediately. It's Aspen.

Her hair is tangled, and she's covered in soot and blood. Her knees and elbows are scraped up, and there's a laceration running from her shoulder down her arm. Her marching band uniform is in complete tatters, hanging limply off her body in charred strips of cloth. With dazed green eyes, she stares at me, her head rolling from side to side. She looks like a zombie, and although it sends a chill through my body, I know I can't just leave her there.

I throw open the door and exit the vehicle. Tigger continues to bark as I rush over to her. She continues to stare at me, but her eyes won't focus. They lazily roll around in every direction. Oh no. Does she have a concussion? I think she has a concussion. I place my hands on her shoulders and force her to look at me.

"Aspen, come on, let's go."

Her mouth moves but no words come out. I take her blistered hand and lead her to the car. All of a sudden, Tigger launches himself at the window, snarling and slobbering—I've never seen him like this before.

"Tigger! Stop!"

But he continues to snarl and snap, his eyes wild. I throw the door open and push Tigger into the backseat, then help Aspen inside. Her body is limp like a noodle, and she doesn't even move to buckle herself in; I have to do it for her. Her eyes flutter, and almost immediately, she falls unconscious. That can't be good, but I've got bigger problems to worry about.

I hear a thunderous crack behind us, and when I glance over my shoulder, I can see the wildfires racing ever closer. I scramble to the driver's seat, climb inside, and hit the gas. Without even bothering to look in the rearview mirror, I peel out and race for the freeway.

Day 1 - Early Morning

ABOUT AN HOUR PASSES before the night sky returns to its normal shade of navy blue and black. The smog disappears, and the stars become visible once again. Surrounding us is nothing but the open road and the bountiful yet eerie wilderness of Maine.

On the opposite side of the road, emergency vehicles race past us, sirens wailing, heading in the direction of Little Brook. My mind circles back to the homecoming game earlier that evening. A rival football team had come from hours away to play…I wonder how long it was before their parents and school figured out what happened.

What a God-awful nightmare this is.

For the first thirty minutes of the drive or so, Tigger snarled at Aspen, but now he's dozing in the back. Aspen sleeps soundly in the passenger seat, curled up in a ball. She looks like hell, and smells like it too. I know I shouldn't let her sleep, in case she has a concussion, but there's nothing else I can do and if she's still breathing, well, that's good, right?

When we drove by the hospital, it was also on fire.

The silence is uncomfortable for me, but there's nothing else I can listen to except my tires bouncing along the road. I never got an adapter, so I can't plug my phone into the truck to play music. And for whatever reason, no matter how hard I try, the radio won't work. I've tried AM, FM—everything is static. Which is bizarre because the truck still has an antenna. I guess it's just that old. I thought I'd hear at least snippets of something. Maybe the haunting voice of one of those midnight-radio preachers or the canned audience laughter of bad talk radio shows. But nope, nothing.

As the hours stretch on, my eyes grow blearier. I try to stay awake by drumming my fingers on the steering wheel and counting the number of signs we pass by. But it's not helping. The muscles in my arms are aching, and my legs are sore. I've never driven for this long. Even when Mom and I were trekking cross country, she never let me drive for more than two hours at a time.

Mom. My eyes well with tears, and I swallow back the lump in my throat. *She's probably dead.* I try to resist it, but the realization sinks in and fills me with dread. If she was safe, she would've answered her phone when I called her. Mom can be careless, and yes, she's irresponsible, but she would never abandon me in a time of crisis. She would've come back for me if she could. But everything north of Main Street was engulfed in flames, and Titan Tech appeared to be the source of the fire. The tears blur my eyes and before long, I'm sobbing, hunched over the steering wheel, barely able to see inches in front of my face. Aspen remains asleep, but Tigger nudges me with his nose. When I see a sign for a rest area, I pull off the road, tears still streaming down my face.

The rest stop is quiet, empty except for a couple of raccoons digging in a tipped-over garbage can, full of greasy fast-food wrappers. They scuttle back into the undergrowth when my truck pulls up. A sole streetlight illuminates the space with its bleak fluorescent light. Mayflies and moths dance in its thin rays.

I don't bother to turn off the truck when I exit. I throw the door open, and stumble out, nearly crumpling to the asphalt. My tears burn as they run down my cheeks and drip onto the ground below, and my head throbs with each sob escaping my mouth. My body is tired, and yet I continue to shake; electric, alive, juiced-up. Questions flood my panicked mind, and suddenly everything around me is too loud— the crickets, the breeze, the buzz of the streetlight. I entered panic mode when I escaped the fire, but as the adrenaline leaves my body, my composure goes with it. My mind circles back to the fire, the sirens, the screams. There was no hope for survival, and now, there's no way I can stop the tears or escape the fact that Mom is most likely dead.

My mom died.

She died tonight, and I didn't even bother to text her back.

The minutes pass, and they feel like hours. By the time my sobs finally subside, my throat is raw and hoarse. I turn and glance at the car. Aspen is still asleep. Tigger is staring at me with those soft sad eyes of his. It's like he's also realized what's happened. Dazed, I reach into the car and grab his leash. He squats on the ground and does his business before nervously retreating to the backseat.

When I return to the driver's seat, I check my phone. Time reads three a.m. My battery is at twenty-one percent, and there's no service…I can't even call my dad. I slump over and rest my forehead against the steering wheel. I have no idea what to do. I know what I want to do, and that's bawl my eyes out and get some sleep, but honestly, I'm too creeped out to stay here. This rest stop is so old and backwater it looks a piece from the set of *Deliverance*. I half expect a guy to pop out of the bathroom and shoot me with a shotgun.

Something flashes in my rearview mirror. Headlights. Another car. I raise my head, confused. There's been no one behind me for miles... I have no idea where they've come from. Have they just been sitting there? My chest tightens. I wonder who it could be. The car parks in a spot directly behind me, making it difficult to see. It's one of those new SUVs that has headlights so ridiculously bright, you think they're high beams. Hell, maybe those are high beams. The driver could be that kind of jackass.

The weird thing is that the car just...sits there, headlights fully on. And it doesn't do anything. No one moves or exits the vehicle. I can't even see if anyone is inside. Something isn't right here. I shift the car into reverse, and to my surprise, the car starts to creep forward. My breath hitches in my chest and my heart throbs. True crime story taglines race through my head. *Traffickers Kidnap Girls from Rest Stop*. But why else would there be people all the way out here?

I shake my head. No time to keep thinking about this. I shift gears, spin my wheels, and slam my foot on the gas pedal, accelerating back onto the freeway. Tigger stumbles off the backseat and onto the floor. Aspen moans a little in her sleep.

"Sorry, boy."

Tigger sighs, then climbs up and tries to fall back asleep. I glance in my rearview mirror. The car doesn't seem to be following me, but I'm going to keep cruising. The speed limit sign reads sixty-five, but my speedometer is at seventy-five—and for now, I'm going to keep it that way. If Mom was here, she'd harp on at me for driving so fast. She always snapped if the arrow on the speedometer ever so slightly moved over the speed limit. I can almost hear her bitching about it—

—I can hear her.

I can hear her.

Tears stream down my cheeks once more, but I firmly shake my head, willing them to disappear. *Stop, Riley.* You can't think about that. Mom isn't here. And Mom's not going to be around to save you from whatever weirdo attacks you at a rest stop. From here on out, or at least until I can get in contact with Dad again, I'm on my own.

I glance at my gas tank and wince. I'm a little less than halfway down. This truck gets decent mileage for being old as ass, but I'm going to need to stop somewhere soon. And this stretch of highway is next-to-endless, with very few signs along the road. Besides, I'm a little afraid of stopping somewhere by myself in the middle of the night. Aspen is completely conked out, and although Tigger's here, he's not going to be much use. Can't exactly fuel up the car when you're trying to keep your dog from scarfing down moldy, trampled hot dog buns at the pumps.

Sunrise. When is sunrise? I'm hoping it's more like five a.m., but honestly, it's probably closer to six or half past, given the time of year. I don't know exactly how long our gas tank is going to hold out. If I drive for at least an hour, that should be enough to put the weirdos behind me, right?

Up ahead in the distance, the faintest shimmer of orange light rises above the horizon. Excitement floods my body and I eagerly grip the steering wheel, leaning forward in my seat. But a moment later, I'm hit with a realization—it's only three a.m.—followed by the stench of something foul. I recognize the smell. I was only driving through it hours earlier.

Smoke.

As we drive closer, the horizon expanding, the fires burn brighter. Bewildered, I stare at the signs to make sure I didn't drive back in the opposite direction. But no. I don't recognize this town, and I don't recognize any of the other landmarks. I mean, I'm driving on the correct side of the road for Chrissake. There's no way I got rerouted and made it back to Little Brook.

I pass a smoldering metal sign—*Lichfield*—and head under an overpass. The flames are alive; flickering orange sparks float through the air and crackle against the torn-up asphalt road. The night sky is turning a different color once again. The city surrounding me is in total ruins: ash, crumbling buildings, charred…oh God, what *are* those? I shake my head and focus my attention back on the road. It's suddenly sweltering in the truck; my clothes dampen and stick to my body. I turn on the AC. Tigger starts whining in the backseat. I glance out the window, and I notice a sign—Titan Technologies Transport. The building, sitting high on the hills, is in ruins; a blackened shell of what it once was.

What the hell is going on?

MAINE ISN'T LIKE CALIFORNIA; it's not known for having wildfires. It's known for Stephen King novels and spooky shit, like the ghosts of dead ladies coming out of lakes or wendigos hiding in the woods. I mean, I guess this *is* spooky shit. Why are two Titan Tech laboratories and their surrounding cities, entirely engulfed in flames? Is it a bizarre terrorist attack, or is it the work of disgruntled employees?

Did they have some kind of self-destruct button that would explode every facility?

This is unreal.

I rub my eyes and sniffle, trying to clear the smell of smoke from my nostrils. We left the second town about half an hour ago, and yet, I can still smell the flames. I'm so tired my eyes feel like they're bleeding. I check the time on the clock: four a.m. My gas tank is getting low, but thankfully, a gas station has appeared near an overpass on the horizon. What's even better is that it doesn't appear to be on fire. Bonus points if they have halfway decent restrooms.

I glance in my rearview mirror, and while I can see a few other cars full of people—either escaping from the last town, or just doing their morning commute—I don't see the car that tried to trap us at the rest stop, but that doesn't necessarily mean that they won't catch up to us. I can feel my anxiety setting in; making my nerves feel all prickly. Or maybe that's just the exhaustion. Jesus, I never thought I would want to sleep this much. I feel like if I went to bed now, I wouldn't wake up for a week.

I move off the freeway, and head toward the gas station. It's painted a bright, blistering orange, and a little polar bear statue waves to passing cars at the side of the road. The statue would be charming if not for the fact its paint job has been ruined by years of rain—the little eyeballs have bled together in a swirly mess of black and white that drips down its cheeks. It's vaguely demented, not exactly hospitable, but I don't have the luxury of being picky.

When I pull in, a bunch of cars are piled up in the parking lot. Every single parking space is full. In fact, I have to park at the back of the lot, away from the other cars. Some of the pumps are open, but I want to let Tigger out first. He's already whining and scratching at the door by the time I come to a complete stop.

I park the car, kill the engine, and grab his leash before hopping out. I lead him to a patch of trodden grass and let him do his business. Technically, it's a little early for his breakfast, but I'd rather he got some food now, since we may not be stopping again for a while. I dig into the truck, retrieve his food container, and pour it into his bowl. He ravenously gobbles up the kibble and then expectantly looks up at me. At that moment I realize that I forgot to pack his water bowl, and also, I don't have any water. Shit. I'm going to have to buy some at the gas station. I wonder if they even sell bowls or containers.

A weird murmuring catches my attention, and I notice Aspen's hand hanging out of the window. Tigger growls again, and I tug on his leash, glaring at him. He averts his eyes.

"Yeah, that's what I thought, tough guy." I walk over to the truck and look inside.

Aspen stares back at me, fully conscious, but completely dazed. Some of the scars and scratches on her face have scabbed over. Streaks of dirt stain her pale face. The skin around her eyes is sunken in; hollow. She's slept all night but she still looks fatigued.

She blinks. "Uh… hi."

"Hi."

For a moment she appears flustered. Red floods her cheeks and she looks away. She twists strands of singed hair round and around her finger.

"I know you might not remember what happened, and t-that's okay."

I try to place a reassuring hand on her shoulder, but it feels clammy and awkward. She shrinks away from my touch, and my stomach does a somersault. Is she in shock? I mean, God only knows what she saw in town last night.

"Aspen?" When I say her name, her eyes focus on me sharply. Her pupils appear long and thin for a moment; constricted and reptilian. It's a jarring image, but when she blinks again, they look normal. "Aspen, are you alright?"

"Uh…," her cheeks darken to a beet-red. "Y-yeah."

"Yeah?" I'm unconvinced.

She runs her fingers through her hair and bites her lip. "Uh…what was your name again?"

As soon as she asks the question, she looks away again. My shoulders sink. *Oh.* She has no idea who I am. I guess that makes sense. We never really talked one-on-one like this before. I've said her name plenty of times, but I don't think she's ever once said mine.

"I'm…Riley. From English class."

"Oh!" she squeezes her eyes shut and nods. "That's right. For some reason I thought it was Ramona."

"Ramona?" I wrinkle my nose. "Like the books?"

"What books?"

"The Ramona Quimby books? The ones by Beverly Cleary?"

She stares back at me blankly.

"Never mind, look, it's not important. Are you feeling okay? You've kinda been passed out for the past…" I sigh. "I can't do math right now. My head hurts. You've been passed out since last night. I have no idea if you have a concussion or not."

She rubs her head, as if that's a sufficient way to check. "Nah, I don't think so. No bumps or anything."

"You're sure?"

"I mean, if I haven't slipped into a coma by now, I'm assuming I'm fine, right?" She looks around, perplexed. "Where the hell are we?"

"I don't know."

"You don't know? You brought us here."

"I've been just…driving. Everything is on fire."

Her eyes widen. "What do you mean, everything is on fire?"

"Like…every place that we've driven past that's owned by Titan Tech? It's on fire. This is the first place we've been that doesn't look like it's exploded. Also, we're almost out of gas and my dog has to pee."

As if on cue, Tigger starts growling at Aspen again. She doesn't flinch or shrink away. She stares down at him, not smiling.

"You have a dog."

"Yeah. This is my dog, Tigger. Tigger, stop." I tug on his leash, trying to get him to heel. He stops growling, but the intense look in his eyes remains. "I'm sorry. I don't know what's gotten into him."

"It's fine. I've never really gotten along well with dogs. I mean, they're cute and all, but I think they know I'm more of a cat person." On the last word of her sentence, she coughs, loudly and hoarsely. Her eyes water and she places her hand against her throat. "Sorry. Little parched."

"I guess driving through smoke for hours will do that to you. I didn't pack any water, but…" I nod toward my backpack. "I have a credit card in there. That should get us everything we need."

Aspen reaches for the backpack and fumbles inside it. She grabs Mom's credit card and stands on the running board but almost immediately, her wobbly legs give out beneath her. Tigger barks like he's about to go in for the kill.

I catch her by the wrist just before she falls. "Aspen!"

"I'm fine." She holds up a hand, and slowly pulls herself to her feet. "I think my body's just a little…weak right now."

"Okay, well…" I look down at Tigger, who continues to growl. His tail is stiffened and bristly. I can't give her his leash. What if he bites her or something? Then we'll have a bigger problem on our hands.

Aspen passes the credit card to me. I walk around to the opposite side of the truck and open the door. Tigger hops into the cab, and mournfully looks at me when I shut the door.

"Sorry, buddy. If you can't behave yourself, you're going to have to chill here." I look at Aspen. "I'll buy a pack of water bottles. Do you want a breakfast sandwich or anything?"

"Sure."

"Okay. Any dietary stuff?"

"Dietary stuff?"

"Y'know. You're not a vegan, right?"

"Even if I was, I don't think I really can be picky. You think they serve vegan food at a gas station?"

I shrug. "Sunflower seeds are vegan, right?"

"Actually, certain kinds have bacon salt on them."

"Ok. Are you a vegan or not?"

"No. Egg and cheese sandwich is good, if they've got it. Otherwise, I'll take a hot dog."

I nod and walk into the building. I thought being surrounded by people again would feel comforting, but it's just as eerie as the black smog in the sky outside. These folks look like ghosts, wandering through the aisles, adding more snacks to their already-full arms. Some people are sitting on the ground in front of the cashier's counter, sipping water and wolfing down hot dogs.

I make a beeline for the restroom first. It's full. A disheveled mother tries to scrub the soot off her young daughter's face. The kid's maybe five or six. Other women slowly wash their hands, their haunted eyes staring endlessly at their reflected figures in the mirror. One woman scrubs her hands over and over again underneath the piping hot water, until they appear almost blistered. Someone has to pull her away and help her dry her hands. The trash can is filled to the brim with wet paper towels, like the employees have given up attempting to clean. Supplies of toilet paper and paper towels are sitting in boxes at the back of the room. I patiently wait my turn and finally go to use the restroom, which, as you can probably imagine, is absolutely filthy. I grimace as I use the dwindling toilet paper to wipe up the seat as best I can before doing my business. As I'm washing my hands, the little girl starts to cry, and her mother tries to comfort her, whispering gentle words into her ear. For some reason it makes me feel nauseous, and I hold back tears as I hurry to exit the bathroom.

Come on, Riley. Now isn't the time.

I head toward the back of the gas station, where the water bottles are. The cheap bottles are completely gone; all that's left are the fruity waters and the giant bottles of Evian. Grimacing, I grab about four of the biggest water bottles, and then waddle over to the hot bar to grab whatever food is sitting out. Spinach-egg white with Canadian bacon. Gross. Who the hell wants freeze-dried spinach from a gas station? But it's the only thing sitting out, so I grab two of the sandwiches and walk over to the counter.

The cashier is a woman in her late fifties, maybe early sixties. She's got obviously graying hair which she's tried to dye an orange red, an unfortunate reminder of the flames. She stares down through her thick owl-rimmed glasses and pops her gum. Above her head is a TV, which is tuned into the news. My jaw drops slightly when I see the bulletin scrolling on the lower part of the screen. EMERGENCY EVACUATION: LITTLE BROOK... TAYLOR'S FALLS... SALSVILLE... All these names are accompanied with images of the burning towns. I recognize the Little Brook football field, its turf burnt to a smoldering, blackened crisp. Another set of words flash on the screen: TITAN TECH UNDER ATTACK?

"Twenty-two, forty-three," the cashier says slowly. I jump, startled. She offers a kind smile. "Sorry, sweet pea. Didn't mean to scare you, but I gotta keep the line moving."

"I'm from there. Little Brook, I mean."

Her eyebrows raise. "You are? Hmm. That's a first. Most of the people coming in are from the surrounding areas."

"I...I don't know if anyone else made it out. It was really bad." I swallow back a lump of tears in my throat.

Goddamn it, Riley, stop crying!

"You're the only one who made it out?" Her voice is soft, but she's not being kind. She's scared.

Everyone in here; we're all terrified by what's happened. Numerous wide eyes shift over in my direction. People are whispering to each other. Another mother is trying to comfort a crying child.

"I brought my friend Aspen, and my d-dog, Tigger. But I can't...I don't know where my mom is." I shake my head and suck in air, hoping I can force the sobs back inside my body. I hold out the credit card to her, but she waves me off.

"Don't worry about it, baby. You got someone you can call for help?"

"I haven't had cell service."

"There's service here."

Service. Thank God. I can call Dad!

I thank the cashier profusely before sprinting out of the building. Aspen stares back at me with doe eyes when I hand her the food, and then I reach for my phone on the dash. After quickly unlocking it, I watch the three little bars at the top of the screen struggle to connect to the signal. Phone held up to the sky, I circle around the car desperately as if it will somehow help. Aspen stares at me as she cracks open a water bottle and takes a sip.

Finally, my phone starts to vibrate. Text after text floods my phone, and then a message pops up on my screen. Fourteen missed calls, eleven voicemails. My inbox is full. Throughout the entire night, my dad has been trying to reach me. And Khalil and Caia have both called me too. I dial my voicemail, and when I listen to Caia's latest message, it's just incoherent sobbing.

A lump rises in the back of my throat. *Jesus. Everyone thinks I'm dead.*

I quickly dial Dad's number and pace anxiously. Aspen offers me a sandwich and I shake my head ferociously. She tentatively takes another sip of water, watching me with an oddly careful intensity. Dad answers on the first ring.

"Riley?" he cries out, his voice hoarse, and he starts to cry. "Riley, sweetheart, is that you?"

"It's me, Dad." I wipe at the tears streaming down my face, and then break down sobbing. For a few minutes I stand there, sobbing into the phone. I desperately want a hug. I want Mom here with me. I want a shower. I want to feel safe. "I don't know what happened."

"Are you okay?"

"No…!" It's the truth, but this—understandably—causes my dad to panic even more.

"Are you hurt?!" he shouts into the phone.

"No, no, Dad, I'm fine. But Mom…"

"Where's your mother?"

"I don't… Dad, I don't know…" I sob, my shaking knees giving out underneath me. I sit on the ground, clutching my phone as waves of panic rack my body. "Everything was on fire, Dad, we didn't have much time… S-she never came home from work."

"Jesus." I can hear my dad sob as well. "Lorraine."

"Dad, h-help. Help me. I don't know what to do."

"I'm trying, honey, but I can't get you a plane ticket. The whole east coast is on fire."

"On…fire?"

"Every town or city on the East Coast with a Titan Tech facility is on fire. They think it's some coordinated terrorist attack. All air travel has been grounded. I'm trying to think of something."

"Do you want me to drive to Seattle?"

"You can't make that drive by yourself."

"It's not like we have a choice, is it?" I swallow, blinking tears from my eyes.

Dad's voice is stern. "No, Riley. It's dangerous for you to drive that far alone."

"I'm not alone. I've got…Aspen."

"Aspen? Who's that?"

"Classmate. Found her when I was driving out of town." I glance over my shoulder and look at her. She's still sitting in the passenger seat, munching her breakfast sandwich.

"Does she have a license?"

Shit. She has *no* belongings with her. I'm the only one who has a valid driver's license. Meaning I'm the only one who can drive.

"I mean…if we don't get caught, it's fine, right?" I laugh a little, sniffling.

"Honey. You cannot drive from rural Maine all the way to Seattle, or Portland for that matter."

"I can't stay here, Dad."

No way in hell. The entire coast is on fire. I guess they're gonna be rolling out relief workers and the National Guard to help, but why would I want to stay in the middle of this chaos when my family is on the other side of the country?

"Okay, wait a minute, wait a minute." I can hear the panicked shuffling of papers across the desk, then fingers clacking away on a keyboard. "Let's meet at a halfway point, and then I can make the rest of the trip back with you."

"Where?"

"Minneapolis. Upper Midwest."

"O-okay, but Dad I have a car. I mean…if you drive there and I drive there, what are we going to do with the second car?"

"What car are you driving? Your mom's?"

"It's my truck."

"Yeah, no. I'm driving. We can tow that damn thing back if it hasn't fallen apart by the time you get there." Dad lets out a shaky sigh and sniffles. "W-what about this Aspen girl? Does she have friends? Any family that you could stay with?"

"If they did...I mean, they're gone. *Gone*," I whisper, glancing over my shoulder at her again. She's oddly...calm? She just keeps eating and staring at the ground. It's like she's on autopilot. But maybe that's just shock?

"Okay, if that's the case...that's fine. Talk to her, bring her with you; we'll figure it out once we meet up. It'll be safer if you travel together than alone, anyways. People get...crazy in times of crisis."

Yeah, Dad. You don't have to say it. I'm already scared shitless.

"Do you have money?"

"Yes. I have some cash in my wallet, and I-I took Mom's credit card."

"Are you sure you've got enough to make it to Minneapolis?"

"I'm sure." Unless Mom hit her credit limit. But it's not like a couple hundred dollars' worth of gas is going to put us there...right?

"I'll make a deposit to your checking account. Just to make sure you have a backup to pay."

"It's fine for now, Dad. Look, I have to gas up the car, and I have to...try to get some rest. I've been driving since last night."

"Jesus. You poor thing. Riley, I'm so sorry. I'm so..." He chokes up again, and my heart feels like it's breaking.

"I will call you like every other hour, Dad. I promise."

"As long as it doesn't drain your battery. Please, for the love of God, don't let your phone die."

"I won't. I love you, Dad."

"I love you too. So much."

It feels painful to hang up on him first, but I have to. Establishing Minneapolis as the goal feels like lifting a weight off my shoulders. There's an end point to this hell, and I just have to make it there.

I quickly plug the city into Google Maps. *Woof.* It's trying to route us through Canada, and I don't know whether or not we need papers. If we do? We don't got 'em. So that's not an option. We'll have to drive southwest, cut through Ohio, and then move up from there. Which will take...

... a little over twenty-four hours.

Shit.

No, Riley. Do not panic. I spent maybe six hours driving last night. I had to slow down, obviously, since I was driving through towns with literal *fire* running through them. I've already made it to New Hampshire. If I do three eight-hour days, or four six-hour days, we can make it. If the east coast is in a state of chaos, I'm probably not going to be able to drive as long as eight hours, but six is something I can aim for. And little by little, I can make it to Minneapolis.

I glance over my shoulder and look at Aspen, still just eating. I stand up and walk over to her, then show her my phone. She blinks.

"So, my dad lives in Seattle. And he wants me to meet him in Minneapolis."

"Okay," she says quietly, nodding her head.

"Are you...do you know of..." I sigh heavily and lean against the truck. Tigger whines a little. "Look. I don't know...if anyone in our town made it out, right? I mean, if they have, they're probably hours ahead of us. So, to stay on the east coast, especially if it's on fire—"

"—it's on *fire?*"

Oh yeah. She might have missed that part of the conversation. I nod slowly as her eyes widen with shock.

"Yeah. Apparently, all the Titan Tech labs have blown up. My dad thinks it's a terrorist attack."

She leans over and vomits. She does it so fast that I don't even have time to pull back her hair. When she finishes retching out the contents of her shitty breakfast, she wipes her mouth with the back of her hand and shakes her head. I'm feeling a little...weird about this whole situation. Is she nauseous because of shock? Because the sandwich is just as gross as it looks? Or...was what Nathan said yesterday accurate? Is Aspen experiencing morning sickness?

"Sorry." She takes a sip from her water bottle and shakes her head. "I really don't feel well."

"I mean...yeah," I say. Like a stupid person.

We sit in silence for a few minutes. Aspen rubs her stomach and tries to drink a little more water. Beads of sweat form on her forehead and slowly run down her face, she wipes them away with her hand. The same hand that she used to wipe the vomit off her mouth. Gross.

"Here." I lean in, open up the glove compartment, and pass her a bottle of hand sanitizer. "Use this. The bathrooms in there are a bit of a mess. Almost out of soap."

"Thanks." She squeezes out a bit and rubs her hands together. "So. The entire coast is on fire. You're going to Minneapolis."

"*We're* going to Minneapolis. Unless you...have family or friends that you want to stay with?"

Aspen shakes her head. For the first time this morning, she appears to not be in a neutral state of shock. Her expression is sad. She blinks rapidly, as if trying to hold back tears.

"Everyone I knew was back in Little Brook. And if they're all gone, then…" She exhales slowly, shaking her head again. "I think I *may* have a relative, like an a-aunt or something who lives on the west coast, but…"

"Do you know where?"

She bites her lip. "California. San-something or other."

"San…Francisco?"

"I don't think it was that."

"Are there other cities in California that start with San?"

"Uh, yeah. There's San Jose, San Diego, San Luis Obispo… You lived on the west coast, didn't you? Shouldn't you know better than me?"

"Wait a minute. I thought you didn't remember my name. But you remember that I'm from the west coast?"

She shrugs her shoulders. "I mean, yeah. We just all kinda called you Portlandia."

"*Portlandia?*"

She shrugs again, as if that's a sufficient response. Being nicknamed after a mediocre variety show—which most Portlanders *hate,* by the way—is super insulting. It's weird to think that just yesterday I saved someone from literally burning alive, and she apparently never bothered to learn my name. Actually, it's not just weird, it totally sucks. Because now I wonder how often they all made fun of me, and if she just played along with it. And now I'm about to be stuck in a car with this person for days on end. Wonderful. Fantastic. Life couldn't possibly get any better.

"So…to answer your question…I don't have anyone else that I could go to, other than that aunt on the west coast. So, I guess I'm going to go with you to Minneapolis. Are we flying there?"

"Flights are grounded."

"Wow, really?"

"Yeah." I drag my hands over my face. "So…I'm going to gas up the car, maybe let Tigger out one more time, and then we gotta get going. Because if we're fleeing the east coast, I'm sure thousands more will be too. Traffic's going to be insane."

"Okay." She folds up her sandwich in her tinfoil and sets it on the dash, then looks at me expectantly. "Do you mind if I maybe get something else to eat? I think I'd prefer a hot dog instead."

"Uh, yeah, sure, knock yourself out." I pass her the credit card. "Grab me one too, while you're at it."

"Toppings?"

"Just ketchup and mustard. No relish or anything."

"Okay."

As she walks into the gas station, I hop back into the truck and turn on the engine. Finally, some of the cars have begun leaving, and there's an open spot at a pump. I pull up alongside, park, and fill up the tank. Since Aspen's got the credit card, I charge it to my debit. Woof. Almost fifty bucks worth of gas. I really wish that Mom had gotten me that little used Prius like I asked her to.

By the time I finish refueling, Aspen walks back, carrying far more than just a couple of hot dogs. She has Cheetos, coffee—yuck, to go with *hot dogs?*—and a few bags of lemon drops. I arch an eyebrow at her.

"Cheetos are supposed to help with nausea."

"I don't have any…uh…oh, wait, maybe we should get a trash bag or something? Just in case…?"

"Good point." She opens the passenger door and sets the food on her seat. "I'll head back inside and see if they got any."

"Cool. Uh, Aspen…?" I wince, trying to get her attention before she walks away again.

I can't help it. What if she's *actually* pregnant? Isn't it really bad to be pregnant and inhale a ton of smoke? What if her life is in danger and we don't even know it? Should we try to find a hospital to get her checked up? What would happen if we went to a hospital without a parent? Would they just call DHS? Would I not be able to drive back and meet Dad?

"Yeah?" She turns around and places her hands on her hips, a little impatient; or nervous.

"Uh…you sure you're feeling okay, right?"

She stares. "No. Not really. Our whole town burned down last night, I smell like a wildfire, and I just threw up in a gas station parking lot, so I'm not really doing that well. Thanks for asking, though."

Why is she being such a shit? I'm genuinely concerned about her. And look, for as much as I hated Little Brook, it's not like I wanted it to be razed to the ground. Or for my mom to…

No. Stop thinking about that right now. "I'm just wondering because…like…I mean. Are you sure you don't have morning sickness?"

Her eyebrows raise. "Excuse me?"

"I…uh…"

She tosses her hair over her shoulder and shakes her head. "You know, you really shouldn't believe everything you eavesdrop."

"I wasn't eavesdropping. It's not eavesdropping if someone makes a comment loud enough for you to hear in a public place."

"It's eavesdropping if it's a conversation that doesn't concern you."

"Why are you getting so defensive? I'm not going to judge you. I'm just saying, like, if you *were* pregnant, then…we have to worry about your health a little bit more."

"I'm not pregnant, Riley."

"Okay, but like, are you *sure* though?" I clap a hand over my mouth to stifle my word vomit. I'm so tired that my filter has been turned off.

Aspen stares back at me coolly, and for a moment, I could swear that her pupils shrink in size. But then she blinks, turns on her heel, and stomps back into the gas station. As I start to clean off my windshield, a feeling of dread fills my stomach.

Aspen isn't the nice, quiet little person I thought she was. She's actually kind of an asshole.

And now I'm going to be stuck in a car with her for God knows how long.

Awesome.

Day 1 - Afternoon

WE DRIVE FOR MAYBE three more hours until finally, I feel like I can drive no more. I finished all my coffee, but not even the turbulent swirly feeling of the gas station hot dog digesting in my stomach is enough to keep me awake. In fact, I might be the one that needs to puke into a trash bag soon.

Aspen's been sitting in silence most of this time, just staring out the window. Occasionally, she'll pick up my phone to give me directions, but otherwise, things have been pretty shit. Tigger growls at her basically every time she moves, and I can't really do anything about that.

I pull off the freeway and head toward a motel which is, understandably, very crowded. I glance over at Aspen, who looks back at me with that sharp gaze of hers.

"I'm really tired. We need to stop for a while."

She nods. I pull into a parking space and quickly call Dad. I give him my location, the name of the hotel, yadda yadda, just so that he doesn't panic. He actually praises me for stopping.

"Getting some rest will be good for you. You're going to need it for the drive."

I grab my backpack and head inside to talk to the front desk staff, who are disheveled and upset. There're tons of people milling around in the lobby, sipping from water cups and carrying stacks of towels. *Towels. Showering.* Just the thought of a nice hot shower and a nap is luxurious to me, even at a motel as skeevy as this one. Hopefully I don't catch anything funky from this place.

Since I'm underage, I can't rent a room by myself, so I pass my phone to the receptionist so that he can talk to my dad and get his permission. Normally, I'm pretty sure that this wouldn't fly, but I've got a credit card, and this is a bit of a national emergency. The receptionist finishes the call with Dad and passes the phone back to me, along with a set of key cards.

"Checkout is at noon," he says, waving a hand dismissively. Just as soon as I step away from the counter, another group of people approach. Poor guy. This is probably the busiest this place has ever been.

Outside, I find Aspen leaning against the truck. She's examining the dirt underneath her fingernails. Tigger whines in the car, and barks urgently. I quickly help him out of the truck, and pass Aspen a key.

"What room are we?"

She checks the keycard envelope. "Uh… Either A153 or A163. This handwriting is worse than mine."

We wander the lower floor of the building until we reach A153, which just happens to be the last room available on this floor. We unlock the door and step inside. Almost immediately the smell of musty curtains and carpeting hits my nostrils. Oh God. Wait a minute. The carpet is also *on the walls?*

Aspen looks around the room with an expression as dejected as mine. "I feel like I stepped onto the set of *American Hustle,* and it's incredibly underwhelming."

"American *what?*"

"Bradley Cooper, Jennifer Lawrence. 2013. *American Hustle*," she repeats, as if those words are supposed to mean anything. I watch as she walks over to a bed and cautiously sits down. She lifts a pillow and peers curiously at the sheets below, then yanks the mattress off the frame and sticks her head under it.

"Oh God. What are you doing?"

"Checking for bed bugs." She bounces up and down a little bit. When the bed springs squeak, they sound like distant screams. "Wow. This mattress feels awful. Almost prefer sleeping in the passenger seat."

"Almost?"

"The passenger seat is lumpy as hell. This is at least a solid, flat surface. Flatter than I'd like it to be, but oh well."

I sit on the bed and Tigger jumps up beside me. The beds are covered with raggedy quilts that look like they're from a demented Grandma's house. The nightstand and headboard are made of glossy walnut. The longer I sit here, the more I can smell the heavy fumes of lemon-scented furniture polish. At least there's *one* thing they keep clean. I stand up and flick on the TV, but of course, it shows the news, which is all fire and brimstone. I immediately turn it off.

Aspen looks over at me. "You could've just changed the channel."

"Be my guest."

She tries to press the buttons on the remote, but nothing changes on the screen. She flings it down on the bed in disgust.

"Why is this so greasy?"

"Is it furniture polish?"

She shakes her head at me, her eyes wide. If I wasn't so pissed at her, I would laugh. She's had a shitty attitude since this morning, and I was just trying to help her out. Would it have killed her to make conversation with me, or maybe even just say thank you? I feel like it's the bare minimum she could do. But then again, I don't know what to expect from either one of us. We just lost our family and homes. She lost her friends. The last major "tragedy" I could say I experienced in my life is when my Grandma Wanda passed away—and to be honest, I didn't even know her that well. I don't think I know how to grieve. One minute I'm crying and spiraling out of control, the next I feel like I'm having an out-of-body experience, and that my actions aren't really my own. Maybe that's what it's like for her, too?

Aspen pulls back the covers and crawls under them. She stares at the ceiling and drags her hands over her face. I don't know if I should say anything to her right now. Maybe it'd be good to give her some space. Plus—and I don't know if I've emphasized this enough—I really need a shower. I leave her in the room while I walk back outside to grab my duffel, and some of the water bottles we picked up at another gas station about an hour ago. When I get back inside, she's still cocooned in the mess of nasty blankets.

In the bathroom, I flick on the light. It sputters for a minute, and then finally, illuminates the tiny space. It's floor to ceiling pink tile; the toilet *and* the bathtub. Speaking of the bathtub, on the two little shelves meant for soap and shampoo bottles, there's melted candles. They're so old that there's no wick left on them. They can't honestly have recycled these candles over and over again, right?

You know what? I better just stop asking questions I don't want to know the answers to.

With a heavy sigh, I set a clean change of clothes on the toilet and look around. This motel is so dingy it doesn't even offer complimentary shampoos. In my rush to leave my house, I didn't bother to pack my own so I'm still going to smell nasty, but hopefully I'll at least feel a little cleaner. I peel off my greasy, smoky clothes and throw them on the ground and turn on the water, which like the light, sputters before springing to life. Thankfully, the water pressure here is nice, and the heat is amazing. Within moments there's steam covering the mirror.

The hot water hits my skin, scalding me, so I turn down the temperature, and finally, get it adjusted. My shoulders are so stiff and sore that when I massage them, I can feel the individual bulging muscles struggling to pull apart. This road trip is going to do a number on my body. Even when I've finished rinsing my hair, I remain under the water for a few more minutes, until I can actually feel my body relax.

When I step out, I grab a towel and carefully shake it out before wrapping it around my body. No bugs, thank God. The towels are still old and ratty though. It makes me miss the ones we have at home. Fluffy, soft, warm to wrap around your body. Although Mom was in total control over our move to Maine, she at least let me pick out the towels and the décor for my bathroom. We spent an entire day wandering through Bed, Bath, and Beyond, laughing at those tacky wooden signs that say things like *"Bless This Mess"* in Papyrus font and caressing sheets of all different thread counts. The happiness of that memory causes my eyes to water once more. Leave it to me to cry over a friggin' towel. After drying off my body, I put on my clean clothes: fresh underwear, a new pair of jeans, and a t-shirt.

When I exit the bathroom, Tigger is snarling. He's standing across from where Aspen sits, the hair on the back of his neck bristling. I scold him and grab his collar, trying to pull him away from her. Aspen watches me soberly. When he finally relaxes, she gently stretches her hand out to him. I open my mouth in protest, but she shakes her head.

"He's gotta get used to me, right? He just doesn't trust me."

Tigger continues to snarl as her fingers inch closer to his face. I keep my grip tight on his collar so that he doesn't suddenly lunge forward and bite her. When her hand is dangling in front of his nose, he tentatively leans forward and sniffs, his lips still drawn back. She places her fingertips right against his nose. Slowly, but surely, he begins to relax. He even licks her politely. At that moment, I let go of his collar, and he pushes closer to her. She strokes his head slowly and soothingly. A few moments pass. She smiles.

"Good boy."

"I guess he just doesn't like strangers."

"Well, that, and I probably reek."

"You said it first, not me."

She smirks. "I'd shower but I don't have a change of clothes."

"Oh." I say, feeling very stupid. That's right. I'm the only one with any belongings. How do I keep forgetting that? "Do you want to try to borrow some of my stuff?"

"I don't think we're the same size." She averts her gaze. "No offense."

Why do people always say that when they know that it doesn't make it any less offensive? I mean, I get her point. She's tiny, rail-thin; the envy of every 1990s model. I'm taller and as my mom liked to put it, "curvaceous." I call it "half-assed thicc," because my hips are wider than my shoulders, and yet somehow my ass is flatter than a pancake. Maybe it's from sitting on a bike for so long. I have a tiny waist and flat stomach, which is nice, but my boobs are big. I can't fit into any one size—my pants range from eight-twelves, and my shirts are either too-tight mediums or loosey-goosey large. I think I have the most awkward body type in the world.

"What do you want to do?"

She yawns and stretches. "I don't know. There's a strip mall on the other side of the road. We could look through there. See if there's anything. You don't mind buying me some clothes, right?"

"N-no. It's fine. We can go over and take a look. It's just I have to take Tigger. I can't leave him here all by himself. He's anxious enough as it is."

She nods. "I guess when I go in the store you can just stand outside and wait for me or something."

"Sure. Sounds good."

I unwrap my hair from its wet towel, let it fall to my shoulders, and take in my reflection in our room's full-length mirror. Black-blue rings of exhaustion line the undersides of my swollen eyes. I feel like shit, and I look like it too. All the more reason to get these errands done as soon as possible.

I grab Tigger's leash, clip it to his collar, and we head out the door.

THIS LITTLE JUNCTION IS filled with some of the most random highway stops I think I've ever seen. Across the street from the motel, as Aspen said, is a strip mall. It's filled with various random stores: a kitschy Thai food restaurant, an antique shop, and one of those overpriced indoor kid party places that have inflatables. The parking lot is decrepit; chunks of asphalt are torn from the ground and lie on the sidewalks. Various cars are lined up bumper to bumper outside of the McDonald's and the Jack in the Box.

Aspen locates a thrift shop at the end of the mall, and while she goes inside to look for clothes, I take Tigger on a walk around the outskirts of the parking lot. He's looking a little moody, his head hanging low to the ground. I can tell he's missing our morning run. He keeps sniffing at the grass with this pathetically sad expression on his face. Poor Tigger. Poor me. Poor us.

When Aspen emerges from the thrift shop, she's wearing a new pair of bell bottom jeans, an off-the-shoulder white crop top, and an oversized color block button-up. Even in the most bizarre clothing choices, this girl looks like a fashion icon. She passes the credit card back to me and boinks Tigger on the nose with her finger.

"What'd you do with your old clothes?"

"I asked the owner to throw them out. I mean, they're all covered in dirt and blood and stuff. I don't need to hold onto them." She runs a hand through her hair and glances in her bag. "I got some pajamas, another pair of jeans, and some other shirts. I think we'll be good enough."

"What about a sweatshirt?"

She smiles. "Feel this." She grabs my hand and places it on her button-up shirt. It's thick and somewhat rough to the touch. "It's corduroy. Durable. Warm. Don't need a sweatshirt when I can lounge around in this all day." She runs her hand through her hair again, shaking her head. "Wish that they had a hat or something though. Scrunchies. Anything to get my hair out of my face."

"I think the gas station probably has hair ties."

"True." She looks around the parking lot, then back at me. "So, what do you want to do?"

"Get something to eat. Sleep. Try not to cry."

"Sounds like a plan." She exhales slowly. "But our options seem to be a little backed up right now." She points to the Thai food place next door. "Want to try it?"

"Do I want to get sick, you mean?"

She frowns. "Don't be mean. Just because it's a strip mall doesn't mean the food is bad."

"That's exactly what it means when a restaurant is in a strip mall."

"Or maybe it just means that this is where they could afford to set up shop. Look, do you want to eat here or not?"

I want her to check her attitude. But instead, I bite my tongue and nod slowly. I'm assuming that these next few days are going to be filled with eating fast food. It'd be nice to get something to eat that's hopefully fresh.

"Can you go inside and get a menu? I'm going to have to stay out here with Tigger."

She nods and within two minutes she returns with not just a menu, but a staff member who has a fold up table and chairs. He smiles at us apologetically.

"I'm sorry about what happened. It's just truly awful."

I know he's being kind, and while I was grateful for that sort of kindness this morning at the gas station, I now feel awkward for being pitied. He ducks back inside and returns with a paper bowl and a bottle of water, setting it on the ground for Tigger.

"Let me know if you have any questions. I'm going to grab those bubble teas for you real quick."

I look at Aspen, who is looking through the menu with a coy smile. I stare at her.

"Bubble teas?"

"They make them in house. Oh, sorry. I ordered one for you. Green matcha. Now…" She lays the menu flat on the table and points to some of the highlighted specials. "They've got a Massaman curry here. Delicious. Pad Thai if you want to play it safe. Ooh, and these fresh little shrimp rolls."

"How do you know so much about Thai food?"

She stares at me. "You know that there was a Thai restaurant in Little Brook, right?"

"Seriously?"

"Yeah. It was run by the…" Her voice grows quiet. "The Saelims. Their daughter Kannika was in our grade."

"I don't think I knew her."

"I don't think you really knew anyone." Aspen's expression is cold. She lifts the menu back up and sifts through the pages. "You kinda kept to yourself. And apparently eavesdropped on all of our conversations."

Okay, *now* I'm pissed. "Again, can you call it eavesdropping when you have those conversations in public, out loud? It's not like you and your friends ever whispered about anything. Everyone could hear you."

"But only you chose to pay attention."

"If you think I was the only one, that's really rich, Aspen. No one could tune you and your friends out."

She blinks, and I see tears form in her eyes. But she doesn't burst out sobbing. She swallows, and her voice is low and thin.

"Well now you don't have to worry about that anymore, do you?" She slaps the menu on the table and stands. "I'm going to use the restroom."

"Aspen—" It's too late. She's already run back inside. I stroke the top of Tigger's head and try to ignore the tears rising in my own eyes. I know that I should maybe try to be nicer. We're experiencing the same kind of losses, and maybe hers are slightly worse because that was her actual hometown. But I can't help but feel…*used* isn't the correct word. I guess I had this perception that she was nice and innocent, but apparently, she was just one of many people making fun of me behind my back. I felt nervous moving to a new school; worried that I wouldn't fit in. And I was right to be worried, I guess. Her biting remarks about my loneliness and inability to make friends just cut a little too deep.

In two minutes, the waiter returns with the matcha bubble tea, and I'm grateful for the sugary drink. I take a sip or two and munch on the tapioca balls. My friends and I used to grab bubble tea every Friday after school, before going to hit up a movie or play games at someone's house. *Oh shit.* Caia. Khalil. I forgot to call them.

I immediately dial Caia's number, and as soon as she answers, she's sobbing into the phone. For a few minutes, we both sit there, her crying, and me trying to reassure her.

"You asshole, why didn't you call me?" she sobs, gasping for air. "Oh my God, are you okay?"

"No." I hear my voice warble, but I quickly shut that shit down. I'm so tired that I can't cry anymore today. "My mom. She…"

"Oh my God," Caia sobs. "Riley, I'm so sorry. I'm so, so sorry."

"I'm trying to get back to the west coast. My dad is going to meet me in Minneapolis and we're driving back to Seattle together."

"Did Tigger make it?"

"He made it." I smile a little. "He was at home with me all night, so…"

"What the hell happened?"

"I can't even explain, Caia. I just…" I squeeze my eyes shut. "Jesus, it was… I don't even know if what I saw was real or if it was an illusion."

"Was it a terrorist attack?"

"I mean, if it was, it's unlike anything I've ever seen before." Images flash through my mind. The fires. The roar. That fire truck somersaulting over the buildings on Main Street. "It wasn't a human."

"What? What do you mean? Didn't the lab blow up the town?"

Aspen approaches the door and stares at me as she takes her seat. She takes a sip of her tea and avoids making direct eye contact. Her eyes are blotchy and red.

"I mean the lab blew up, but I don't think that's what…" I shake my head. "Caia, I don't…"

"What do you mean? What happened?"

"Caia, I'm really sorry, I have to go, babe. I've been driving since last night, and I'm trying to grab food with a friend."

"A friend?"

"She was in the same class as me. I'm so sorry, I can explain more later, but right now, I gotta eat so I can get some rest."

"No, it's fine. Please don't apologize. Jesus, Riley. If anything, I'm the one who's sorry." She laughs a little, and then cries. Her sniffles sound staticky. "Please. Please just keep me posted, okay? And if you need anything, anything at all…"

"Could you tell Khalil and the others that I'm okay? I've kinda had shitty service, so I can't post on Insta or Snap right now."

"Yes, yes, of course. I love you."

"I love you too. Please stay safe."

When I hang up the phone, oddly enough, I feel a little better. I was worried that hearing her crying would send me into a panic, as it usually does, but it didn't. I sit there and sniffle and stroke Tigger's head and do my best to calm down. Each deep breath I take sends a shudder down my spine.

Aspen looks up at me, and for the first time, her expression softens. But she doesn't bother to say anything, not until after the restaurant worker brings us a plate of the shrimp rolls Aspen pointed out earlier.

"A relative?"

"No. My friend. My best friend." I sniffle and take another sip of my tea. It suddenly feels too rich on my empty stomach, and I have to take another deep breath to keep the nausea down. "From back home."

"Oh." Aspen takes a long sip through her straw. "That's… nice."

"You don't have to make small talk with me if you don't want to."

Aspen rolls her eyes. "Okay." She glances at her menu and places her palms flat against the table. Takes a deep breath. "I'm sorry… if I…" Her eyes water, and she chokes on her words. She looks at me, solemnly. "I feel like I'm in a nightmare and I have to find a way to wake up."

We both start drinking from our teas, furiously trying to blink away the tears in our eyes. I have no idea why, but when I'm drinking something, it's like I can't even cry. We sit there, pathetically sipping our drinks, until our waiter returns to ask us our orders. I pick the Pad Thai, Aspen the Massaman curry. When he leaves, we finally manage to look at each other again.

"I don't remember what happened last night," Aspen says flatly, quietly. "But I heard you say something to your friend. Something about…"

"You're going to think I'm crazy. Honestly, I probably *was* crazy."

"What do you mean?"

"Like…" I laugh nervously, rubbing my hands together. "You know how when you're scared—when you're traumatized—your brain tends to like, make things up? Create things that aren't there?"

"It's never happened to me before."

"Me either. And here I thought I lived a sheltered life."

Aspen stares at me. "What did you see last night, Riley?"

I swallow down more of my tea; chew on some of the boba. Her gaze is unwavering, intense. Part of me wonders if she heard it too, and is just trying to figure out what I am trying to figure out: was it real? Or was it an illusion?

"Well, at first I didn't see anything. But…I heard something. This giant roar." I drum my fingertips against the tabletop, trying to find the words. "When I was standing outside on my front lawn… I-I could see Main Street from there. And I watched this fire truck come racing down the road, and then it disappeared behind a building, and then it just went flying."

Her eyes widen. "Flying?"

"Flying. Like it was launched into the air w-with a springboard or something. It flew above the buildings, and then came crashing down."

"An explosion."

"N-no, Aspen. Explosions don't sound like that. It didn't sound anything like the other explosions I heard yesterday."

"Morbid."

"Huh?"

"That you've heard enough explosions by now that you know what one really sounds like." She folds her hands together, and takes a deep breath in. "That's terrifying."

"And you didn't hear it? You don't remember anything?"

She shakes her head; leans back in her seat. "No. I…remember going to the game. I remember…Helena and Bennie…uh…doing their hair in the bathroom. Bennie was trying to get her stupid ponytail to curl, and she kept dropping Helena's iron in the sink. And that's…that's all I remember."

"Something…happened to you."

"What do you mean?"

"I don't…I don't know. I was on my way out of town, and then you suddenly stumbled out into the road like a zombie. It was fucking scary. Your clothes were all tattered; looked like you had gotten in a fight with Wolverine."

"Bold of you to assume that I would lose to Wolverine." It's a joke, but she doesn't smile. Just takes another sip of her bubble tea and shrugs her shoulders. That catatonic look returns to her eyes…glazed over and harsh. "I don't remember anything after going to the game and getting ready for it with my friends. But if something did happen to me, I guess it's better to not remember it."

At first, I'm confused by the coldness of her statement: the matter-of-fact way that she dismisses that something *really* bad happened to her. But then the tears water in her eyes again, and she buries her face in her hands and sobs for a few minutes. When she looks up at me, she smiles through eyes full of tears.

"I'm glad I don't remember what happened. Because then I can just remember them as we all were. Laughing and bitching about stupid shit." She sniffles, nods affirmatively, and wipes her eyes again. "I'm glad."

She places her shaking hands on the table, and I reach across to hold them. My fingers loop through hers. Delicate. Small. Fragile.

"I'm sorry for your loss."

She swallows back a lump of tears. "I'm sorry for yours."

Day 1 - Night

AFTER EATING LUNCH, WE trek back to the motel room. While I flop down on the bed in a state of exhaustion, Aspen makes her way to the bathroom, and takes a shower. I lay there for about fifteen minutes, trying to sleep, but instead, listening to the running water. Tigger lies on the bed beside me, equally exhausted and already asleep. I make a mental note to remind myself to feed him dinner once he wakes up.

THUNK! "Shit!"

I raise my head from the mattress and shuffle over to the bathroom to knock on the door.

"Everything alright in there?"

"Yeah, uh…sorry. It's slippery in here."

She opens the door, and a cloud of steam escapes the room. Her blond hair drips down her shoulders, and she struggles to keep her towel wrapped around her body. Almost instinctively my eyes trail downward, but my leering is stopped when I hear her sharp voice.

"Do you have a tampon?"

"Oh shit. Uh, yeah, lemme check." I rifle through my backpack to find a few tampons and pass them to her.

She glares at the yellow wrappers. "Ultra-light absorbency?"

"I don't like tampons." Maybe I'm just a baby but using those has always felt kinda uncomfortable. Also, every time I've used one, I've been hyper aware of it, simply because I'm afraid of dying from toxic shock syndrome. Personally, I'd only ever use a tampon if I was going swimming.

"I'll walk over to the gas station and buy some later." She turns and faces the mirror once more, and I notice something strange. On her back, curling around her shoulder, a piece of skin; thin and gray like a fish flake.

"Aspen, you got something on your…"

She twists her head over her shoulder. "What?"

"Like…skin?"

She reaches her hand around and touches it. "Oh." Her fingernails dig into her shoulder, and she gently peels off the long strip. "I get really bad sunburns sometimes."

"Oh."

Aspen stares at me. "Riley."

"Yeah?"

"Can you let me get changed?"

"Oh. Y-yeah, sorry." I shut the door, and heat floods my face instantaneously.

I stumble back to my bed and groan into my pillow, wishing I could shrink underneath the covers and disappear. Subtlety is not something I do well. I was totally checking her out and she *knew* I was. At least she didn't yell at me—although she would have had every right to.

She opens the door again, and I can see from the icy look in her eyes that she's still tense. My heart sinks to the bottom of my stomach, knowing that I've likely just made everything even worse. How typical of me: to ruin something just as it's getting better. She straightens out her shirt and looks at me.

"Are you gay?"

"Me? Gay?" Playing dumb is not my strong suit either, and clearly Aspen already knows that. She rolls her eyes and pops her lips, then shakes her head.

"I'm just letting you know you're not my type."

"Well, duh. You like dudes, right?"

Aspen's lips form a teasing smile. "And girls."

"A-and girls?" I don't know why, but I'm a little taken aback by her confidence. I grew up in Portland—very much its own gay haven—but even there I hesitated to say I was bi, stammered through my sentences when asked by Grandma Lucy if I found any boys cute, and dodged questions about my sexuality when talking to my aunts and uncles.

Coming out as gay is one thing, coming out as bi is a whole other playing field. People feel more comfortable talking shit to your face and hypothesizing reasons why you are the way you are. For example, my Aunt Mildred told me I was bi because I was raised by indecisive parents, and my Uncle Ben—who is actually gay—told me that I was looking for attention. In fact, I think the only extended relative who readily accepted me was my Aunt Cheryl, Mom's sister, who had (perhaps a bit too enthusiastically) offered to plan a coming out party for me. But here Aspen is, having grown up in the middle of rural conservative nowhere, and replying so confidently; proudly. I'm jealous.

"You weren't the only queer person in Little Brook, Portlandia." She musses up her still damp hair. "Or are you one of those 'bi people don't exist' assholes?"

"No, actually, I'm bi too. Just barely."

"Barely?"

"Like…I *mostly* like girls. Some boys. But mostly girls."

Honestly, I'm somewhat hoping that I grow out of the attraction to men—I'm sure if I admitted that out loud though, Aspen might lecture me and say I have internalized biphobia. Honestly, it's not that I hate men—I had a lot of guy friends growing up and got along with them really well. And I'm definitely, 100 percent, attracted to at least some of them. But my relationships with men have left a lot to be desired, and my attraction for women is just so much more intense. Sometimes the attraction to men feels…inconvenient. It doesn't mean that I'm ashamed of who I am or anything like that, but I'd be lying if I didn't wake up sometimes and think being a lesbian would be easier. At least that way I could be rejected from one gender within the dating pool, rather than literally all of them.

"Still bi."

"I know, I'm just joking…" I shake my head. "I wasn't checking you out."

"Good, because it's impolite to stare." She smirks and flops down on bed.

"Weren't you going to get hair ties?"

"I'm too tired. Weren't you going to get some sleep?"

"Yeah."

It's funny; I've felt so exhausted, but now when faced with the chance to sleep, I'm almost afraid. My heartrate is picking up and my palms are clammy. Even when I sink underneath the cool covers, and when she shuts off the lights, my mind still races. After laying in the darkness for thirty minutes, I think I can smell smoke. I sniffle and take in deep breaths, over and over again. I look over at Tigger, fast asleep, and rub my hands over his belly. If Tigger feels safe, then I should too. I know that the smoke isn't there. I take a deep breath and close my eyes, but my face feels hot; and orange lights flicker in the darkness. My heart is pounding so hard that it feels like I'm going to throw up. Hot tears force my eyes open, and I sit up in bed.

Aspen rolls over and looks at my phone on the nightstand. She passes it to me.

"Unlock it."

"Why?"

"Just do it."

I unlock it and pass it back to her. She types in something, pauses, and then suddenly, I hear the sound of quiet rainfall. Thunder echoes in the background.

"Sometimes you just need something that can drown out all the noise."

"Just…thunderstorms?"

"Yeah. There's also some with fans or white noise machines. I almost always slept with a fan on back home." She fidgets. "When your brain gets *that* loud, you gotta drown it out."

I rest my head against the pillow again and listen to the soft sounds of the rain. Almost immediately, I feel relaxed. I run my hand over Tigger's body again and close my eyes.

WHILE SLEEP CAME EASILY, it also came fitfully. In my dreams I pictured myself running through the woods behind my house, and that everything around me was on fire. I remember how the closer I came, the further away the houses were. At the end of the dream, I could see Tigger and my mom in the bedroom windows. Tigger scratched at the window and barked, and Mom wouldn't stop screaming my name. But just as I got to the house to rescue them, Aspen came traipsing around the corner. Her skin cracked, her eyes white; zombified. The last thing I saw was her face, pressed close against mine, and her cold hands, electrifying like ice, cupping my cheeks.

Tigger's growling snaps me out of the nightmare. It takes me a few moments to realize that I'm in the motel room. Tigger's ears are pulled back flat against his skull, and his eyes are glinting maliciously in the light. *Wait.* Light? I turn my head toward the window. Aspen's bed is empty. Outside, through the blinds, a small white light bounces around.

I lean over to flick on the lamp, but a familiar voice stops me. "Don't."

Panicked, I look around in the darkness and notice Aspen crouched beneath our window.

"What're you doing?"

She presses a finger to her lips and shakes her head, staring out the window. I don't know if it's because of the flashlight or what, but I could swear her eyes are glowing. The light eventually bounces away, and I breathe a sigh of relief.

"Keep the light off."

"What's going on?"

"I got up to pee and saw someone looking through all the windows."

"Thieves?"

"Thieves would've broken in by now."

I swallow a lump of fear rising in my throat; pull the covers closer to my face. "W-what do we do? Do we call someone?"

"No. Whoever they were, they didn't find what they were looking for." Aspen carefully crawls over to her bed and climbs in.

My mind trails back to last night. The rest stop. The people in the SUV. They couldn't have followed us here, right? That wouldn't have been possible?

Tigger jumps off the bed and wanders over to the door. He whines a little. I check the clock. Two in the morning. Poor boy. He hasn't peed for hours—and I just remembered that I forgot to feed him dinner, because he fell asleep right away. I grab his leash off the nightstand and wander over to the door.

"Riley, what the hell?"

"He has to go out."

"Someone is trying to break into the motel rooms. Don't leave."

"He can't pee on the floor."

"Smell this place. Many people have peed in here, *many* times."

"Aspen, *stop*." I clip the leash to his collar.

She throws back the covers. "Fine. Shit. I'll come with you."

I don't protest—I'm kinda freaked out. We both slip on our shoes and shuffle outside. The air is crisp and cold; my breath fogs as I take in a few shuddery breaths. Although I've been sleeping since early afternoon, my body is still sluggish and sore. I yawn and rub my eyes, and carefully lead Tigger over to the grass. Aspen follows close behind.

After sniffing around, Tigger stops to do his business on a trampled patch of grass. I look out toward the parking lot, and instantly, my heart stops in my chest. SUV. Brand new. Sitting in the motel parking lot. I know it wasn't there earlier. I tug on Aspen's sleeve.

"We gotta go."

"What?"

"We gotta pack up the car and go."

She stares. "Right now?"

"Right now. I think someone followed us here."

"What?"

"Last night, w-we were chased out of this rest stop by this brand-new SUV. I *know* that's the same car."

"You're sure?"

"Look at the parking lot. A-all the cars here? Dirty. This is the only clean one."

Aspen glances over her shoulder at the car again, then shrugs and turns back to me. "Okay. Let me handle it."

"What? How?"

"I'm gonna go talk to the front desk and let them know. Head back to the room, okay?"

"O-okay."

My grip tightens on Tigger's leash, and Aspen takes off in the direction of the front desk. I don't know why I agreed to split up, but I'm too freaked out to do anything other than panic. My head is pounding. I slowly creep back to the room and open the door with my keycard. Once inside, I gather up my things; check the bathroom to pick up any misplaced toiletries and cram them into the backpack, and before I leave the room, I shake out a little food and water into Tigger's bowl. He graciously wolfs down the kibble. There's a knock at the door and I look over at the window. My heart throbs. I swallow and approach the door, fists clenched, and look through the peephole. But it isn't Aspen that I see.

A tall man, long and slender, dressed in a black suit, peers back at me through the hole. His mouth and nose are obscured by a mask. I clap a hand over my mouth to stifle my scream. Tigger is immediately on his feet, barking, the fur on his back and tail bristling. The man pounds on the door again and shines his flashlight through the window. I scramble over to the phone by the nightstand and press the button for the front desk. But there's no dial tone. I sit on the bed, my entire body shaking. A light flicks on outside, and the man stops pounding, his shadow moves away from the window. I can hear the confused murmurings of other motel guests. Briefly, I stand, but my shaking knees bring me to the floor. My lip wobbles, and I start crying.

Aspen opens the door. "What happened? Are you okay?"

"H-he tried to break in. Some guy. In black. Mask."

"Where did he go?"

"I don't know," I sob, gulping back tears.

"Okay. Get our stuff and get in the car." She comes over, firmly grasps my arms, and effortlessly lifts me to my feet. "Give me the keys."

"Y-you don't have your license on you—"

"*Riley. Keys. Now.*" Her voice is an urgent, low growl. I have never heard her speak like that, ever.

She grabs the food bowls along with Tigger's leash and urgently ushers us out the door. Motel guests are standing around, watching us, their faces a blur. Aspen says nothing to them; only keeps pushing me toward the truck. She whips open the car door and places me in the passenger side, shoving Tigger in the back.

But she doesn't get in the driver's seat. Instead, she stomps away, and I see her pass behind me in the rearview mirror before she disappears. Tigger whines urgently and I can hear the blood rushing in my ears. What in the hell is she doing?

Within a few moments, she comes sprinting back to the car, and hops in the driver's seat. She tears out of the parking lot fast, and as we exit, I see the SUV. In the glint of the streetlight, I notice that its tires are deflating. Huge, gaping holes.

I look over at with wide eyes. "What the hell did you do?!"

She doesn't respond; just grips the steering wheel and leans forward. I glance over my shoulder, and I can see not one, but *two* men in black sprint over to the SUV. They throw up their arms, clearly pissed off.

"You slashed their tires, Aspen!"

"Because I didn't want them following us, RI-LEY." She barrels for the freeway entrance ramp. "Get your phone up. Get Maps up. You gotta tell me where to go."

I fumble in my backpack for my phone and plug in the destination. "Stay on this. Exit's not coming up for another twenty miles."

"Alright. Let's hope we can put those assholes behind us."

"I should be driving—"

"Riley, seriously, *stop!* Just let me drive for a while, okay?"

"You don't have a license and if we get pulled over, we are fucked. So yes, I have to drive!"

She scoffs, shakes her head, and presses her foot down on the accelerator. The speedometer climbs higher and higher. She's pushing eighty. The engine grinds, and Tigger whines fearfully. Aspen's eyes, narrowed into angry slits, glow in the faint light. Her fingers tightly curl around the steering wheel, her knuckles as white as the moon looming overhead.

"ASPEN! Pull over! Right now!"

She slams her foot down on the brake, and swerves for the shoulder. She pulls to a stop, leaving a plume of dust behind us. I throw open my passenger door and Tigger whines anxiously. Aspen, huffing and puffing, gets out of her seat and winds around the front of the car.

"I've had it with your shitty attitude."

"Same here."

"*No.* I tell you that someone followed us to the motel; you run away. You left me, *twice*, when someone dangerous is trying to break in. And then you slash their tires—we'll be lucky if they don't call the cops on us!"

"I was trying to help!"

"*I'm fucking scared, Aspen!*" I screech as tears fall down my cheeks. "You can't leave me! Not when I need you! And you *have* to stop fighting with me!"

I hate to admit that I need her. But I do. I can't make this trip by myself. I can't escape a bunch of creeps by myself. I need her, and I need her help, but I'm so tired of feeling like every conversation is an uphill battle.

Her face softens. She gives a stiff nod and looks at the ground. "I'm sorry." She looks back up. "But we gotta go."

I nod and climb into the driver's seat. She buckles up and leans back with a heavy sigh. I signal, and pull off the road, heading toward our destination. I glance over, and I notice her picking at her fingernails. There's blood underneath them. She pushes back her cuticles, and attempts to dig out the fresh, bright red blood. Weird.

"How did you slash their tires anyways?"

She stares out the window. I think she's pretending not to hear me. But I'm not going to bother her. I think I'm too afraid to ask again. I shift my eyes back to the endless road.

Day 2 - Morning

AS THE SUN SLOWLY crawls over the horizon, my exhaustion sinks in again. Through bleary eyes, I struggle to see the road ahead of me. Aspen, who's been curled up on the passenger seat, instantly notices when I start to drowsily swerve to one side of the highway.

"Riley. Please let me drive."

"I can't."

"I will go the speed limit; I promise. But we have to keep going," she says, sitting up. She points to a road sign as we pass. "Pull off here. We can get breakfast and change places."

I don't argue with her; I'm way too tired to. I flick on my turn signal and peel off the highway, then pull into a nearby gas station. This gas station is conjoined to a diner, an old-school one with a red and white checkered exterior. I can't look at it for too long otherwise my eyes will bleed. I park the car and flop back with a heavy sigh.

"Come on. Let's get you something to eat, and then you can nod off."

I roll down the windows and sluggishly drag myself out of my seat; I walk over to try to let Tigger out, but Aspen intercepts me.

"Go in and sit down. I'll take him out."

I place my keys in her hand and shuffle inside the restaurant. It's a sit-yourself establishment, kinda hazy, with lots of steam wafting out from the kitchen. A woman, presumably in her twenties, with smudged black eyeliner pops her gum and smiles as I walk past.

"How many?"

I hold up a peace sign. Too tired to speak. She rolls her eyes and nods, then follows me over to a booth covered in crumbs. She wipes them off with her bare hand. When I glance down at her chest, I can see her nametag: June.

"Guess night shift 'forgot' again," she mutters to me, handing me a wrinkly, laminated menu. "Want anything to drink?"

"Apple juice?"

"Apple juice it is. Where's your friend?" She peers out the window and smiles. "Aww! Cutie! That your dog?"

"Yeah. But we'll leave him in the truck."

She shrugs. "Bring him in here. I don't care."

"Isn't that like…a health code violation?"

"I won't tell if you don't."

I smile. "Thanks."

"You bet. Any idea what your friend would like?"

"Probably some coffee."

"I'll be right back. And I'll let her know to bring the dog in."

I watch as our waitress exits the restaurant and eagerly bounds over to Aspen. She drops to her knees and immediately begins petting Tigger, who is all too eager for affection. She guides them back inside the restaurant and over to where we're sitting.

"I ordered you a coffee."

"Dope," she says, sliding into the seat across from me. "This is so comfy."

"Compared to the truck? Yeah."

I pass her one of the menus and she eagerly flips it open, scanning over the possibilities with eager eyes.

"They have a Monte Cristo."

"Never had one."

"What are you getting?"

"Probably pancakes."

"Pancakes sound awesome. But I'm feeling a little more carnivorous than usual today."

Our waitress returns with our drinks, along with a small bowl of water for Tigger. She places her hands on the table, smiling.

"So, where y'all from?"

Aspen and I both exchange a look before turning back to her.

"Small town in Maine."

"Oh, *Maine*? Like where those explosions happened? Well, I mean they've been happening everywhere, but that little town in Maine had the worst of it."

She stares at us for a couple of moments while we sit in dead silence. Recognition slowly spreads across her face.

"Oh no. Oh, I'm so sorry."

For some reason—maybe it's from the way she lost her smile, or how her brown eyes are full of pity, but I instantly tear up. To my surprise, Aspen reaches her hand across the table and squeezes mine. She looks up at the waitress.

"We're just trying to find our families."

"Oh. Oh my God, all by yourselves?"

"We're meeting up with my dad. So…all we gotta do is make it to Minneapolis."

For a moment, Aspen's eyes flash, but she shakes her head and looks up at June with a tight smile before ordering our food. June rushes off to put the order in, leaving us alone. Aspen smirks at my drink choice.

"Apple juice. Solid. Like the Jessie Reyez song."

"Like who?"

"You gotta get out more." She tears open a tub of creamer and pours it into her coffee. "You didn't get my *American Hustle* reference either."

"What?"

"*American Hustle.* Jennifer Lawrence. Bradley Cooper. That lady from *Enchanted.*"

"You mean Amy Adams?"

"Okay so you know who Amy Adams is, but not *American Hustle*, arguably one of her biggest roles."

"I've only ever seen her in *Enchanted.*"

"Oh Riley." She sighs dramatically. "You wound me."

"You're not a film nerd, are you?"

"Is it time for me to come out of the closet?" She blinks, leans in, and whispers, "I'm a film nerd."

I laugh. I have no idea how she has so much energy at six in the morning—oh wait, yes I do. Because she's been napping for most of the three hours we've been driving today.

"So, do you want to be a critic? Like Roger Ebert or something?"

"Girl, no. I want to direct. I wanna be the next Kathryn Bigelow. But for like, horror movies and shit."

"Horror?"

She smiles. "Yeah. Why?"

"You…seem too sunshiny of a person to be into horror."

"Sorry. I left my Goth clothes at home." She flinches. It's a funny joke, but it reminds me exactly how hard it is. Everything feels like we're walking on eggshells right now. But I appreciate her trying so hard. It's like today she's making an effort.

I chuckle. "So, what are your favorites?"

"*Ginger Snaps, The Blair Witch Project, Pulse,* and *Jennifer's Body.*"

"Ahh yes, *Jennifer's Body.* Every bi girl's sexual awakening."

"Not mine. *The Mummy* trilogy.

"Never seen it."

"*Riley.*"

"What? I've never seen it."

"Oh my God. Wait a minute. How many queer movies have you seen?"

"Few and far in between."

Aspen spreads her hands. "Okay. *But I'm A Cheerleader?*"

"Is that the name of the movie?"

"Oh Jesus. *Riley.* Okay. *Moonlight?*"

"No."

"*Pariah?*" Each question builds with more desperation, and although I know that I'm sure to disappoint her, I keep going.

"No."

"Okay we're getting nowhere. Which ones *have* you seen?"

"*Blue is the Warmest Color.*"

"Oh no."

"What's wrong with it?"

"We can't talk about that right now."

"What? Why?"

"There's too much to unpack." She shakes her head again and takes a loud, long sip of her coffee. "I can't believe you watched that. It's like, X-rated, y'know."

I shrugged. "My mom didn't care about that. She was letting me watch R-rated movies when I was nine."

"My dad wouldn't let me watch anything above a PG rating in our household."

"Your dad?" I don't know why, but my throat runs dry. *Her dad. Her family. Dead like my mom.* I don't know much about Aspen's family—if she had any siblings, or what her parents were like. I think I only saw her dad once, and that was during summer orientation. He looked like the dude from that sad farmer and wife portrait. What was it? *American Gothic.* That's kinda how the dude looked, but with a little more hair, and dressed in a far more expensive suit. Obviously, Aspen didn't get her looks from him. Thank God. Oh wait, shit, he's dead. I shouldn't think those things. Or is it because he's dead that I can get away with thinking those things?

She nods. "Yeah. He was always kind of a hard ass. 'Course, when I got older and he got busier, he loosened up a lot. Or ignored me. I don't know."

"You...weren't close?"

There's something off about the way that she looks back at me. "Both unfortunately close, and yet, distant."

June swings by our table again and drops off our food; she also brings Tigger a plate of scrambled eggs. He eagerly wolfs them down before I have a chance to stop him.

"Oh, it's okay! Dogs can eat eggs. Plain eggs, of course. They're good for their coat. Makes them shiny." She smiles, her eyes twinkling. "Let me know if you need anything."

Aspen rubs her hands together eagerly and pulls apart her sandwich. She stretches her hand across the table and waves one half of the sandwich in my face.

"You've never had it before, right? Take a bite."

"What's in it?"

"Just take a bite."

I bite down, and immediately, my mouth is filled with juicy, cheesy goodness— with a sweet kick from the raspberry jam. "Oh my God. That's amazing."

She laughs and takes a big bite out of her sandwich. I cut apart a piece of my pancake and place it on her plate. She smiles back at me with pursed lips, a blush on her cheeks—like she's trying her hardest not to giggle with a mouthful of food.

"For as much shit as we've been through, we've at least been eating good."

We eat in silence for a few more minutes, but I can't help but notice her nails. Still dried with blood. I wash down my bite of syrupy pancake with some juice and clear my throat.

"About last night... You slashed the tires of the car."

"I did. Yeah."

"How?"

"Does it matter?" She shrugs her shoulders. Her tone isn't hostile, but her eyes seem nervous.

"Well like...you're not..." I lower my voice and lean in closer. "You don't have some kind of secret weapon that I don't know about, right? Like a knife or something?"

"I have a knife, yeah." she nods unconvincingly. Takes another sip of her coffee.

I take a deep breath. "Aspen. Can you be honest with me?"

"I have a knife, Riley. That's what I used to cut the tires. See?" she digs into the pocket of her pants and sets a small multitool on the table. She pushes out the knife to show me, then retracts it and sticks it back in her pocket.

"Why are your nails so bloody then?"

She rolls her eyes. "I don't know, Riley. I think I slammed them in a door or something while we were on our way out of the motel." She dips half of her sandwich in the sauce that's puddled on her plate. "You don't seem to trust anything I say."

"What? What do you mean?"

"You think I lied about being pregnant. Which I'm not. I've never even had sex. Unless you count a regrettably boring hand job in the back of Jared's mom's Yukon, I'm a total virgin."

"Further than I've gotten."

"Further than I wanted to go." Her voice has a hard edge to it, and I could swear her eyes are watering, but then she glances down and I can't see. "Why I dumped Jared."

"Oh shit. Aspen, I'm sorry."

"It's okay. I'm okay. It's just…" She takes a deep breath. "I'm not pregnant. I was nauseous that morning because I felt sick, because I knew that Jared was going to be a total dick to me. There's no big conspiracy here."

"Well…I'm glad you're not pregnant. That would suck."

"I don't think I even want kids anyways. *Ever.*" She wipes her hands off with a napkin; averts her eyes. "Too much bad family health stuff I don't care to pass on. Like whatever the hell was wrong with my dad."

"Your dad?"

"He was just…he was always busy with work, to the point where he hyper fixated on it, and…"

"What, was he a lawyer? That would explain why he wears a suit everywhere."

"A lawyer?" She smirks. "You don't know?"

"Don't know what?"

"My dad's the head of Titan Tech."

"The head of…" I trail off, completely surprised. Her weirdo dad was the CEO of an international corporation?

"Anyways, something was…wrong with him. I don't know, Riley. It's complicated." She laughs a little, but sounds exasperated. "Can we switch the subject?"

For the rest of breakfast, we go back to talking about films. My profound lack of film knowledge, coupled with the fact that I've never seen *Goodfellas,* is somehow deeply emotionally devastating to her, but makes her laugh her ass off. She prattles off about watching *Scarface* for the first time and her collection of Studio Ghibli. At one point, she asks June for a pen and records a list of movies that I have to watch on a napkin. By the time we finally finish breakfast, my exhaustion is gone. Talking to Aspen is easy, at least compared to yesterday. She's witty, and unusually hyperactive. Not at all like how I thought she was.

June circles back to our table. "How was breakfast?"

"*Amazing.* I have never had a Monte Cristo that good. Thank you so much."

"How much do we owe you?" I ask.

"Oh no." June shakes her head. "It's on the house."

"Oh no, June, we can pay," Aspen protests.

June waves her hand dismissively. "No. Don't worry about paying for food. Trust me when I say that $13.50 isn't going to make or break this place." She bends down to pick up our empty plates. "But…couldn't help but hear you talking about movies. On the gas station side of the place, there's a ton of movies and CDs, things like that. I know kids like yourselves probably just stream things all day, but…"

"Come hell or high water, I will find a DVD player, and make this girl watch *The Mummy.*"

"I don't think we have that one, but there's a copy of *13 Going on 30* in the bin."

"Equally a classic; Riley, let's go."

I grab Tigger's leash and migrate over to the door that separates the diner from the gas station. The shelves inside are unusually bare, but the fridges at the back of the store are crammed to the brim with alcohol. *Nice.*

Aspen makes a beeline for the CD and DVD bins and begins digging through. She finds the copy of *13 Going on 30* and hands it to me, along with copies of *Clueless* and *Fried Green Tomatoes.* The DVDs are clearly used, but at least they're cheap. She rubs her hands together excitedly before digging into the CD bin.

"What're you into? Looks like we got some rock, Motown…ooh!" She picks up a Bee Gees Greatest Hits CD.

I stare at her. "Disco?"

"Okay, hear me out: the Bee Gees slap. They *slap*. Oh, they've got ABBA too!"

"Oh God. Okay. We can get a few of those CDs, but what about the rock music?"

"Coldplay."

"Nice."

"Elton John. Oh my God. Oh my God. Hootie and the Blowfish."

"I have literally never heard of Hootie and the Blowfish."

"Then we're getting it. Also, Rob Thomas. Also, Train. We're getting all of these."

We cruise around the store and pick up some drinks and snacks. After paying, Aspen turns to me and hands me the keys, saying that she has to use the bathroom. I take Tigger and lead him outside, over to the truck. He darts off to the nearest patch of grass, and immediately poops. I roll my eyes and reach into the car for a spare plastic bag. He wags his tail and pants; almost looking like he's smiling. I bet he's proud of himself.

As I tie off the bag, I hear tires rolling into the parking lot. I glance over my shoulder, and I immediately regret doing so.

The SUV.

I have no idea how or why it got here so fast. I don't know how long it takes to change out a tire, much less four of them. I scramble behind the truck, along with Tigger, and look toward the store. Two men climb out of the SUV with something in their hands. *Guns.* Pistols. One of the men presses a finger to his ear, like he's got some kind of piece in it. He winces and speaks into it loudly.

"Healey. We've tracked them here. Proceed?"

A moment passes. He nods, as if confirming that he understood the message on the other end of the line. Before I even have a moment to react, they burst in through the doors of the diner.

And I hear gunshots fire. *Pop-pop-pop.* Fireworks, somehow smaller, but still earth-rattling. Tigger opens his jaws to bark, but I hold his mouth shut. He keeps wrestling with me to try to get his mouth free, but I hold him as best I can. The man who worked the gas station register starts screaming, and I hear another pop, as blood splatters against the window. A hand presses up against the glass and slowly slides down. Jesus Christ. I'm listening to people die; watching them die. An eerie roar echoes out, tearing through the air, and I instantly recognize the sound.

It's the same sound I heard the night we fled Little Brook.

I hear the men shouting, I hear more gunfire, but then suddenly, silence.

Eerie, eerie silence.

I wait behind the truck for what feels like forever, bile and tears building up in the back of my throat. But no one comes out. *They're waiting for me.* They have to know that I'm here. The truck is right outside. Tigger won't stop barking. Are they baiting me? Waiting for me to enter the diner so that they can shoot me? To make their job easier?

Then something bursts through the doors. It's not a man. It's not a woman.

It's a monster.

It's large, black, and slithery; with several arms protruding from its hunched back. It has razor thin, reptilian eyes, and a jaw lined with rows upon rows of bloody teeth. I can see, crammed in between the teeth of its oversized maw, a hand. I have no idea whose hand that is. As soon as Tigger sees it, he starts barking, but it slithers around the edge of the building and disappears.

Again, I wait. But I don't hear the monster anymore. And I don't hear anyone inside. I slowly rise to my feet and walk over to the restaurant. Inside it's a massacre. Blood splattered on the checkered tile. Dishes smashed against the floor. And then I see it: June, dead on the ground. Her eyes and mouth wide open. Laying haphazardly on the floor as blood pools beneath her. I scream and clap my hands over my mouth, turning away from the scene, but just as soon as I do, I spot the cashier from the gas station, dead as well, a bullet hole between his eyes. I don't know where the two men went, but I'm guessing they were eaten by the monster. Tigger immediately pees on the floor, just as traumatized as me. He rigidly stands there, shaking. I collapse to my knees and bury myself against his neck and hug him tightly.

"Riley."

I turn around, and Aspen, drenched in blood, is stumbling from around the corner. She wipes blood from her mouth. Her hair is straggly, and she looks a little bruised, but otherwise, unscathed. She rushes over to me, and I hug her tightly. We cry into each other's shoulders. I'm just so relieved that she's safe; that she's here with me.

"What happened?" she asks, holding me at arm's length.

"Y-you were in here; didn't you see it!?"

"I was in the bathroom, a-and I heard the gunshots, and they were screaming, and…" She shakes her head. "What did you see?"

"A *monster*. A giant, big black monster. It looked like a Komodo dragon, but the size of a grizzly bear and it can stand on its hind legs—Aspen, it's the same thing that I heard the night we left Little Brook. The *same* sound."

"What do you mean?"

I swallow. "I think we're being hunted."

Day 3 – Afternoon

EVERYTHING AFTER THE MONSTER attack is a bit of a blur. I remember finding the cook, still alive, but unconscious in the back. I remember briefly arguing with Aspen about whether or not to call the police and crying so much I couldn't see straight. I remember her giving Tigger a kiss on the nose and wrapping me up in a blanket as she helped me into the passenger side of the truck. After that, only sleep. Hours and hours of sleep. Voices. Fire. Blood on my hands.

When I wake up the next morning, Aspen is still driving, looking surprisingly alert. I glance at my phone and check our route on Maps. From what I can tell, we're somewhere in between Buffalo, New York and Erie, Pennsylvania. We keep passing signs for the Allegheny National Forest.

"Did my dad call?" I ask hoarsely, rubbing my eyes.

"He did."

"What did you say?"

"That you had to get some rest. He was pissed, but like, what's he going to do, you know? You can't do this all by yourself." Aspen brings her knuckles to her mouth, gnawing on them.

"Anyone else?"

"Your friend…not the one you spoke to before, but…the dude one."

"Khalil."

"Yes. Why do your friends have similar-sounding names?"

"They're cousins."

"Oh, no shit."

I sit up in my seat, and glance over my shoulder. Tigger is snoring softly. Aspen nods.

"Don't worry. I fed him. How are you feeling?"

"Head hurts."

"Probably dehydrated. You want to stop for a bit? Maybe get some air?"

I shake my head and then stare at her. "You haven't stopped since yesterday, have you? You've been driving straight through?"

"I stopped for food a few times, you were sleeping. But yeah, the more distance we can put between us and them, the better."

"Is there still a…them?"

"I don't know. But there's an 'it,' right? A giant monster chasing us?" She grips the steering wheel so hard I think it might snap off.

My mind circles back to yesterday. Our conversation at the dining room table. Her father, being the head of Titan Tech.

"What…you said about your dad, yesterday…"

"Yeah?"

"Does…does he have…anything to do with this?"

"I wouldn't be surprised if he did," Aspen responds curtly.

"What did they…do at Titan Technologies?"

She glances over at me. "If you're trying to ask me if my father is capable of making a giant monster and why he would do it, the first answer is yes, and the second answer is that he's never seen *Jurassic Park*. Scientists don't read much aside from abstracts."

"So…so you believe me?"

"I don't know what you saw, Riley. I don't know if it's a monster or a mutant or what. But there was no way that a human could do what was done to those bastards back there."

"What do you mean?"

"The hand torn clean off."

My mind flashes back. The hand sticking out of the monster's throat. "Yeah. Not human."

"Exactly. So…" Aspen sighs. She rubs her eyes, and now she looks sleepy.

"Do you want me to take over?"

"We should probably get some rest, honestly."

"Alright. Let's pull over for the night, then."

We peel off the highway, and head toward the nearest hotel. I unload the car, call my dad, and we get the room. Dad sounds relieved when I tell him that we're stopping.

"I'm just glad you'll both be getting some rest. At this rate, you'll get there sooner than I do. Has Aspen been able to contact her aunt at all?"

"Again, Dad, I don't think she has her number." I rub my eyes. "Anyways, I gotta put Tigger in the room, and unload the truck."

"I love you."

"Love you too."

Aspen looks at me when I hang up the phone. "Mind if I go shower while you unload?"

"Yeah."

I hand her Tigger's leash and one of the room keys, then exit the building. There's a lot of trash we've tossed into the backseat: empty water bottles, food wrappers, and some of Tigger's kibble spilled out onto the floor. I take my time cleaning it up and open up all the doors to air out the car. While I'm cleaning, I reach my hand into the pocket behind the passenger door and feel something soft and leathery. It wigs me out and I immediately pull back. I grab my phone, turn on my flashlight, and peer inside.

There's a small leather book.

Slowly, I pull it out, and look at the cover. It's a journal, its cover emblazoned with the previous year in gold, sparkly font. When I open it up, I recognize my mom's handwriting. Not that I can really read it at first. She always writes—*wrote*—in this bizarre cursive. Dad joked that she had a signature just as good as a doctor's. For a minute, I wonder, how the hell did it end up in my car? But then I remember Mom had to drive the truck a couple of times to get it maintenance after she bought it…and she kept everything in her purse.

I immediately close the book. Suddenly I feel nauseous. I shut the car doors, grab my backpack and duffel bag, and head for our room. When I enter, the shower is running, and steam wafts out from underneath the door. Tigger lays on the bed, bored.

The bed.

The single.

Bed.

Oh shit. They gave us the wrong room. I gently set the journal down on the mattress, and set my bags on the ground, then peel out of the room. The receptionist—a new one, not the one we spoke to when we checked in—is on the phone when I show up. She holds up a finger, mouths, *"Wait,"* and then places the caller on hold. She looks at me with the deadened eyes of someone who's worked one too many years in customer service. I already know this isn't going to go well.

"Yes?"

"Uh, we were supposed to have a double?"

"A double."

"Two queens."

"We're fully booked." She dismissively waves her hand, and I stand there, stumped.

I found a random journal with my mother's handwriting. And now I have to share a bed with Aspen, a girl I find *extremely* attractive. The emotional agony. The absolute audacity of the universe to create this situation, on top of all the other bizarre, traumatizing situations.

Dazed, I stumble back to my room, wondering what ethereal being I must have pissed off to grant me this much grief. It's not just that Aspen is hot, it's just that…that I don't know how I feel about that level of cliche bad fanfiction intimacy.

The bathroom door is still closed. I sit on the bed and pick up the journal, running my hands over the grooves on the binding. When I lift it close to my face, I can smell my mom's perfume. It makes my eyes water. I open the first page and look down. There's a date, nearly illegible, followed by an entry:

Dr. Hamar encouraged me to write in this journal and keep track of my thoughts and feelings. It's funny, but I don't think even writing them down will help me keep track.

For the past few months, people have been dancing around the question: "Why?" "You and Ivan had such a good relationship." "I never even realized things were bad." "Have you considered counseling?" "Things aren't always set in stone." Everyone is bewildered, and I can't blame them— I didn't want to be in this position. But when people say all these things, I know what they're really implying: that I am crazy. I'm crazy for breaking off things when I don't have a backup plan. I'm crazy for doing this to my daughter when she's so close to graduating high school. I'm the bitch either way I go: if I tell the truth, or if I refuse to play answers. I can't win. I don't even want to try.

I'm so tired.

Bewildered, I set the journal down. Mom didn't want the divorce. Something happened between her and dad that caused it. My mind immediately goes to cheating. Did Dad have an affair? How could he have the time for that when he was so busy with work? Did he sleep with a coworker? If he did, how did Mom find out? How long had it been going on?

It takes a few minutes for me to realize, but the water is still running. Tigger raises his head, curious, but not growling. I look in the direction of the door. I hear a soft cry of pain.

"Aspen?"

Another one, an urgent, shrill whimper. I knock on the door. No response. I knock again and try the handle.

"Aspen, what's going on?"

"N-nothing. I cut myself while shaving."

She has a razor? My mind floods with dread, and I don't even want to think about it. I stand up on my tiptoes and feel around for a spare key. Sure enough, there's one at the top of the frame. I insert it and jiggle it open.

Aspen is slumped in the bathtub, exhausted, trying to wash away blood. She's wearing her bra, and her pants have been rolled up to above her knee. My mind floods with fear, scanning over her body. She lifts a hand. So many tiny ribbons of blood, cascading down the drain. When she leans forward to hug her knees, I finally see it: a slice between the center of her shoulder blades.

"How in the hell did you cut your shoulder?" I rush over and turn off the water, ignoring the stiff faucet's squeals of protest.

"I get hair up there sometimes," she says woozily. "Riley, I'm fine. I'm going to be fine."

She groans in pain, and her eyes roll, and the closer I get, the more I can see. This isn't a simple cut. It's a deep gash; intentional, with shredded skin lining the sides. The blood bubbles up at the surface; gushing and racing down her back in ragged red rivers.

"A-Aspen, this wasn't an accident. Why did you do this?" Does she self-harm? I never noticed any scars on her before. Is this how she copes with trauma? How am I going to take us across the country *and* prevent her from hurting herself?

She buries her face in her hands, too tired to engage. "Riley, please."

I hear the soft clicking of nails on the tile, and when I look over my shoulder, Tigger is standing there, his head bent low. He whines, clearly anxious, and approaches cautiously. He sticks his head over the side of the tub. I glance back at Aspen's face. I see the dark circles; the pruny wrinkles in her fingers. She's too exhausted to climb out of the bottom of the shower tub. She sits there panting, her face buried in her hands.

"Riley, get out."

"No. I can't leave you."

"Riley. *Leave*."

"Aspen, I—"

She coaxes me. "Riley, please, I'll be out in just a minute."

With what little strength she has, she reaches for my hand. Squeezes it. Looks at me with those deep green eyes of hers and smiles weakly.

"I'll be out in a second, okay?"

I don't respond. My eyes follow the trails of blood. And then I see it. I almost mistake it for a razor blade; so small and metallic and bloody. But then I realize that it's not nearly long or flat enough to be a blade. Before Aspen has time to react, I've picked it up. It crumples like ash between my fingers. I twist it around and around in the light, and then I finally see it.

A tiny, blinking red dot.

I look back at Aspen, my eyes wide, wondering if it truly came from her. But Aspen can't look at me. She bites her lip, and rolls her eyes to the ceiling, as if she's begging for mercy. I take a deep breath, and with shaking hands, hold it out to her.

"What the hell is this?"

Day 3 – Night

HER PARCHED LIPS SEARCH for words she doesn't know how to say. She stares back at me, her arms wrapped around her knees. Water droplets roll off of her chin, down her long strands of hair.

"It's a tracker."

"What?"

"It's a tracker."

"In your *body?*"

"Yeah."

I blink, stupefied. "And you *knew* this was there?"

She sighs and at first, moves to slump against the back of the tub, but then winces and leans forward again. "Not exactly. But I figured it out."

"Did your dad…?"

"Do you have to ask? Yes. Yes, he did it."

I don't know what to say. I don't know how to respond. The wheels in my brain are turning but no answers can be found. After a few minutes of stammering and staring, I finally muster up the only word I can say.

"Why?"

"Because my father was a controlling piece of shit, Riley. He was a real piece of shit."

"He *put* something inside you. He cut you open, a-and put this inside of you." Worse, he put it between her shoulder blades—probably to make it intentionally more difficult to remove. *Why?* Why would any parent do that to their child? And yet the thing that disturbs me the most is how calmly she's responding to all of this. She literally performed surgery on herself to get it out, and her attitude is so nonchalant.

What the hell did this man do to her?

"Riley…"

"I…I don't…understand," I stammer, running a hand through my hair. "He…how did you…then…then the guys following us have something to do with Titan Tech?"

"Maybe?"

"Like they work for Titan Tech?"

She sighs. "Or they're… rivals. I don't know exactly, Riley. I just found it weird that we were being followed. And I had a hunch that it had something to do with me."

"But what do they want with you?"

"Who knows? If they're competitors, maybe they think I know company secrets or some shit. I probably do. My dad has done hella illegal, fucked up things. This isn't even the worst of them." She winces in pain, gritting her teeth. "Can you help me?"

I grab all the towels I can find, and I wrap them around her body, trying to blot the blood dry. But it won't stop flowing, so I move her into the bedroom and have her lay down on the mattress. I take a clean towel and firmly press it down against her back, trying to soak up as much as I can. Red blossoms through the fabric, and I switch out for another one. Finally, the wound stops bleeding, and I look at its dry, sinewy surface.

"Stay here."

I run out to the car, grab the first aid kit from the dash, and race back in. Inside the kit there's a small bottle of hydrogen peroxide, along with a few cotton balls and butterfly bandages.

"This is going to sting," I murmur apologetically as I dab some of the peroxide on her wound. But she doesn't even flinch, just hisses through clenched teeth. I clean the wound a few times for good measure, and then apply the bandages, along with wound dressing to cover it completely.

She rolls onto her back, and for a minute she lays there, taking deep breaths. Her hands move to cover herself with a sheet. Blush rises to my cheeks.

"Pajamas?"

She nods. She presses her hands against her eyes and continues to take deep breaths. I fumble through our bags until I find her an oversized shirt to sleep in. She pulls it over her head and stiffly, carefully, sits up. Tigger wags his tail and rests his chin on her lap. She gently strokes his head, her eyes far away, and once again, I have no idea what to say. I sit down beside her, and she leans her body against mine. She feels cold, so I wrap my arm around her waist; careful not to touch her wounded shoulder.

"Tonight's diary entry is gonna be an interesting one."

It takes me a minute to register what she's talking about, but then I see her eyes on the book.

"It's not mine. It's…my mom's," I murmur quietly.

"Your mom's?"

"I found it in the seat pocket thingy. And yeah. It's her handwriting. Apparently, she was keeping a diary because of her therapist."

Aspen eyes it suspiciously, her green eyes glittering in the faint light. "How do you feel about…finding it?"

I know she's trying to distract me from what just happened, but when I'm reminded of the diary, I can't *not* talk about it.

"I don't know. Apparently, my dad did something."

"An affair?"

"I don't know. I don't know if I want to know."

She nods. "Then don't read it."

"What?"

She shrugs her shoulders; runs her fingers through her wet wispy hair. "Don't read it. Not until you're ready."

It seems stupid, but the thought hadn't crossed my mind. I feel like when you find things, mysterious things, the immediate option is to open it, read it, embrace it. But maybe she has a point—maybe I'm not in the right headspace to read this right now. To learn about Mom's most private thoughts. If she wrote it in this diary and didn't share it with me, then that means she didn't want me to know at all, right? Should I respect that? If a person dies, and you read their diary, is that still a violation of their boundaries? Does that even matter anymore?

"Do…" I trail off, biting my lip. "Do you think that's appropriate?"

"What do you mean?"

"I mean, like…these could be my mom's last words."

She stares. "Do you really want to traumatize yourself even more right now?"

"I…." No. I know that the answer is no. I can't handle it right now. The idea that I'm driving across the country to a man I've known my whole life, but didn't know at all, is too terrifying to think about. More terrifying than the blood circling our bathtub drain.

Because it means that I might not have a home.

And I already don't have a home.

My eyes water with tears. Aspen shakes her head. She says nothing as she leans forward and grasps my hands. Her fingers, spindly and small, loop through mine. Her palms are warm. She pulls me in closer, hugging me tightly. The smell of her strawberry shampoo permeates the stench of iron-blood, still stuck in my nostrils. I take a deep breath. And then another. And then another. And then I realize I'm not breathing but sobbing, and the sobs are wracking my body so hard that I can't even see straight. My eyes are a blurry mess of dim halogen lights and ugly brown paisley patterns and tangles and tangles of Aspen's blond hair. I rest my head on the pillow and Aspen curls up beside me. She runs her fingers through my hair, down my shoulder, over the dips of my hips. She murmurs to me, in that voice sweet and slow like molasses.

But even lying beside her, I don't feel safe. I don't feel safe. I don't feel safe. The words are coming out of my mouth, and I don't feel safe. I don't feel safe. My voice climbs louder and louder as the sobs rack my body, and she hugs me tighter against her, till not even the dust rising off the comforter can push its way between us. Her lips, pressed against my ear, her voice, like a haunting lullaby.

"You will. You will. You will."

Day 4 - Morning

ASPEN WAKES ME UP the next morning. She offers me a muffin and a hard-boiled egg, and says good morning, but my head feels like it's underwater, so her voice comes out in bubbles. I don't have to explain. She can tell from the look in my eyes that I'm not really here. My sleep was punctuated with nightmares of bloody hands and slithery claws and vacant eyes. Tigger whines to go out but I don't move from the bed, so Aspen does it for me. I lay there, catatonic, floating in the mass expanse of starchy brown blankets and Aspen's strawberry smell, left on the pillow. Funny how last night I was so panicked by the thought of sleeping in the same bed as her, yet none of that fear registered when I was having a breakdown. I only felt her radiating warmth, and the softness of her body pressed against mine.

When Aspen returns, she forces me to sit up. She grabs a hairbrush and starts to comb out the tangles in my hair and I remember that I forgot to bathe last night. I must smell disgusting, but I can't even feel ashamed right now. I let her take care of me, like I'm a doll.

"Let me drive today," she says quietly. The bristles tear through a particularly tight knot and I wince. "Sorry."

I don't argue with her. I try to tear off a chunk of the muffin, and I manage to chew it, but for some reason, its sugary taste gurgles uncertainly in my stomach. I set it back down on its paper plate.

"I don't want to eat."

"You have to eat something."

"I feel sick."

She sighs. "I can get you a bagel. That'll be easier on your stomach."

I nod slowly and gently pat Tigger's head. She sets down the brush and begins to twist around strands of my hair.

"What are you doing?"

"Want a fishtail braid?"

"I've never had one."

"No?"

71

"I don't know how to braid hair. I don't exactly brush it often."

My hair isn't curly, but it's definitely not straight. My mom called it messy-wavy; my dad called it beachy and said that every woman on his side of the family had hair like that. He teased me about it when I was little. *Beachy, beachy, like a breeze.* I can barely be bothered to take care of it most days—I mean, usually when I do try to brush it or blow dry it, it looks like shit, so I try not to do much. My mom didn't really know how to braid hair either; she always had a sporty soccer mom bob cut. The last time her hair was long I was a baby.

Aspen braids my hair and it actually looks lovely. A few strands refuse to cooperate, but the fly-aways look nice, and frame my face.

"How's your shoulder?"

"What do you mean?"

I blink. "Your shoulder?"

"Oh. It feels fine."

"Are…are we going to talk about your dad putting a tracker inside of you?"

"I mean…I don't know what there is to say. It's not like I remember when the thing was put in or anything like that."

"Were you a runaway? Did you run away a lot? Not that that justifies anything, but…I mean…"

"Tried to." She leans back against a pillow. "I was going to try to see if my mom was out there somewhere. Was really determined to do it. One time I actually convinced a dude to sell me a bus ticket to get to Portland."

"Oregon?"

"No. Portland, Maine."

"Oh."

"Yeah." She smirks and sighs. "She left when I was a baby. She used to send me letters when I was younger, and my dad would hide them from me. I get the sense she wasn't all there."

"Not all there…?"

"I found them in my dad's office as a kid when I was looking for pocket money for the school book fair. He had them all stuffed into a file cabinet. Letter after letter. Always handwritten and smudged. Could barely read the damn things. But yeah. She sent me letters every year on my birthday, and he hid them from me. There were always different addresses on the envelopes. So, I'd try to collect all the different-addressed-envelopes that I could and try to find her. I thought if she sent me the letters, maybe she would love me enough to take me away from there." Aspen sighs again and shakes her head. "Any place would have been better than growing up with him. Even if she was like, not all there mentally and, living in a rundown trailer at the side of a highway or something. At least she seemed to care."

"But you stopped trying to find her?"

"I mean, yeah. I can't figure out where the hell she is. She bounced around so much."

"Would your aunt know where she is?"

"Probably not." Aspen shrugs her shoulders. "My aunt is on my dad's side, so I doubt she would've stayed in contact with my mother."

I think about how vindictive her father was. How malicious, to put a tracker in your daughter; to physically invade her body when she's unconscious. Simply because she tried to find her mother. And I think about Aspen's behavior—her tendencies to be dodgy, to be pissy, to be weirdly distant. All defense mechanisms. Coping mechanisms. I understand her more, but I'm not sure I want to. Not like this.

"How about that bagel?"

"Sure." I sniff the hard-boiled egg she brought me. "Yeah. This is just about inedible."

"It's a good source of protein."

"So is cream cheese."

She laughs and leaves the room. I shuffle into the bathroom to wash my face and pee. When she comes back, I'm in the middle of drying my face. In the trash can there's piles of pinkened white bandages. The bandages that I put on her last night.

"Did you put on more bandages?"

Aspen stares at the trash can, and glances back up at me. "Yeah. They got a little dirty."

"You did it by yourself?"

"Yeah. The wound kinda closed up a bit overnight, and wasn't leaking as much, so I slapped on a fresh one. Now come on. You gotta eat breakfast and we gotta hit the road."

I LET ASPEN DRIVE this morning. We're heading further away from the east coast. We cycle through our CD collection as we drive along the nearly empty highway, passing by tractors and farmlands populated with smiling yellow flowers. The unfamiliar but lovely sounds of Hootie and the Blowfish fill the car. I close my eyes and feel the warm sunlight radiating against my skin. I can't remember the last time I felt this warm and cozy.

"Hell yes!" Aspen bangs her hands on the steering wheel. "This is my *jam!*" She glances over at me. "*Hold My Hand.*"

Her voice has a deep bass vibrato, rich and warm as the sunlight I bathe in. She rolls down the windows and Tigger eagerly sticks his head out, his tongue flopping around in the breeze. I nod along to the song, laughing as Aspen does the absolute most when she sings. I don't know any of the words, so I can't sing along.

Midway through the chorus, she reaches across and loops her fingers through mine. She does this so easily; not even bothering to look my way. She squeezes my hand as she continues to belt out all the lyrics. And I can't stop laughing, but I also can't stop staring. The way her blond hair catches the sunlight, bathing her in a gossamer glow. That mischievous, gorgeous smile. Infectious. Pulling in the sunlight. Pulling me in. Pulling us together.

When the song finishes, she restarts it, and finally turns to look at me.

"How long does it take you to learn lyrics?"

We stop for a late lunch at a strip mall off the highway. We're passing through one of the small towns—I think we're almost on the Ohio-Pennsylvania border. The complex only has a Walmart, a burger joint, and a questionable sushi restaurant. Aspen being the bougie eater she is of course wants to stop there. I try to convince her otherwise. She convinces me to think about it more, and I finally give in.

"If I get the shits, it's your fault. And you have to clean up the toilet of whatever place we're staying at tonight."

"I would expect you to do the same for me."

"The sushi is *your* idea. You have to face your food poisoning alone."

She rolls her eyes. "Fine."

"Do you want to get us a table while I go to pick up some food for Tigger? We're running low."

"Oh, let me do that. Since you feel squeamish, I'd rather you figure out if you want to eat here first. I would just order everything." She extends her hand, and I give her the credit card. "What brand is it again?"

"Purina."

"Gotcha." And she's off, her hands tucked in the pockets of her color-blocked jacket. I kinda want to giggle at the way she walks. When Aspen's confident or happy, she tends to take wider, almost bow-legged steps. It's like an old school musical theater swagger; like how the T-Birds did in *Grease*. And the best part is I don't think she notices.

I enter the sushi restaurant with Tigger's leash wrapped around my hand. The inside is a lot nicer than the outside; it's got a waterfall that cascades down onto some black lava rocks. Each of the booths have fake ivy and flowers threaded around their barriers. Everything looks nice, except for the hostess, who immediately glares at us.

"No dogs allowed," she says.

"I can't leave him in the car. It's too hot outside," I reply apologetically.

"No dogs," she repeats, shaking her head.

"Do you have a takeout menu?" I would just leave, but I know that Aspen really wants to eat here. And I would be fine to wait outside on the curb until the food is finished. I don't need to have a nice sit-down meal.

She rolls her eyes. Glares at me again, but this time her eyes survey my entire body. Her nose wrinkles in disgust and waves a laminated menu in front of her face.

"You can't eat here. You stink."

My face flushes. My clothes are old, and while I've been bathing, I haven't exactly had any access to a dryer or a washer for the past few days. I shuffle in place nervously.

"I'm sorry. We've been travelling from Maine for the past few days—"

"—What part of you can't eat here don't you understand?" She makes an honest-to-God shooing motion with her hand. I'm stupefied by her rudeness, so I don't immediately react. Her eyes bug out.

I tighten my grip on Tigger's leash, and sluggishly exit the restaurant. I stand on the curb awkwardly, not knowing what to do. I guess I'm in a state of shock. Most people we've met have been kind and understanding; they never told us to our face whether we smelled bad or not. I can understand her not wanting Tigger inside, but to not serve us at all? Not even let us order takeout? I don't think I have ever felt this dirty—not in my whole life.

Across the parking lot Aspen is loading dog food into the back of the truck. She frowns when she sees me, and jogs over. Just as soon as she hits the sidewalk, the door behind me opens, the bell ringing wildly.

"Hey!" The lady barks, her eyes narrowing. "Don't bring your ragamuffin friends over here! I said leave! Do you want me to call security?"

Aspen glares at her. "Can you chill out? I wasn't even going inside."

"We were just leaving."

She snorts. "You better."

"What the hell is your problem?" Aspen sneers at her.

The lady's face grows redder, and her cheeks puff up, almost as if she's holding back a scream. She speaks through gritted teeth.

"You filthy girls and your disgusting dog need to get the hell out of here."

"Or what? What're you going to do, *bitch*?"

My eyes widen in horror, and I stare at Aspen, who surprisingly is undeterred by this woman's anger. She even takes a step toward her, squaring her shoulders.

"How dare you—"

"—no, how dare *you*. Our hometown was set on fire. We are literally refugees. The least you could do is not be a piece of shit and start threatening us. Or you know what?" Aspen glances over at me. "I'm a local guide on Google Maps. Would be a damn shame if I was to, I don't know, leave a bad review for the restaurant, and let everyone know exactly what an asshole you are? And that your food gives everyone the shits?"

"Aspen."

She holds up her hand, motioning for me to stay quiet. She stares intently at the woman, whose face is flushed. She averts her eyes. Aspen laughs haughtily, crossing her arms. There's something terrifying about her—the defiant posture, the cool iciness of her green eyes. She speaks calmly, but her demeanor is threatening. The hostess shrinks into herself.

"Hey, the least you can do now is apologize." Aspen glances at me once more, then back at the lady. "You gonna apologize to her?"

The woman glances over at me, her eyes still downturned. She mumbles an apology, and Aspen rolls her eyes. She reaches for my hand and squeezes it, then leads me back over to the car. My stomach feels fluttery. That was kinda…*hot*. No, Riley, stop it. Bullying Karens is a great personality trait, but you should by no means read that as hot. God, you have set the bar low for yourself. Although I'm staring at her, she doesn't immediately look at me. When she finally notices me again, she smiles.

"Burgers sound better anyways."

I smile. "Yeah. They do. But you didn't have to, like, boss her around."

"Sometimes bitches need to be taken down a peg." Aspen rolls her eyes. "Can't believe she started screeching like that. That was unhinged. Would've made for a good meltdown TikTok."

"Maybe she's afraid of dogs."

"So? Doesn't give her the right to start ranting about how stinky we are."

"Do I smell that bad? I didn't bathe last night."

"If you stink, then I stink. And it's probably because we've been driving across the country in a hot stuffy car for the past…what, two days?"

"Yeah. Two days." I chuckle weakly. "Feels like it's been weeks."

We reach the burger place, which has a drive-thru packed with cars. Some kids in baseball uniforms sit on picnic benches outside. Aspen and I snag the only free table available, which is unfortunately dirty. She heads inside to grab some napkins and a cup of water for Tigger.

"So, it's your standard burger faire here. Quarter pounder with or without cheese. Double bacon. Uhh they do have something called Onion Death."

"Onion *Death*?"

"Yeah. It's got a ton of sauteed onions and a couple onion rings on it."

"I kinda want that."

"I kinda do too."

"I mean, we're already stinky. What's an Onion Death on top of that?"

She chuckles. "So, two Onion Deaths, two fries, and two milkshakes…?"

"What flavor?"

"Oreo?"

"Fabulous. Yum. Love it."

Aspen smiles and heads back inside to place the order. I sit outside with Tigger and listen to the laughter of the children nearby.

Everything here feels…weirdly normal. Vibrant. Full of life. As if what happened not less than a week ago had never happened at all. A few of the little kids are looking in my direction nervously, no doubt disturbed by my disheveled appearance. One petulant mother snaps at her son not to stare, and he twists his head back around so fast, I think he's going to get whiplash. I resist the urge to giggle—can't draw too much attention to myself around here.

Aspen returns with the food, and we dig in. It's greasy and sugary and salty and fills every inch of my arteries with its goodness.

Once we finish up with lunch, we get back on the road, and drive for a few more hours, until we finally cross the border from Pennsylvania into Ohio.

Aspen has been sleeping most of the afternoon. When she's in a deep sleep, she rests her chin against the seat belt holder, and her mouth opens slightly. Her eyelids twitch and I wonder what she's dreaming about. She wrinkles her nose and mutters under her breath. Uh oh. Nightmare.

"Aspen."

"Hmm?"

"Wake up."

"Huh?" She rubs her eyes and sits up.

"Having a nightmare?"

"My entire waking life is a nightmare. Why shouldn't I have nightmares when asleep?"

"Because that's depressing and awful?"

"But at least it's consistent." She smirks and chuckles, stretching. "You think you want to buckle down for the night and rest?"

"We probably should, shouldn't we? We got to change out your bandages."

"My what?"

I laugh. "Your bandages. Remember? You dug a fricking tracker out of your body last night?"

"Oh. That. Yeah, I guess we should stop." She laughs a little, but I detect something odd—nervousness? "I keep forgetting about that."

"It doesn't hurt?"

"Nah. I heal, uh, kinda quick."

We pull off the road and start looking for hotels. We pass Wyndhams, Come-on-Inns, Quintas, even Holiday Expresses—but each place we go, the parking lots are packed, crammed to the brim.

Aspen runs inside each place to check to see if there's an open room, but there's nothing. Frustrated, we continue back on the highway and try the next exit—same issue. We drive around for around an hour and a half, stopping by three exits; completely unable to find any place to stay. The orange sun eventually eclipses behind the cityscape, painting the sky shades of inky black and blue, and it starts to sink in that we are in deep shit tonight.

"What the hell?" Aspen grumbles, scratching her head. "What's going on?"

As we pass a billboard, I see it: a sign for a comic convention. We both notice it at the same time and groan. Of course, that's why it's busy and there's no rooms—everything around here is probably booked for miles. We're not going to find anywhere to stay. We pull into the parking lot of another hotel, and Aspen once again sprints out to check. This time she returns, but with an excited smile on her face. She waves a single piece of paper around in a sporadic happy dance.

"The hotel called around and asked for available rooms. There should be a few at this one place, but it's going fast." She quickly plugs the address into my phone, and we're off once again.

When we stop by the place—a seedy little motel that looks like it could be owned by Norman Bates—it's crammed too. Even the pool, with its murky pseudo-green water, is full of kids and middle-aged women tipsily sipping margaritas. But at this point, Tigger needs to go out and potty, so I park the car at the back edge of the lot. Aspen runs inside to check and returns moments later with a disappointed look. I don't even have to ask her how it went.

"What are we going to do?" I ask.

"I don't know. Do we swap out and keep driving?"

"But we're both exhausted. That's dangerous."

She spreads her hands. "I don't know what else to do, Riley. But you can buy me a couple of Red Bulls and I can see how far we get."

I shake my head. "I don't think that's a good idea. We really need to change out those bandages."

I notice a couple exiting the doors—a middle aged bald man and woman, hand in hand. The man wears a buttoned up Hawaiian shirt, the woman a knee length purple muumuu. They spot us and immediately float over, the woman clinging tightly to the man the whole way.

"Hey, did you girls manage to get a room?" the man asks in his booming, Brooklyn-accented voice.

Aspen shakes her head. "Nope. Booked up full."

"Are you both travelling by yourselves?" his wife asks. Interestingly, she has a different accent than he does. It sounds vaguely...Russian? Looking at her up close, she's long and slender; mysteriously beautiful. She has golden-brown foxlike eyes and laugh lines around her mouth. Her husband on the other hand is stocky, somewhat fat, and broad shouldered. Opposites attract, I guess.

"Yeah. We're on our own," Aspen says to the wife.

I shoot her a look, but she doesn't seem to notice. While we're travelling together, I know better than to tell two complete strangers that we're on our own. No matter how friendly or quirky they seem. The woman places her hand against her chest, deeply concerned.

"Oh my goodness. It's ten o'clock at night. How much further do you have to go?"

"A couple days," Aspen replies vaguely. "We're headed to Minnesota."

The man shakes his head. He smiles sympathetically, and there's a slight twinkle in his soft cerulean eyes. "We wanted to get ourselves a hotel too, but I guess we're just going to have to spend the night with my brother in town. If you ladies need a place to crash for the night, you can come with us. I don't think he's got enough beds, but you're welcome to park your car. Give you a few blankets."

"That's...so kind of you." Aspen replies cautiously, a sweet smile on her face. "Well, we'd love to get some rest. If we wouldn't be a bother."

The wife laughs. She shakes each of our hands, her bracelets clinging together musically as she does. "No, you wouldn't be. We have two daughters—much older than you girls—but if they were travelling around at this age, I would hope someone would help them. I'm Karine, and this is Enzo, my husband."

"Were you in town for the convention?" I ask.

"Oh no. We're visiting my folks." Enzo smiles. "So, ladies, I can give you the address if you'd like?"

"That would be great."

I reluctantly exchange phone numbers with Enzo and Karine, and she texts me the address of the house. They walk back over to their car, and when Tigger finishes doing his business, we hop back in as well. I anxiously grip the steering wheel and look over at Aspen. She glances back at me.

"What?"

"You don't think that that was...weird?"

"It's a nice older couple."

"You don't think that this is like…a human trafficking scheme?"

"What?" Aspen laughs.

I glare at her. "I'm not crazy, Aspen. You know they do that kind of thing now. They pair a dude up with a woman to look for vulnerable people. And like, there's a convention in town. That's prime human trafficking time."

"Should I be suspicious that you know all these things about human trafficking?"

"What? Aspen, don't joke with me."

"Riley. Look." She pulls up the house on Google Maps and shows it to me. It's a simple one-story suburban ranch house, right next to other houses. It's got bright red brick and a navy-blue roof. Quaint. "This is not the house of a human trafficker. And plus, you can just text the address to your dad. Tell him it's an Airbnb or something."

"Can you do that? I'm going to get us over there."

"Sure thing." She settles back in her seat, and we set off.

Day 4 - Night

THE NEIGHBORHOOD IS HUMBLE and quiet; flickering streetlights cast their hazy golden hue onto pothole-riddled roads. Tigger whines as we bump along, and I slow down so we can take it easier on the tires. Google Maps beeps at us, signaling that we've arrived at our location. We roll up on the street just as Enzo and Karine's car pulls into the driveway. A man flicks on the outdoor light and it sputters to life. He shuffles outside to greet them, and looks at our car. Aspen gives a friendly, awkward wave. We exchange looks and move to exit the car.

Karine makes a sweeping gesture toward us. "So Emile, these were the girls we told you about. Here they are. Remind me of your names again?"

"Aspen, and this is my chauffeur, Riley." Aspen flashes a beaming, wholesome smile, the kind that makes parents melt. They laugh in response to her joke.

The homeowner bears a striking resemblance to Enzo. It takes me a second to register they have to be twins. The only major difference is the homeowner has a scraggly beard. He shakes our hands.

"Well ladies, hate to break it to you, but I don't have any spare beds. But uh, I do have a tent that you can pitch in the backyard. And that'll be better for your dog, too." His nose wrinkles with disdain.

"Not a big fan of dogs?" I shrug my shoulders and tousle Tigger's floppy ears. "That's totally fine. I get it. He's a big boy."

"I've noticed. What kind of dog is he?" Enzo asks.

"Great Dane mix."

"Simply gorgeous. And well, better to have a mutt than a purebred."

I nod. "Yeah. Great Danes tend to have a lot of health problems thanks to their size. Thankfully Tig is a lot smaller."

"That's his name? Tig? Tig Notaro? Like the comedian?" Karine asks.

"Like the who?" As soon as I ask the question, Aspen releases a heavy sigh. "Uh, he's named after Tigger. You know. Winnie the Pooh."

"Oh, that's so cute." Karine smiles politely.

From her tone of voice, I don't think she actually believes what she said. She looks in the direction of the men and ushers them off to get the tent. Aspen and I migrate to the backyard. I encourage Tigger to do his business, but he teases me: eagerly huffing and snuffling the grass, stopping every few inches to inhale deeply, then moving forward again.

"See?" Aspen smirks. "And you thought they were human traffickers."

"We still haven't seen what's inside the house, y'know. Wonder if they have a secret basement."

"Riley. Stop. Have you watched *Hostel* one too many times or something?"

"What?"

"Oh my God. How have you survived for this long, babe? How?"

I feel my heart pang at the way she said it. *Babe*. Not tenderly or croony, like you would in a rom-com or how my dad used to do to my mom when he was mildly annoyed with her, but matter-of-factly. Like the word just fits. It's so simple and natural it throws me completely off guard, but she doesn't notice.

We circle around the yard a couple of times. It's fairly normal. Nicely manicured, for a middle-aged man who seems to live alone. Hydrangeas and plushy peonies line the flower beds along the back. Manicured grass, like someone had just trimmed it that morning.

There's a small fire pit nestled in the corner, scorched and old, along with some of the lawn chairs. Nestled at the base of one of the chairs is a small bin filled with toys; it looks like old Hot Wheels and toddler-sized Legos.

Emile opens the back door. "Ladies! If you need to, you can come inside and use the bathroom. Dog is welcome too."

"I'm gonna go pee. Brush my teeth. Shower. All of those things. You cool to stay out here with Tig?"

I nod, and I watch her go inside. Karine steps out just as she enters. She reaches into her purse and pulls out a cigarette, then carefully lights it. She watches as Tigger squats down.

"Thank you again," I tell her, feeling awkward. "We're really happy we have a place to stay."

"Happy to help." She takes a long drag and blows a circle of smoke into the air.

When Tigger finishes peeing, I walk over to her. She smiles and reaches back into her purse, then pulls out a carton of cigarettes. She flips the lid open with one fluid motion and extends the box to me. I lean in to stare at it, but then realize that she's actually trying to *offer* me something to smoke. I stare at her with wide eyes. She arches a brow.

"No?"

"Uh, no."

"I figured most girls your age would be vaping. Vapes are dangerous, though. They can cause your lungs to collapse."

"I thought you had to vape a lot to do that."

She laughs. "Or just be unlucky."

I don't know why, but it's the way she laughs that offsets me. As she takes another drag of her cigarette, something stirs deep in my stomach. *Danger.* But I tell myself no. I grew up with kids whose parents would offer me alcohol at small parties; offering cigarettes isn't that much different. We're at a house on a residential street. There are children's toys in this yard.

There are...

There are children's toys in this yard.

Is there even a toddler here?

"What's the matter, dear? You look a little pale."

"Oh, just a little tired." I laugh, trying to hide my nervousness. I look out toward the garden. "This yard is so pretty, though. Really nice plants."

"He really should be watering them more. But I'm glad you think so."

She takes another long drag, and then drops the cigarette on the ground. She grinds it beneath her heel and looks back up at me, nods towards the sliding glass door. "Shall we?"

No. *No.* But I can't run away. Aspen's already inside. I have to get her, and we have to go. Each step toward the threshold of the house feels heavier and heavier, and when I place my foot on the orange shag carpet, I somehow feel electrified. Again, normal house. Cute house. Quaint house. Safe house? There're finger-painted family portraits tacked to the fridge. A highchair. I nod slowly, appreciatively, even as the panic rises in my body. A sinking, odd suspicion creeps inside the pit of my stomach, and I silently pray that it's just anxiety, but as my eyes survey the room, I see the dreadful evidence:

A family photo.

Young. Blond. Mother and father. Daughter and infant son.

This is not this man's house.

The sliding glass door clicks softly shut behind me. I know without looking that the hair on Tigger's back is bristling. Still, I remain calm. I don't even tighten my grip on the leash. I silently coach myself. *Good girl, Riley. Don't panic. Not yet.*

"Cute…family," I say, my throat suddenly hoarse.

Karine laughs. "You're a smart girl." She walks up next to me, and stares directly at my face. Her eyes are big, golden and bulging, like an owl's. Then she smiles. "Sorry you had to be brought into this."

My mouth is parched. I can't find the words to speak. I want to beg for my life. I want to beg for Aspen's. Tigger's growling is my only source of strength. I'm pretty sure I'm going to piss my pants. This woman isn't a trafficker. I know without her saying it that she's with the men who were chasing us. The men who were killed by the monster at the diner. There's more of them, and they tracked us here.

A door squeaks open. Aspen walks out into the hallway. She immediately notices the panic on my face, the crazed look in Karine's eyes.

"Riley, what's going—"

And suddenly, Enzo and Emile pop out from around the corner. One pulls Aspen back by her hair, the other affixes a piece of cloth over her mouth. She struggles, and to my surprise, fights valiantly. Throws an elbow back that's deflected; tries to slam her foot into a guy's knee but he manages to knock her off balance. Tigger barks, growling and snapping, lunging at his leash. And interestingly, Karine makes no move to stop him. She simply watches on, as I cry silent tears and beg them to stop.

Eventually, Aspen stops struggling. Her eyes roll into the back of her head, and she falls back on Enzo. Enzo wrinkles his nose in disgust and throws up his hands. He steps backward, and she falls clumsily to the floor, banging her head against the cold tile of the kitchen. I sob, and as soon as I do, the men look up at me.

I rush back over to the door and throw it open, and immediately Karine tries to pull me back. I fight her off as best I can, and wriggle Tigger's leash off my wrist. I kick him out the door, and he yelps in surprise, but thank God, he's smart. By the time they go to grab me, he's fully outside, his leash out of reach.

The stench of the chemicals are sickly sweet as they hits my nostrils.

WHEN I AWAKE, I feel so sore, yet my muscles won't stop shaking. It's like I've carried a fifty-pound boulder above my head uphill. I lay there for what feels like half an hour, continuing to shake and convulse. I wonder if I'm having a seizure, but then I realize: the ground is just really cold. My hand moves against its smooth surface. It's concrete. I blink rapidly and try to raise my head, but everything feels heavy. There's a zip tie around my wrists. My vision doubles, no, triples, variations of objects spraying out in all different colors; a chromatic aberration of chaos. Slowly I try to uncurl my body, but my ankles are also tied together, so the best I can do is lay in a crumpled-up fetal position. Eventually, my eyes focus, and they trail to the back corner of the room, where I see them.

Bodies. Four blond-haired bodies. None of them Aspen's. But still horrific, boated and gray and brown. They stare wide-eyed at the ceiling. A gaping bullet wound, scabbed over with dried blood, rests between the mother's eyes. The toddler's limp body rests lifelessly in the corner, like a broken toy. The foul stench drifting from that corner is enough to make me throw up, but even when I gag, nothing comes out.

Over by the wall opposite me, I see her. Aspen, dressed in a medical gown. I wriggle in my bindings and attempt to scoot across the floor, but my body hurts, and waking up from a drug-induced coma is apparently harder than expected. Unlike me, her wrists and ankles aren't zip tied together. They've chained her down.

I look around the room once more. I can't tell where we are. I would say it's a garage, but the ceiling is too high. Long, rusted metal beams run from wall to wall. Computer monitors have been mounted on a wall, their screens filled with spreadsheets and odd 3D models. My vision is still blurry, so I can't make out anything specific. In the center of the room is a stainless-steel table, bolted to the floor. A roller cart filled with scalpels and other surgical utensils is next to it. On the second shelf sits a buzzsaw. It appears that this room is some sort of lab.

I grit my teeth and wriggle around to face Aspen again. "Aspen, get up."

No response. I dig my shoulder into the ground and push myself upright, even though every part of my body is on fire, screaming in pain. I look down at the zip ties around my wrists and remember seeing TikTok videos about how to break out of them. I bend down and try to tighten them with my teeth—but I can't get a grip. They cut the ends too short. Guess they saw the videos too. *These Gen Z wannabe bastards.* Still, I try to bring my arms over my head, and break them against my hip. But I'm moving so slowly, my body feels so heavy. I only succeed in bruising my hip bone and hurting my wrists.

There's no way that my body feels this way from just chloroform. They drugged me. They had to. But what they want, I don't know. Are they from Titan Tech?

I look over at her again. "Aspen! Aspen, wake up!"

My throat feels like it's on fire. My voice comes out a shaky, cough-filled croak. But I try again and again, calling out to her, begging her to wake up. She winces but doesn't open her eyes. Down the hallway, I hear voices; muffled, low, un-urgent. The click of Karine's heels against the floor slowly approaching.

"Aspen, please," I cry out softly. "Please get up!"

Her eyelids flicker, but her eyes don't open. As the door swings open, what little hope I have left sinks lower and lower, the depressive thoughts come spilling forth like a torrential flood, one after the other, simultaneous voices sobbing and screaming inside my head.

We're going to die here.

They're going to cut us open and harvest our organs.
We're going to be dumped in that pile of bodies in the corner.

I'll never get to see Dad again.

I'll never see Tigger again. Is Tigger even safe? God, please let him be safe.
    I promised Caia I would make it home safe.
I'm so sorry Dad. I'm so sorry Grandma. Grandpa. Tigger. Caia. Khalil. Aspen.
    I don't know what's waiting for me on the other side.
Mom, Mom, are you there?
        Mom, Mom, Mom.

Catatonic, I watch them walk into the room. Enzo, his brother, and Karine. All dressed in white laboratory coats. The men wear medical grade gloves, and they lift Aspen into their arms. They lay her down sloppily on the table and strap her down. Karine interrupts them.

"Wait a minute. Lean her forward. I think I saw something."

The men obey Karine. She examines Aspen's neck, and pulls down the back of her gown, exposing more of her shoulders. My eyes widen. There are no bandages on her back. Just flaky, molting skin. A small scar. Gone is the inflamed red skin and the deep wound.

What the hell is going on?

Karine clicks her tongue with disapproval. "So, she really did it. Admirable. That must've hurt like hell."

"We'll put a new one in."

"No need." Karine waves a dismissive hand at Enzo.

Enzo stares. "Healey won't be happy if we don't do it now."

The name sends a chill down my spine. *Healey*. Where have I heard that before? It takes me a minute to register it, but then I remember. The diner. The men at the diner were speaking with a Healey on their earpieces. My suspicions were right. These people are all connected, and they all have something to do with Titan Tech.

"Healey's never happy. Besides, this'll be over soon enough."

"Who the hell are you?" I rasp, sitting up. "What the hell do you want from us?"

Karine scowls at the sound of my voice. She turns her eyes in my direction. A familiar smirk returns to her ruby red lips.

"Like you don't know what you're dealing with."

"What?"

Karine glances over at the men, and they exchange some sort of silent communication. They roll Aspen onto her stomach, and undo the strings of her gown, exposing some of her back. From the roller cart, Enzo grabs a massive syringe—with the longest needle I've ever seen in my life—and begins to extract some kind of fluid from her lower back. But it's not red like blood or yellow like plasma, it's…green. Bright, electric green; almost neon.

I look pleadingly toward Karine. Even though she's my captor, she's apparently the person in charge here, and the only one not preoccupied with the hellish task at hand. When she locks eyes with me again, she smiles, stares at me for a few moments, then falters. She glances back at the men conducting their work on the table. Enzo looks at her, then at me. They both grin, like there's some inside joke I clearly don't know about.

"What the hell is going on?" Suddenly my face is hot, boiling even. I ignore the pain in my muscles and wriggle myself into a seated position.

"She doesn't know?"

"It would appear so."

"Why are you doing this to her?"

Tears rise like a lump in the back of my throat. My eyes water and burn. But I don't break down sobbing. I glare ferociously at Karine, wishing that my gaze would light her aflame. That stupid, pretentious, bitchy smirk is replaced with faux pouty lips and a pitiful gaze. She approaches me and crouches down, extending a hand, as if to place it on my cheek. Instinctively I snap at it, but Karine recoils just in time.

"Brave," she praises. Then she delivers a resounding slap across my face, sending me to the floor again.

There's a gasp from over by the table. I think it's Enzo. "*Karine.*"

"Did you see her try to bite me?"

I wriggle on the ground, trying to sit up once more. Karine stands and straddles my body, watching with amusement as I try to right myself. It's infinitely humiliating. She places her hands on her hips and *tut-tut-tuts*.

"Where was this energy before?" she asks, her voice curious. "You only decide to start fighting for your life *after* you're captured? Not the best move."

"Karine, come on." Emile snaps. "Let the girl be. We have work to do."

Karine doesn't take her eyes off me. "A little slap or two won't kill her. In fact, it might cure her of being an annoying little shit."

"We're not supposed to be roughing up civilians."

"I've had enough of taking orders from people who can't even track down two teenage girls. I mean, really, Emile. How hard is it to look at traffic cams? We've had the license plate for forty-eight hours."

The license plate. My truck. That's how they found us. And somehow these assholes have access to traffic cams. Plus, people stationed everywhere. We were never safe, nor were we going to be safe. It was just a matter of time before they found us.

"If you're going to kill us, the least you could do is explain to me what the hell is going on!" I rasp.

Karine rolls her eyes. "Kill you? Why would we kill you?"

"T-those men at the diner shot at us!"

"They did?" she sounds somewhat surprised. She looks back at Enzo and Emile, as if waiting for them to respond. They don't answer. Her eyebrows narrow, and she shakes her head a little. Her eyes dart back and forth, as if she's performing some complicated calculations in her brain.

"Yeah, they did. And now you expect me to believe that you won't kill us?"

She snaps out of her trance. "Maybe I should. You're quite annoying."

Again, she crouches beside me. She hugs her arms to her chest and lays her head against her knees. Her pose is almost childlike. "So deeply insufferable. When we found out about you, we combed through what we could find. Insta. Facebook. Twitter. You're like one of those... Enzo, what were those called again?"

"Memes?"

"Memes. That's it. You're like one of those *I'm Not Like Other Girls'* memes." she giggles. "You think you're so much cooler than everyone else. I was like that when I was young."

"What, thirty years ago?"

"More like twenty." She frowns disdainfully before rising to her feet. She looks back over at the table. "Boys, are you done yet?"

"Don't call us boys."

"I'll call you whatever I want, Emile, so can it. Don't we have blood to draw?"

"What's wrong with Aspen?" I beg, frustrated beyond belief. "Why can't someone just explain anything? Just explain something! Just one thing!"

Karine shakes her head. "I'm afraid I can't do that, *mon cherie.* You'll just forget it anyways."

"Why?"

"Because we're going to wipe your memory. See..." She glides over to a table that rests beneath the wall of computer monitors and picks up some kind of gadget-thingy? It looks like a metallic spider, with sharp metal legs with needle-pointed ends. "We've got this little device here. I know it looks scary—and it is. Could potentially lobotomize you, but not to worry, I'm fully trained. It's supposed to wipe your memories. Can go back as far as two weeks. Pretty remarkable. Won't that be nice? To forget all of this?"

I throw my head back and scream. My voice boils deep in my gut and rips out through my throat, echoing through the air. Karine watches me in amusement, but the men stop and glare at her in frustration.

"Karine!" Enzo shouts. "*Handle it!*"

"She's not stopping you from doing your job, is she?" Karine sets the device back down on the table and walks over to me. I brace myself for another slap, but to my surprise, she doesn't hit me. "Sweetheart, just so you know, this basement is soundproof."

"Soundproofed? Why is this—"

"—Courtesy of the scientist who lived here. He happened to work from home a lot. And his sort of work was the kind that required the utmost privacy." She folds her arms across her chest. "So, to recap: soundproof, and the houses on this block have been evacuated."

"Evacuated or slaughtered?"

"Slaughtered? I don't…" She looks at the bodies in the corner. For a moment her expression softens, and she averts her gaze quickly, like it's too much for her to handle. "Oh. Yes. An unfortunate necessity. Collateral damage. But they knew too much. You know how it goes."

"H-how?"

"Y'know, you've been asking an awful lot of questions. I'm surprised you've had the time to ask them." She rolls her eyes and with a heavy sigh, looks back toward the men. "How hard can this be? Haven't you done it at least a thousand times?"

"With other patients," Enzo snaps. "This one has some weird kind of coating around her spine. It's gonna be next to impossible to get anything out of her."

"How much have you gotten?"

"Half a vial," Emile responds.

"*Half a vial?*" She groans with frustration. "Good God, we're going to be here all night."

"Make yourself useful then. Wipe that girl and dump her ass. We don't need to be listening to her bitching all night." Something snaps, and Enzo throws up his hands in aggravation. "Goddamn it!"

"What's wrong?"

"Needle fucking broke. Goddamn it," he repeats through clenched teeth. He wipes the sweat from his forehead with the back of his hand and reaches for the buzzsaw, then looks at Emile. "Help me plug this in, will you?"

"What are you doing?"

"We have to break through the coating to get the fluid."

"Aren't you going to damage the spine?"

"Maybe, but isn't that for the better?"

"Enzo, *stop*," she hisses through clenched teeth. "That's not a part of the plan. We can't cause unnecessary damage to the specimen."

"Of course, *you* would be worried about that, Karine."

"I am," Karine says, her voice unshakable. "You are not to damage the specimen. This was supposed to be quick and easy. You cannot hurt her."

"Based on what she's done, I think she can take a beating."

Her eyes widen. "That's not part of the plan!"

"It's not a part of *your* plan."

"What's that supposed to mean?"

"Jesus, Karine. You're not slick. We know what you're up to."

Karine stares back at them as if in shock, and then her expression darkens menacingly. Enzo rolls his eyes dismissively and looks toward Emile, who plugs in the buzzsaw underneath the table. It jitters and sputters into life, whirring loudly. But just as it does, Aspen's eyes flash open. They're different this time. The green is electrified, glowing like the liquid in the syringes; her pupils thin and reptilian. She wriggles her body ferociously, like a fish flopping on a deck. The table creaks underneath her weight, some of the screws pop out of place, ricocheting across the floor. I narrowly dodge one that comes flying at my face.

Aspen's mouth opens, but not in a humanoid way. Her lips peel back vertically, and her jaw widens into a monstrously large slit that curves over the side of her face, inching toward her neck. Her eyes narrow into slits and bulge as her mouth inverts, peeling back her epidermis to reveal an iron-black, scaly surface underneath—and then her actual skin seamlessly melts and recedes into the scales. The gown tears apart as several spikes, in varying lengths, emerge from Aspen's back.

And then I finally realize.

The monster…it's her.

Aspen is the monster.

Day 5 – Midnight

I CAN'T EVEN SCREAM.

Can barely think.

My mind races.

I think I can feel my heartbeat

In my throat

I can't

Focus

Panic

Deep breath Riley

Deep breath again

Inhale

I can't hear

It's too loud

Why won't they stop screaming   Stop it stop screaming

Breathe Riley breathe

Inhale

Hold

Exhale

Hold

Inhale

Enzo and Emile are screaming, racing toward the opposite wall. Karine watches on and I think she's in as much shock as I am. Her face is pale, and her smarmy smile is gone. But I'm much too terrified to be glad about that.

Enzo reaches inside his lab coat. He withdraws a pistol, takes aim at Aspen, and fires. It bounces off her body like a ball, ricocheting back at him. He narrowly dodges it. Emile reaches into the panel and grabs another weapon. Wordlessly, Karine brushes past me. It's bizarre how calm and orderly she seems. She makes a beeline for the door, and Enzo glares at her. He shouts at her, nearly frothing at the mouth.

"You can't leave us here, you bitch!" he roars, firing another shot.

It misses. She releases a roar—a terrible, all-too familiar roar. Like a tiger's spliced with a fox's scream. And yet underneath all of it, I swear I can hear her. Aspen's voice, hoarse, tired, afraid. But while there's fear in her voice, she wastes no time sprinting forward, her horrible maw open and full of razor-sharp teeth. One bullet, two, three. This time she swallows them like pills—and goes in for the kill. She clamps onto Enzo's arm, and he screeches in pain, twisting and wrenching around in a hapless attempt to pull away from her. To his credit, he does successfully tear away, leaving his arm a ragged stump. Through the spurts of ruby-red blood a hint of bone glistens, but to my surprise, it disintegrates. A bubbling black acid sweeps down his arm, and he screams, his eyes white, convulsing in pain. His screams are guttural and high pitched, ear-piercing. He doesn't stop to take a breath as his skin shrivels and bubbles away. When his arm has nearly receded into his shoulder, Aspen moves and takes the final bite, crushing his skull between her massive jaws.

With shaking hands Emile fires off two rounds, but Aspen is blind to them. Her mouth retracts further, and Enzo's body goes sliding down her massive gullet, like an anaconda swallowing its prey. Emile locks eyes with me, and I say nothing as he races over, aggressively pulling me to my feet. He pushes me in front of him, and at that point, I realize he's using me as a human shield. But with my ankles still tied, he can't move fast enough. He digs his grubby little fingers into my shoulder and yanks so hard, I scream in pain.

Aspen stops. She slowly slinks around to face us, her spiked tail curling around her feet. Enzo's feet disappear down the back of her throat. Something soft surfaces in those reptilian, predatory eyes—or at least, I'm trying to convince myself of that. But it's gone when Emile places the gun against my temple and I scream in protest, sobbing. He shakes me ferociously, screeching curse words into my already-ringing ears.

"Shut up!" he roars. "Shut the hell up!"

Snot and tears dribble down my face as I stare at the monster that used to be my friend. My friend with her gorgeous green eyes and sun kissed blond hair. My friend who loves nineties music and watches way too many movies. My friend who held me last night while I was crying over my dead mom. The person who over the past four days has been one of my few reasons to smile, to laugh, to hold onto hope as we search for safety.

Is a monster.

A bloodthirsty, hungry monster who is probably going to eat me without a second thought.

"Aspen," I cry out, and she roars in response. I shout back at her. "*Aspen!*"

"Shut up!"

Emile presses the gun harder against me. I hear the click of the bullet in the chamber. My body feels warm and damp with sweat, but I also think I've pissed myself. Aspen approaches us, her long slinky body slithering over the floor like a cobra preparing to strike. The fluorescent lights bounce off her scales mesmerizingly.

Emile yanks me by the arm, and I howl in agony. But I'm interrupted by a loud, wet *pop!*, and then suddenly, an intense swelling of pain. I glance down at my shoulder. A little knob of bone is protruding from the top of it, threatening to break through the skin. It's dislocated. I fall to the floor, against my other shoulder, screaming in pain. Emile fires another round at Aspen, but she's not as patient as she was with Enzo. She snaps him up between her jaws and ends it quickly. Her teeth sink into his neck and the blood sprays against her body, the wall, and onto the ceiling. A few stray droplets splatter on my face as I helplessly wriggle about on the ground, in complete agony.

Panting and sobbing through gritted teeth, I try to sit up again. Aspen doesn't bother to tear into Emile. She lets his bloody, lifeless body drop to the floor. His empty eyes stare menacingly, accusingly at me, and I squeeze my eyes. I hear the pattering of her wet, heavy feet as she inches closer. Can feel her hot, putrid breath against my bare skin, making it sting at the touch. Her guttural hisses fill my ears as she circles me. She paces for what feels like an eternity.

"Aspen, please," I whisper, tears dripping down my cheeks. "I-it's me. Riley."

No response. I open my eyes and stare at my bruised feet. My head is pounding, and my shoulder is throbbing, but if I want to get through to her, I know I have to try. And if I'm right—if I could actually hear her voice in her layered, anguished screams—she's somewhere in this mass of inky-black flesh and wild bloodthirstiness.

"R-remember?" I ask her. She circles me, her claws—long and sharp like a hawk's talons—scraping against the cement floor hesitantly, as if she's debating whether or not to attack. "You asked m-me about queer m-m-movies. I-I just remembered, I saw one. *Love Simon?*"

A hiss. I can't tell if that's good or not. I raise my head and meet her emerald gaze. Cold, but something alive underneath the surface. Yearning to break free.

"Have you seen that one?"

She stops. Stares. I sift through each of my fearful thoughts, trying to think of something that could get through to her. The song. Yesterday's song. I hum the opening notes, my voice shaky and sure to crack. I sing it from the beginning, through to the first chorus. At that point, her eyes begin to flutter, as if she's suddenly sleepy. Her body nestles into the floor, and she lowers her head. I watch her, my voice carrying its lullaby, until finally, her eyes close. Her massive body shrinks into itself, as her peachy-porcelain skin cells resurface above the black scales and her face takes shape once more. The monster recedes and the human returns. Her scales remain around her torso and pelvis, clinging to her human skin like a wetsuit. For a few moments, she lays on the ground, remaining still, and then her eyes open. She looks at me.

"Why're you singing?"

I didn't realize I hadn't stopped. I laugh a little, wiping my tearful face against my good shoulder. Aspen sits up, scrubbing a few drops of blood from her mouth and stares at the little red stains on her fingers.

"Oh. Oh my God." She leans forward and buries her face in her hands. "Oh, holy shit. What did they put me on?" She looks at me and her eyes widen. "What the hell happened to your…oh shit." She scrambles over to me, and gently pushes me down onto the floor. "We gotta pop this sucker into place."

"Pop it?" I reply hoarsely. "Shouldn't we go to a hospital?"

"With us looking like this?" She stares at me with big bug eyes, then winces.

In an unnatural way, she opens her mouth and reaches inside, removing a bleached, curved chunk of bone, then shudders in disgust and tosses it to the side.

"Can you not do that right now?"

"Acid reflux."

"Please stop talking."

"Sorry. But we can't go to a hospital for this."

She grabs onto the arm of my affected shoulder, twists it up and out, and I grit my teeth. She pushes, and slowly shoves the shoulder back into place with another loud pop. It's uncomfortable, but surprisingly it doesn't hurt. I stare at her.

"How did you know how to do that?"

"I played softball as a kid—"

"—of course, you did—"

"—and Bennie had bad joints, so she dislocated her shoulder a lot. That's how I learned." She wipes her sweaty palms on her pants, bites her lip and averts her eyes, looking around the room, until her gaze lands on the corpse in the back corner. "Wow. Y'know, I probably could've handled that one better. Where'd the other guy go?"

"You ate him."

"Oh. Right. Duh." She massages her temples, and I can see the tension in her body. The veins in her forehead, the tightness of the muscles in her arms and crunched-up shoulders. She shakes her head. "Riley, I swear, I don't normally forget where I'm at or what I've done."

"Do you?"

"No. They drugged me with something."

"They drugged me too."

"Really?"

"I can't feel my tongue."

"Okay. Maybe you're right. Maybe we should go to a hospital."

I shake my head. "And tell them what, exactly?"

Anxiety surfaces in her expression. Her eyes are sad and watery. She digs her fingers into her knees, and her nails slide between her scales. I don't know why, but I suddenly feel angry. And I'm angry at myself for feeling angry. How could I *not* have known? She was sick, throwing up in class. She was hiding her wounds. She slashed open those tires and her nails were bleeding. She magically reappeared at the diner when the monster disappeared, *with blood dripping from her mouth.* Wasn't it obvious?

But then I think, why wouldn't she tell me?

And then I realize…it's because she's responsible. Responsible for everything that happened. For the destruction of the town. For the death of my mother. For losing Tigger. For the fires, for the terrors, for the running-for-our-lives.

All her.

All because of her.

And I trusted her.

"Riley. I can explain everything. L-let's just get out of here, and…"

She gently reaches for me, but I jerk back, out of her reach. My eyes water. I want nothing more than to go with her and leave this place. But I'm afraid. She looks at my restraints, and I watch as a small reptilian nail emerges from her fingertip. She uses it to cut the zip ties with ease and I rub my bruised wrists, while staring at her.

"There was never an aunt in California, was there?"

She winces, and swallows. "No."

I stare at the ground. "So, I was just…taking you along with me. And you knew that I could be killed."

"I wanted to be free, Riley."

"Is that why you killed all those people? Every friend you ever grew up with?"

"Riley!" she sobs, and her voice is filled with heartbreak. I watch as her sobs wrack her body, as her eyes flood with tears, and her body shakes violently. She tosses her head from side to side. "I didn't *mean* to do it! I just—please, can we just get out of here? Please, I will explain everything."

We slowly stand and inch our way to the door. It feels warm to the touch. Aspen nudges me to the side, forces her way in front, and opens it. Clouds of smoke sift through the gap, and we slowly enter the flaming hallway. Flaming? Oh shit, Karine probably torched the place to burn the evidence. Aspen leads the way, and even when a few chunks of smoldering ceiling fall onto her shoulders, she doesn't burn. Doesn't even flinch. Does she even feel it?

We make our way out the sliding glass door. The house isn't visibly on fire on the outside—just a few flickers of flame dancing in front of the kitchen window. Smoke is starting to drift out the windows, but with the alarms disabled, I doubt anyone is going to notice anytime soon. When we round the corner of the house and look at the driveway, Karine's car is gone.

I hear a woof, and my heart nearly explodes with joy. I call out Tigger's name and throw my arms open, and he races into them. I brace for impact as he tackles me to the ground, showering me with kisses. He nervously approaches Aspen and kisses her too. I feel around in my pocket, and thankfully, the keys to the truck are still there. We approach the truck, and Aspen outstretches her palm.

I stare at her. She gingerly closes her fingers, urgently bidding me to give them to her.

"Let me drive so you can rest. And I'll explain everything, I promise."

And although I'm afraid, I trust her. I put the key in her hand. "Let's go."

Day 5 – Morning

BY THE TIME WE get on the highway, dawn is breaking. I finally take the chance to glance at my phone and I have several missed calls from Dad. I look over at Aspen.

"My dad's been calling all night."

"Do you think you can call him back?"

I shrug my shoulders and dial him. He immediately picks up, and he's pissed. I can hear the echo of the open road as he drives along.

"*Riley.*"

"Hey, Dad," I reply hoarsely.

"What in the hell happened? Why weren't you answering my calls? I was about to call the police and report you as a missing person!" I hear him rev the engine of the car; horns blaring in the background. "Do you realize that?!"

I glance over nervously at Aspen. "Sorry. We were, uh, really tired. We had to sleep outside in a tent."

"A *tent?* I thought you said that these people had a bed!"

"I thought so, but I guess not." I yawn and rub my eyes. I'm surprised at how calm and casual my voice sounds. I guess not even my dad's pissy-ness can scare me at this point.

"Uh huh," he replies, his tone still snotty.

"Whatever."

"*What* did you just say to me?"

"I said *whatever*. I'm sorry. I'm doing my goddamn best."

"Do *not* use that tone of voice with me—"

"—Sorry, you're breaking up." I press the hang-up button and immediately switch my phone to silent. I glance over at Aspen, who stares at me with big eyes.

"Damn."

"If I kept talking to him, I'd probably just start crying. I can't let him know about what happened. He'd lose his shit." I cross my arms. "And you know I can't talk to him right now. Because of that stupid journal."

She nods and taps her fingers against the steering wheel. I stare at her.

"You said that you would explain."

"Right. Yeah." She inhales. "Actually, do you mind if I pull over? I think I gotta just… be sitting still for this."

I nod. We drive along for a few more minutes until we see a sign for a rest stop. We pull off the road. It's isolated here, no other cars. Just a little wood and a weathered brick shack at the side of the highway. She doesn't bother to park between the lines, and I don't have the energy to care. We hop out. I pace around the truck at the edge of the parking lot and she stands at the other end, staring at her reflection in the half-empty vending machines, one of which I'm pretty sure is broken.

After a few minutes, we reconvene. I sit on the edge of the truck bed, not saying a word. Just wait for her to speak. She hasn't taken so much as a deep breath before her body starts trembling. And although I'm mad—egregiously so—I still can't watch her like this. I put my hand over hers. Her fingers are so small and delicate. Hard to believe they can grow into monstrous talons.

"I don't know…what I am," she says quietly. "But I do know that whatever I am was made worse because of my father."

"So…you don't know…"

"I don't know if I'm like, some kind of fucked up spliced genetic experiment or if monsters are real or what. I could never piece it together, and since I could never find my mother, I really don't know." She speaks slowly, carefully. "What I do know is that since I was about four years old, my dad used to take me to a private lab in the basement of Titan Tech HQ, and have tests performed. He started small. Blood tests. Microdoses of prescriptions. And then as I got older, it got harder. Like, I started transforming."

"You call it transforming?"

She nods. "Yeah. In the third grade, we went to a lake, and I transformed there, and I couldn't really change back. That was the only time I ever accidentally transformed in public, and no one even saw but he just…escalated. I have gone on six different diets since I was eight years old trying to control the symptoms. The tests got worse. More painful. Biopsies. Entire parts of my body were harvested."

"What?"

"Yeah, like, I'm missing a quarter of my liver. Apparently, it's the secret for my healing properties. Like how I shed my skin so much and how I can heal really fast. So, he took that for prescription development. When I was twelve, he took some of my…um…" Aspen tears up again, and her eyes grow wide and frightful. I squeeze her hand. "Egg cells. I produce eggs. Like a human woman normally would. If I am one. Which I don't even know."

"Why did he do all of that?"

"He thought I had a gift. That I was special. And I am, but I guess I'm special in the worst way." She sniffles, staring down at her feet. Tigger pushes his head onto her lap, and she laughs softly, stroking his head. "He wanted to trigger a full transformation. So, he kept doing all kinds of shit, but it wasn't working, and I was starting to get really, really sick. Missed weeks of middle school. People were starting to notice that I was always gone and when I was around, I wasn't happy. Then he kinda…relaxed. I tried to find ways to develop my powers on my own without him knowing. Tried to control my hunger on my own. But it was always hard."

"Hunger?"

"Yeah. Like sometimes I just have these cravings for raw meat."

"That's why you kept trying to get me to eat strip mall sushi?"

"Well, sorta, but I also just really love sushi." She smiles. I nudge her softly. She squeezes my hand back and leans against my shoulder. "I… Ok."

"Take your time."

She takes another deep breath, and slowly exhales. She hiccups and tries to gulp back a sob. I don't look at her—it sounds dumb, but I feel like that's the only way I can give her some kind of privacy. I look toward the highway and count the number of cars that drive by. I count five blue, two red.

"So…high school happens. Jared and I start dating. Jared nearly, uh, date rapes me, as you know." She flinches. "I shouldn't call it that. It was a coerced hand job."

"Still sexual assault."

"I mean, technically."

"Technically it is still assault."

"I know, I just…I guess I feel weird acting like it's a big deal. Like, it was awful, but other people have been through worse, and like, there's no evidence that it ever even happened. And now no one except you will ever know, because…"

I don't know how to tell her that I think there is no one on the planet that has had it worse than her. But I also don't want to tell her how to feel. So, I don't say anything.

"I broke up with Jared, and then the week after…I start my period."

"Your *period*? Aspen, how old are you?"

"I'll be seventeen in November."

Seventeen. That's a long time to wait. Caia got hers when we were fourteen, but she told me that she came from a family of late bloomers. I was ten when I got mine, so I used to bitch about her being lucky. It's almost a little hard to believe that Aspen got hers so late, but then I remember the day of the homecoming dance: she was ridiculously nauseous. She wasn't pregnant, she was dealing with *horrible* PMS—and whatever monstrous changes her body was making room for.

"I just thought it was because, well, everything was stressful. Or that it had something to do with the medications my dad put me on over the years, o-or maybe like, my uterus just didn't…work that way? Or that it wasn't supposed to? But I started feeling really weird, and shit got harder to control. I was starting to transform. I couldn't keep down any food. And then… Homecoming happened."

"And…?"

"And… Nathan came up to me."

"Nathan?"

"Yeah. You remember? Jared's best friend."

"No, I know, I'm just having a hard time wrapping my head around why he wanted to talk to you."

Aspen rolls her eyes and wipes away more tears. "It was so stupid. He started off by hitting on me, and then when I told him I wasn't interested, he flew off the handle. Started saying all this shit about how I'm a slut, told me that he knew what I did with Jared; was getting really aggressive. He put his hands on me and I just…Riley, I just snapped."

"Snapped?" I repeat slowly.

"I couldn't handle someone else touching me o-or forcing me to touch them," she says, and she sobs. She sobs so hard that she can barely breathe. I pull her closer to me, rest my chin atop her head. "And I just…the next thing I knew I was rampaging through the field. And I grew bigger, bigger than I have ever been before, and I was *so* scared, Riley, you have no idea. It felt like I was trapped in my own body, and

I couldn't break out. So, I just started breaking shit. Next thing I knew the whole town was on fire."

"So…you don't remember blowing up Titan Tech?"

"Riley, I didn't do that. Think about it. Even if I had blown up the first one, what happened to all the other ones all along the coast?" She shakes her head. "I'm convinced that my dad had something to do with it. He *knew* something. And I think he blew up the labs because he didn't want them to trace the evidence."

"Evidence? Across all the labs…?"

"I don't know for sure, Riley. I only ever had tests done at the main facility in Little Brook. But maybe he sent shit to other people over the years, and they had a record of it."

It's a good theory, but it doesn't entirely add up in my head. Would those sort of top secret—and highly illegal—experiment results just be available on the company cloud? Or rotting away inside a manila folder in a filing cabinet? All to cover up that it was Aspen who destroyed Little Brook? It seems like overkill. Gruesomely violent and financially devastating overkill.

But then again, powerful men have done even worse.

"And…what about…Healey…?"

Her eyes widen. "Healey?"

"The guys who went after us at the diner. And Karine. She mentioned someone named Healey. I think he's behind all—if not most of this. Do you know him?"

Her eyes widen with fear. She presses her mouth against her knuckles and shakes her head. "Healey? You're *sure* that's what they said?"

"Yeah. Healey."

"T-that's my father's right-hand man. H-he's the Head of R and D at Titan Tech."

"R and D?"

"Research and Development." She bites her lip so hard I think she's going to break it open. I can tell from the intensity of her gaze that this is very, *very* bad. "He's…he's been orchestrating the experiments with my dad from the very beginning. I-it'd actually make sense that he's behind all of this. My dad always sends someone else to do his dirty work. But if my dad's dead, then he's probably just covering his tracks."

"*If* your dad is dead?"

"You know how they say that cockroaches can survive nuclear apocalypses? That's my dad. My dad's the cockroach. Even if the whole place went up in flames with him inside—well, it was full of secrets. Not hard to imagine he found a way out. Bottom line is I can't rule out the possibility that he's still alive until I see him dead."

Her voice is cold, and although it's awful, I don't feel creeped out by her saying this. I'm relieved to finally have some answers, but there's still this achy, knotty feeling in my chest.

"So...the entire time, you knew?"

"You wouldn't have taken me with you if you had known. And to be honest..." She pulls away from me. "You made the choice to take me. You found me. And I thought that night I was going to die. I got tired, and transformed back, and could barely navigate my way out of the fire. And when I came to, I couldn't tell you the truth. It was—*is*—too insane."

Well, she makes a valid point. But still... It's hard. My mom is dead, and maybe that's not directly because of Aspen, but it's because of something she's connected to. And she knew, and she didn't tell me. Worse, she wasn't going to ever tell me. Just have me drag her across the country, with scary people chasing us, and let me endure all of that trauma without ever receiving an explanation. I'm not going to lie, while she didn't have a choice, it's still shitty. Sitting here with all this information now feels impossibly heavy. I felt like we were friends, and now I feel used. Discarded. Expendable. To an extent, she was content with that. Holding my hand, singing love songs with me in the car, hugging me until I fell asleep...was any of that genuine? Or just a means to an end? Am I just her escape route?

"Riley. I know you're mad at me. And I promise you, I *promise*, that if I could go back to that night and change things, I would. If someone told me I could've died in that fire, and your mom would be here instead of me, I would be so happy to make that choice. I would do it in a heartbeat," she sobs. "You have no idea how guilty I've felt. But I'm telling you now, I *need* you. You're all I have."

Maybe in my own sadistic way, it feels good to hear her say that. And I feel guilty for feeling good about it. But it makes me hold her tighter, press her head against my chest, and let her cry to her heart's content. And even though I want to cry, for once I don't. Because right now she feels so much more important than everything else that's going on. I'm hurting. But I can't hurt her. I don't have the guts to even hate her. And truth be told, she couldn't control the people hunting us down. Not only that, she's saved my life—twice. To shun her, cast her away? She doesn't deserve that kind of cruelty.

"I had no idea that Healey was going to be *this* aggressive about it. I figured he would send people to find me, but… I didn't know those people last night were with them. Guess I've learned my lesson." She wipes at the tears in her eyes. "We can't trust anyone except each other."

"Can I trust you?" My question is firm, but my voice is soft.

She locks eyes with me. Squeezes my hand. "I promise. You can trust me. I'll be honest with you from now on."

"So can you tell me for certain, can you control your powers, or no?"

"Not…really. Not when I get into that…Komodo lizard mode."

"It's a Komodo dragon."

"But it's a lizard."

"They're called Komodo dragons."

"Well, yeah, I can't control that very much. The little things I can. Like my fingers. My eyes. Uh, I can sometimes control that acid thingy."

"Acid—oh wait, I forgot. You disintegrated that guy's arm."

"Yeah. I've got some kind of gland in my throat that secretes acid when I'm threatened. Which I can kinda control."

"So basically, you and I should never share food or drinks?"

"To be safe, yeah." She smiles. "Probably no spit swapping either. But in my opinion French kissing is real overrated."

I flinch at her joke, and she notices.

"Sorry," she mutters sheepishly, averting her eyes. A blush rises to her cheeks. "Bad joke. But what I said about French kissing is true, though. It high key sucks. I have dated like, three people, and have never figured it out at all. I don't enjoy it at all."

"Three people?"

"Two dudes. One girlfriend, who dumped me because she didn't trust me being bisexual."

"Rough."

"Yep."

I tousle Tigger's ears playfully. He's resting his entire head in Aspen's lap, and he's dozing really hard. "So…you can't control your powers, basically. Small things. Big things no."

"Nope."

"Do you…do you know what you can do in big-boi mode? Besides, like, eat people?"

"Do not refer to it as 'big-boi mode.'"

"Do you know what you can do in Komodo lizard mode?"

We burst out laughing, doubling over so hard that it feels like the wind has knocked the air out of us. She wipes away a tear, and for the first time this morning, I think it's supposed to be a tear of joy. She rolls her eyes and looks at me.

"Well. Not to brag. *Really*. Not to brag. But uh… I think I can breathe fire."

"Like Godzilla?!"

"Godzilla doesn't breathe fire. He has a heat ray. Or Atomic Breath."

"Okay, nerd. You're saying you can kinda do what Godzilla does?"

"Yeah. Kinda-sorta."

"Can you fly?"

"Unfortunately, no, but even if we could, we would *probably* be shot down by the U.S. Air Force. So maybe that's a blessing in disguise."

"Maybe so." I smile at her, and she leans against me.

We sit in contemplative silence and watch the cars go by, not saying a word. My hand wrapped in hers. Wishing that I could protect her forever. But knowing that I can't.

AFTER OUR RESPITE, WE finally get back on the road. We drive through the greater part of northern Ohio, through small dusty towns and one too many billboards about Lake Erie vacation rentals. We cruise through Cleveland's outskirts and manage to beat most of the lunch rush hour traffic. Ohio's Midwestern landscape is oddly flat and framed with golden prairie fields. Every so often it's punctuated with odd little clusters of green spaces, overgrown crab grasses and shady oak and birch trees. Compared to the coastlines, the trees are so much shorter here. Stubbier. Kinda browner? And the horizon stretches on almost endlessly, making this leg of the trip feel even longer than it actually is.

It's weird to think our entire lives blew up only four days ago. Weirder to think about how in just one or two days, I'll be in Minneapolis and reuniting with my sole surviving parent, who may or may not be an asshole that influenced the destruction of my teenage social life, and his own marriage. And I don't know what's going to happen to Aspen at that point. If she doesn't really have an aunt, does that mean she just goes with us? Will my dad let her come and live with us in Washington? Or will he call up CPS and let them deal with her? I don't want to imagine that possibility. We've both been through enough as it is—her more so than me. The idea of turning over Aspen to complete strangers, ones who would potentially abuse her more, makes me sick to my stomach. I know I can't let that happen. I have to convince my father to let her live with us. It would only be for what, two years? Then we'll both be off to college, and we can figure things out from there.

This could work.

"Uh, Riley? What does this mean?"

I lean over and squint at the dashboard. There's a little red light on, but it's kinda faded, and I can't tell if it's referring to the battery or the engine. I check the gas meter—we're all good there, only about halfway down.

"I don't know."

As soon as I say it, I notice something from underneath the hood. Smoke. Aspen and I both look at each other, and she flicks on her turn signal. She begins to pull over, and suddenly I hear a loud *POP!*

The car begins to spin around, and we shriek in terror. We both grab the steering wheel and carefully try to redirect the car over to the shoulder. A few assholes blowing past us blare their horns, and Aspen rolls down her window to cuss them out. I flick on the hazards. We attempt to pull over, but there's a broken-down car in the way.

"You gotta be kidding me!" Aspen shouts, jerking away from the shoulder.

We narrowly avoid the car and move onto the exit ramp. The car barrels down the shoulder, bumpily, until it finally pulls to a stop. For a few moments, we sit in shocked silence. Then we hop out of the car. I lift the hood and a plume of smoke erupts from inside. I cough and wave my arms over it, trying to fan it out. Aspen crouches and looks at the front left wheel—the tire definitely popped. She points to the offending nail that pierced the rubber shell.

"Of course. Just our luck," she grumbles, shaking her head, looking up at me. "What do we do?"

I shrug. At this point, anything that can go wrong will go wrong, and there's no use in stressing out about it. I think I've reached the peak of anxious disassociation. I feel numb to these kinds of problems. *An overheated engine? Oh, no problem. A popped tire? Sure. No money to fix these issues? Yeah.*

"Riley?"

"Yeah?"

"Should we call someone?"

"*Ghostbusters?*"

"While I'm glad you've seen a movie made prior to 2003, I think we need to call someone." She wipes her hands on her pant legs; wipes the sweat from the back of her forehead. "We have almost died so many times on this goddamn trip."

"I'm convinced the truck is a death trap."

"It may be a death trap, but it's the only car we got." She sighs and reaches inside the cab to grab my cell phone.

I look out toward the highway. Dusk is slowly settling on the prairieland. A few passing cars flick on their headlights, paying us no mind. The sky is inky blue and orange, punctuated with a blood red sun. It's a gorgeous, haunting blend of colors. Perfectly morbid, fitting for a day like today.

Aspen fumbles through my phone in search of someone to call. I cross my arms and lean against the truck, stroke Tigger's head.

"You think Karine sabotaged our truck?"

"I wouldn't put it past her, but I think she was more preoccupied with burning the place down." Aspen shakes her head. "No, Riley. I think we just have an old truck. Probably too old to be making a big trip like this."

I look down the road, and I see a red pickup truck. It signals and slowly pulls over, easing up behind us. A woman climbs out of the driver's seat. She has long, wavy black hair that recklessly trails down her shoulders. She wears bright red lipstick, and a red plaid shirt to match. She stretches her arms above her head as she approaches us.

"Hey there," she chirps. "You ladies alright?"

"Define 'alright.'"

"Huh?" she stares blankly back at us.

Aspen smiles and rolls her eyes. "Forgive my friend. We're just a little stressed out."

"I can imagine." She looks at the truck and whistles. "Ooh-boy. What a pickle. I can take a look for you if you want?"

"We know nothing about cars, so be our guest."

She approaches the truck and examines the engine. I watch as her hands fumble around in the faint light with expert precision. There's something so cool about a woman who knows how to work on a car—maybe it's just because that's something that I know nothing about. In Oregon, you can't even pump your own gas. I had to learn on my drive out to Maine. The one time Dad tried to teach me how to do an oil change, I burst into tears from the stress.

She glances up. "Yeah, honey, I think there's something wrong with your engine. Maybe a clogged coolant tube, but it's hard to tell."

"So, it's not going to...cool down anytime soon?"

"Afraid not. You ladies got someone you can call?"

"We were looking for someone to tow the car." Aspen waves the phone a little bit. "But if you mean, a place to stay, the answer is no."

"Oh, well I live about fifteen miles up the road from here. This is my exit. I mean, it's seven o'clock, so I think you're gonna have to leave this here till morning. But I got a guy that you can call."

"Is there like a motel that we could stay at for the night?"

"I mean, there is, but it's not so much as good for sleeping as it is for catching crabs. Don't tell the owner I said that though." She places her hands on her hips. "Well... I guess you're welcome to stay with me for the night, if you want."

At this point, I'm deeply suspicious of anyone who offers us any kind of help. I can't help but cross my arms and appraise her. She's young, maybe in her late twenties. Acne scars on her cheeks, but an otherwise very beautiful face. Kind smile. Wish I could trust her, and from the look on Aspen's face, she wishes that too.

She looks between us and notices our apprehension. "Well, you can't exactly camp out here for the night. Highway patrol might swing by here. I know Hal uses this exit on his route. Trust me, you girls don't want to be spending any time talking to that blowhard."

"You said it's only fifteen miles up the road?"

"Little town called Chester. Kinda close to the lake, but not close enough to benefit from tourism, unfortunately."

"Okay. Well, we don't have many other choices." Aspen squints. "What did you say your name was?"

"I'm Laverne, but most folks call me Fern." She smiles. "It's a long story."

We unload our truck completely since the last thing we need is for someone to rob the abandoned truck in the middle of the night. We decide to sit in the pickup bed, since Fern's backseat is full of groceries and other knick-knacks she got from the antique store earlier that afternoon. Plus, I don't want to risk Tigger jumping out of a moving vehicle. He's never ridden in a pickup truck bed before, and I can tell he's nervous. His claws start scrabbling against the floor as the truck moves, and I hug him tightly to my chest to keep him calm.

"Poor thing. He's been through so much." I kiss the top of his head and try to scratch his ears. "You're going to be okay, boy. Good boy."

Aspen glances over at me. "If this lady turns out to be…y'know."

"Yeah?"

"I'm eating her. First chance I get."

"Are you hungry?"

"Something to note about me: while I'm not always hungry, I can always eat."

"How do you stay so skinny?" I whisper. "Those guys back there were…kinda…"

"Are you fat shaming the dead, Riley?"

"I thought it was only fat shaming when you drag them for being fat. Not for stating the obvious." I elbow her and she giggles.

The road gets bumpier as we continue. The asphalt crumbles away and the road turns to dirt. We drive further and further, away from the open expanse of the highway to a sheltered road populated with trees. Glimpses of sunlight sparkle through the gaps of leaves above us. I don't know why, but it makes me feel nostalgic. Reminds me of the summers my grandparents used to take us camping by Crater Lake.

We drive toward the dying sun till the trees all peel away and we're left with open prairielands once again. A small town rests here, populated with what appears to be a general store, a pizza parlor, and a pharmacy. Small houses, probably half the size of the house we had in Little Brook, line the cracked sidewalks. Little signs hang outside them. *Madame Bourdeau's Psychic Readings. James & Jones Law Office. Erie & Out There Comic Emporium.* Some people sip from beers on their porches and Fern waves to them as we drive past. We head out of the town, up a hill, and back into the forest once again.

We finally reach Fern's house, deep in the threshold of the forest. It sits atop a massive hill. A small creek runs outback. The house is a small ranch style, with a massive porch hanging off the back. As soon as the truck pulls to a stop, Tigger hops out. He flops around in the green grass, eager to scratch his back. He sneezes happily. I smile at him. It's been a few days since he's been able to spend some time on grass that wasn't, like, regulated to a single patch at the side of a roadway. I swat at a couple of mosquitoes flying by my face.

Fern hops out of the truck and then helps us unload our stuff. She points to a shed toward the back of the yard, sitting just above the creek bed.

"That over there is my She-Shed. It's got a loft bed just in case. I'd let you stay in my house right now, but it's a little messy."

"We don't mind at all. And a She-Shed?"

She smiles. "I do a little bit of writing in my spare time. Not for anything that you would know, though."

We wander down the hill and into the She-Shed. It's got a vaulted ceiling, with pine beams running across it. Pink gingham curtains line a particularly grimy window. The space is fully decorated with wood furniture and dioramas of felt animals, which are so lifelike I almost do a double take. It's cute and cozy, like a grandmother's cottage. She points to a squirrel mounted in a picturesque mountain tree.

"That's the kind of thing I write about. Took me a couple of weeks to make that guy."

"It's so cute," Aspen murmurs. Her fingers gently touch the edge of the frame. She points to one of two pandas, cuddling in a forest of leafy green bamboo shoots. "How'd you get into this?"

"It was something I used to do with my daughter."

From the way Fern's smile tightens across her face, I can tell immediately that something is wrong. I look at her again. She doesn't look old enough to have had a daughter who left the house. Fern notices my staring and she glances down at her feet; sheepishly slides her hands into the pockets of her pants.

"She passed away a couple of years ago. I didn't have a lot of money because of the treatment, so I took up felting so that I could make all these little toys for her. Toward the end it got harder for her to grip plastic and everything kinda hurt her hands but making soft toys like this really helped her."

"I'm so sorry."

Fern nods. "I'm learning to make my peace with it." She walks over to the desk and picks up her laptop, then migrates over to the door. "So, there's a bathroom in the basement that you're welcome to use. I'll leave that door unlocked so you can just slide right in there whenever you need to. But if you don't mind, I'm going to keep the front door locked. Even out in the boonies, you can never be too careful."

"Thank you so much, Fern." After all we've been through, I'm hoping that our door locks as well. Clearly, we can't be too careful.

"No worries. Oh, and if you girls get hungry, just holler, and let me know. I think I've got some leftovers in the fridge. Otherwise, if y'all want, you can walk over to the Pizza Parlor and buy yourselves a slice or two. Shouldn't be longer than about twenty minutes."

"Well, we've got Tigger, so...," I trail off, smiling politely. I'm not about to walk up to any restaurant and expect them to let my dog in, ever again. Not after what happened at the sushi place.

Fern nods. "You can leave him here if you want. Or walk back with the pizza." She stops, scratches the back of her head, and looks at us. "Actually, you know what, if you're hungry now, why don't I just take y'all there? What do you say, you want to eat?"

Aspen looks at me. "I could go for a slice."

I swallow back a nervous lump in my throat. I hope it's just pizza. "Sure."

"And we can leave the pooch in the bed of the pickup. I think I got a way that you can tie him up back there. Just bring him some water and some food."

After moving all our stuff into the She-Shed, we load up in the truck once again and head back into town. Things are livelier now— I guess because it's after dinner. Kids run around with sparklers and teenage boys pop wheelies on their bikes in the street. A bunch of blue collared folks stumble out of a bar, laughing hysterically at something that's probably not that funny.

The Pizza Parlor is winding down. The black-and-white checkered linoleum floor is peeling at the edges, and the walls are lined with cracked red leather booths. Stained glass light fixtures brighten the space. It looks like an old Applebee's. It probably is an old Applebee's. A couple exits with a squalling toddler. A teenage couple looks like they're in the middle of a very serious conversation, their hands tightly interlaced in the center of their table.

We approach the register and Fern orders us a large pizza with pepperoni. She cracks open her wallet and fumbles for change, but I whip out my credit card and pass it to the cashier.

"You don't have to do that, honey," she says. "You're going to need to pay big bills for whatever's wrong with the truck in the morning."

"Well, twenty bucks on a pizza isn't going to make or break us. Besides, it's the least I can do for you letting us stay."

The cashier looks at the two of us. He's an older man with thick eyebrows; sorta looks like the dad from *Schitt's Creek,* but with grayer hair and a scraggly beard.

He arches a brow at us and glances at Fern. "Some cousins of yours?"

"Nah. Their truck broke down on the exit leading into town."

"Have you called Will yet?"

Fern's smile strains. "I was going to do that in the morning. These two need their rest."

"Where are you from, ladies?"

Aspen and I look at each other.

"Brooklyn?" Aspen says.

I resist the urge to glare at her. *Brooklyn? Brooklyn, New York?*

Fern arches a brow, but then nods, shrugging her shoulders. The cashier stares at us with a perplexed expression as the register spits out the receipt. He limply passes it over to us with a questioning expression.

"Okay. Gimme fifteen and it'll be out." He pauses, still uncertain. "Want anything to drink?"

"Got any lemonade?"

"Only got water. Soda machine's broken."

Aspen smiles. "Water it is."

We go over to a table. I scooch in next to Aspen, and as I nudge against her, she sets her hand on my knee. I smile at her, and she smiles back. Elvis brings us our drinks and then heads back into the kitchen. Fern plays with the salt and sugar packets on the table for a few minutes, then looks at us. She clenches her tongue between her teeth, the way that you do when you're angry, but you don't want to start yelling. It reminds me too much of Mom. I pick at some of the holes in the leather seats.

Fern leans forward, her voice low and ominous. "I may have grown up in a small town my whole life, but even I know damn well they don't drive trucks like that in Brooklyn."

Aspen takes a sip of her water, her expression cool. "Does it matter where we're from?"

"It does if you're going to stay in my house." A dark expression crosses Fern's face as she surveys us once more. "You girls look a little worse for wear. And forgive me, but there is a little bit of a..." she fans her face. "It's the kind of stench that I'd imagine would be on people who haven't been able to stop at a laundromat—which, you wouldn't be if you were on the run from something."

Holy shit, in another life, this lady would've been a good detective. Aspen and I have been around each other so much, I don't think that we can smell ourselves. We turn to look at each other, silently discussing what we should do next. She nods.

I clear my throat and look at Fern. "Little Brook."

"Little—" she repeats, then stops, her eyes widening.

My voice breaks a little as I repeat it. "Little Brook."

It takes a minute for it to sink in for her. The shock turns to grief turns to sympathy. She takes a sip of water and a deep breath before trying to speak again.

"I can't believe your truck broke down. Seems like you two have just had a lifetime's worth of bad luck," she says softly.

I can see her eyes bubbling with curious anticipation. I know what she wants to ask. *Who did it?* While I haven't been paying much attention to the news these past few days, I'm sure that the conspiracy theorists have already flooded the social media accounts of grandparents everywhere.

"We don't know who did it," Aspen says, anticipating the question as well. "I don't know who would want to blow up all those facilities."

Other than her own father, that is.

Knowing the truth is even more of a burden now that I think about it. Because even if we explained what we knew, we'd be called liars. Survivors and the loved ones of the dead are never going to find the same closure we have. We both know who likely blew up Titan Tech, and we know who the monster stampeding downtown was. But other people are never going to find that out—

—well, if we can help it.

"Such a shame, what happened. I think they finally got some of the fires in Maine under control today. And they're already organizing search parties to see who's survived."

Fern says this hopefully, but I don't even want to entertain the possibility of my mom being alive only to be let down later. Besides, she was at Titan Tech right when it blew up. The fires started from that building and spread outward for days. If anyone survived that, they're not going to be the same. I don't even want to imagine Mom in that state. I take deep breaths as I stir the ice in my drink vigorously. Fern, of course, notices this.

"You okay?" she asks softly.

I nod. Aspen rubs small circles in the area between my shoulder blades. Her kindness, although welcome, just makes me sadder, and soon tears are bubbling up.

"Oh no..." Fern reaches across the table and squeezes my hand. "Honey, you lost someone, didn't you?"

"My mom." I wipe my eyes. "I know I lost my mom. She was working there when it blew up. And I don't—it all happened so fast, and I don't know how I'm supposed to live without her."

The weight of that statement hangs heavily in the air between us. Aspen draws in a shuddery breath. Fern blinks rapidly. Her eyes are wet. She folds her hands in her lap and takes a deep breath. Then she reaches across the table and takes my hands.

"I'm so sorry, honey." She stares at me intensely, with such affection that it makes me want to burst into tears again. "You've both been through so much. And I know that you...that you just met me, but I need you to know..." Her voice catches in her throat. "...you *will* learn. When I lost...when I lost my daughter, I didn't know. And it's going to take time, a helluva lot of time, but I promise you, you'll learn."

Aspen wraps an arm around my shoulder. She squeezes me against her side and lets me rest my head against her.

The cashier delivers a piping hot pizza to our table, along with some clean plates. He stares at our mournful faces with pure confusion.

"Well, I told you it would take fifteen!" He serves the pizza right in the cardboard box—a little odd—and shrugs apologetically. "All the serving pans are being washed. Plus, this way you can take what you want and leave."

To my surprise, he plops a seat next to Fern, who rolls her eyes.

"You should be working."

"You should be too. Don't you got another article to write?" He helps himself to a slice of pizza and takes a big bite. Some of the greasy cheese drips right onto the vinyl tablecloth, staining it orange. He looks over at me. "I'll get you another one, if that bothers you."

"No need," I mumble quietly.

"Oh no, don't sweat it. I'll just give you guys another pizza. You don't want it now? You can eat it when you're hungry again. Maybe for breakfast." He laughs a little, and looks at Fern once more, who appears both amused and irritated. She can't seem to stop smirking. I get the feeling they've known each other for a very long time.

"You'll have to forgive Elvis. He may not be a celebrity, but he's as big-headed as one," Fern says, sipping from her glass of water. "And he just kinda worms his way into everyone's business."

"If people didn't air their business out, then I wouldn't know anything." He holds up his hands defensively.

"They air their business out because you ask invasive questions."

"They don't have to answer."

"Do you have any idea what it's like talking to you?" Fern says, and they both laugh.

Aspen and I glance at each other. She smiles at me and elbows me playfully. It's nice to sit with people who feel trustworthy, who hopefully won't be gunned down by some rogue agent of Titan Tech within the next thirty seconds. Like June from the diner. She was so sweet.

"So, when are you going to call Will?" he asks through another mouthful. "You know the man is busy in the mornings."

She shrugs. "Actually, I didn't know that. But it makes sense as to why he never responds to my texts."

"He's a phone call kinda guy. You know that."

"And I'm not. So." She rolls her eyes.

Elvis tenses up for a minute, but then he looks at us and smiles. He wipes at his hands with a napkin. The grease on his fingers is so heavy that little chunks of paper stick to them. It makes me want to shudder. I don't know why, but I *hate* napkins mostly for this reason. If I want my hands clean, I want my hands clean—not covered in the gristle of too-wet tissue paper. When given the chance, I always opt for a wet wipe or to just wash my damn hands.

"Ladies, I have a game for you. You want to know why my name is Elvis?" he pauses, and in the next breath, answers. "My parents named me after a famous singer. But it's not who you're thinking! It is *actually* Elvis Costello. Not Presley. Costello. Yep. And I bet you don't even know who that is."

"Costello?" Aspen scoffs, shaking her head. "*Alison? Oliver's Army?*"

Elvis arches a brow and purses his lips together. It's like he's trying to hold back his own amusement.

"This one here knows all of the old shit." I elbow Aspen and she giggles.

"Well don't you have a mouth on you!"

"She can say what she wants, El." Fern elbows him.

He rolls his eyes, and smiles at Aspen appreciatively. "That's right. Costello. You know some good music. All Fern ever listens to is Florida Georgia Line."

Fern and I both laugh. I finally help myself to a slice of pizza and lose myself in the conversation. Talking with Fern and Elvis reminds me of when my family were all together; the way my parents used to have friendly banter and bounce off each other when we were eating at the dinner table.

Even if it's just for this meal, it's nice to feel like a part of a family again. But then I think about the journal.

The journal that my mom wrote.

And I wonder how it could've all fallen apart.

Elvis's sudden smackdown of his hands on the kitchen table brings me out of my sorrowful reverie. His eyes glisten with excitement as he looks at Aspen.

"So, you *really* know Elvis Costello?"

"Well, sure, but not too well. Like, I know Johnny Cash better than Costello. You like him? Cash?"

"Again, I'm pretty sure she lives in a completely different decade," I say with a laugh.

"Do you sing? Play music?"

"Me?" A ferocious blush spreads across Aspen's face. "I mean, uh…I was in the marching band. I played the flute. Guitar at home. But I'm not like, the best. And I don't think I sing all that well."

"Oh my God. That is a bold-faced lie. This girl bought so many CDs the other day, and she belts out every single tune."

"You know, I don't know how long it'll take you to get your car fixed, but if you're in town on Saturday night, we do an open mic. And it's a lot of fun," Elvis says with a laugh. "I always love seeing new talent, and I'm sure people get sick of me whistlin' away on my harmonica."

"You have a harmonica?" Aspen's eyes widen with excitement.

He nods. "Sure do."

In an instant, Elvis wriggles out of his seat and rushes to the back, out of sight. He's gotta be in his forties, but the man hustles so fast, you'd think he was our age. Fern pleads for him to come back, laughing and shaking her head.

"El, no!" she calls out to him.

Elvis returns, carrying a gold-emblazoned case and a guitar. Aspen's jaw drops, and I can see actual fear in her eyes. She bites her lip as Elvis approaches the table, holding the neck of the guitar high.

"Want to play us a few?"

"Uhh... has that guitar been tuned?"

"Sure has! Tune it every week after the open mics." He beams with pride, seemingly oblivious to her discomfort.

But to her credit, Aspen nods affirmatively. She glances my way, and smiles. I scooch out of my seat so that she can wriggle out. She grabs the guitar, and a nearby chair, then sits down. Strums a few chords and double checks that it's tuned correctly.

Fern casts a pitiful look in Aspen's direction. She mouths, "You don't have to do this," and the two of us giggle. Aspen nods again and takes a deep breath. She smiles at us. It's like her aura has shifted. Gone is the wisecracker, here is the soft-hearted performer. Even in this tacky ass shop, there's something about her that dazzles me.

"Well, since we've been singing so much of his stuff..." She strums a little. "I'd dig a little Walk the Line. This is different than what you're used to though."

She clears her throat, strums a few chords, and the tempo is slower—much slower than I know the song to be—but the notes are there. Her voice is soft, silky as she sings the first few verses. It's romantic yet hopeful; like she's expressing a hopeful longing she hasn't shared with me before. Her eyes are dreamlike, her eyelids heavy, as she sings tenderly of happiness and waiting for the one she loves. And I could almost swear, by the time she gets to the chorus, she's looking right at me, singing to me.

Day 5 - Night

"SO, I GOTTA ASK. What's the deal with you and this Will person that Elvis kept talking about?" Aspen asks.

We just got back from the parlor. Fern's carrying the box of fresh pizza that Elvis promised us. She glances over her shoulder and purses her lips together.

"Will's my ex."

"Boyfriend?"

"Husband."

"Ohh."

"Yeah. He runs the local auto shop here. He'll be the one to tow your car tomorrow. Don't worry, I'll give him a call in the morning. It's just something that I gotta work myself up to do."

"Thank you so much."

"Okay ladies. I'm going to head in and help myself to a beer. Remember: backdoor unlocked. Just holler if you need anything." She waves goodnight and heads inside her house. Aspen and I wave back.

I look up at Aspen. "You don't think they're going to find us, right?"

"Titan Tech people? Karine? I don't know, Riley." She squeezes my hand. "I hope not. Honestly, maybe our car breaking down was a good thing. Throws us off their tracks. They probably think we're a lot farther along than we really are."

"Yeah."

We go inside the She-Shed. Tigger immediately flops down on the little futon, clearly exhausted from his day. I place his bowl of water and his food on the ground by him. He pays it no mind, so I offer him his reindeer toy instead. His eyes light up and he eagerly takes it from me. I'm so glad I saved that one in the fire.

Aspen climbs up the short ladder to get to the loft bed. "This is cool as hell. Kinda wonder why you'd have a loft bed, though, if you could just sleep in the house?"

"Late nights working. Also, she was getting a divorce," I mumble, looking around the space. I feel like I've learned too much about Fern, more than she would've liked us to. And we told her more about us than we wanted to share. "Probably couldn't sleep in the house. Plus, this place is really cute."

"It is." Aspen flops down against the mattress with a heavy sigh. "Even though it feels a little claustrophobic up here." She glances over the edge of the railing. "Hey, Riley, weren't you going to call your dad?"

"Oh." I stop and take a deep breath.

I look inside my backpack, which is where I shoved Mom's journal. Maybe it's because I—once again—almost died yesterday, but it feels like I can't put this off any longer. It's every explanation I've wanted since we moved to that little town. While on some level, it's an invasion of her privacy, it's also a way for her to tell her story. And maybe Mom deserves that. The whole time, I resented her for moving us to Little Brook. But if Dad was somehow responsible for what happened? Then I want to know.

I hold up the journal to Aspen. She nods.

"You're going to read that first?"

I plop down beside Tigger on the couch. "I guess so."

"Okay. I'm here if you need me."

I crack open the journal, to the last page I'd read. I can smell the faint traces of her perfume on the pages. Trace my fingers across the weathered, coffee-stained paper, look at the familiar loops of her cursive handwriting. I take a deep breath once more. Although I'm afraid, I dive right in.

May 12th, 2021

Tonight, Ivan confronted me. Insisted that our daughter was the real victim in all of this. Told me that he wished that we could work things out.

"That would've been great," I said. "About twenty thousand dollars ago."

I'm so tired of Ivan erasing my feelings. Over and over again. Or worse, he'll do that thing where he brings up Riley instead of us. And Riley is important, but her wellbeing can't continue to supersede my own. Not when I've been making sacrifices for this long! How is that fair? Isn't my happiness important for Riley's happiness? Why am I the one expected to pop a Prozac and grin and bear it, when Ivan's the one causing all of this?

This was what I brought up in my last session with you, Dr. I can't keep feeling like I'm less of a person simply because I'm a mother. And I hate to say it, but ever since Riley was born, that's how he's treated me. We're friendly, of course. He's always been my best friend. But marital life, I swear to God, feels like a chore with him. Every anniversary, pre-planned. Every Valentine's Day. And he was working hard, I know that, so I tried to be flexible. I tried to be gentle. I tried to be patient and kind and understanding and everything my mother bitched at me about and told me to be. Then I found out about the gambling problem.

"Don't worry about it, I've got it handled," he'd say as he went out to the casino once more. I still remember the night he called me—drunk— from that woman's hotel room. Funny how he was the one who insisted on marital counseling but when I brought it up, he shut down. He will do that, and then go home and have the audacity to say that I'm the one who isn't trying, and that Riley is the victim in all of this.

Riley is the victim, but I'm not the perpetrator. Far from it. And I'm not gonna let him twist the narrative anymore.

He got angry at me. "You know if we're going to move forward, you're going to have to let some things go, right?"

But I did let it go. I told him that. The $5,000 spent in Portland. The other $1,200 in Vegas. I let that go. It was when the debt ballooned so high it became too big to ignore that I decided I *would let it go no longer. I want to help Riley when she goes to college, and this is going to destroy all chances of that—not to mention ruin our plans for retirement.*

"And I told you already that it's fine. It's fine. I'm getting the job in Seattle for that reason, remember?"

You need <u>*THERAPY.*</u> *Gambling addiction treatment. Something that you still haven't looked into! You don't need another job, you need to make sure this doesn't happen again!*

An eye roll. A dismissive sigh. Insisting for "another fucking beer." She's going to be back soon, please don't do this. More shouting. Red faced accusations of how I'm just desperate to find an excuse to leave.

Maybe I am. You want me to lie? Lie like you? I'm not like you, Ivan. And I'm pretty damn proud of myself for that. I may be the fucking monster here. But I'm not you. And God forbid Riley grows up to be like you.

I flip through the next few journal entries. They're sporadic. Sometimes in depth. Other times ferocious scribbles of solitary curse words. Sometimes actual scribbles, like she was so upset she couldn't even find the words.

Who loaned you the money, Ivan?

Then, like a fresh breath of air after being submerged underwater, it all comes clear. Their biggest secret, and her reason for everything.

The divorce *had* actually been worse than I thought it was. And Mom moved us across the country, to the most remote and podunk town imaginable, in the hopes we would be out of reach from whoever Dad got that loan from. Mom was trying to protect us, and when her friend had offered her a job, she had jumped at the chance to leave him because she thought she could save me.

And then she died in a fire.

I close the journal with shaking hands. Look up at Aspen. Her eyes immediately meet mine. I don't have to say anything. She climbs down from the loft and sits beside me.

"Bad?" She asks.

I nod. "Really, really bad. Like. Worse than I thought." I drag my hands over my face. I feel like I have lived a thousand years. "I think…he's indebted to a loan shark."

"*What?*" Even Aspen is surprised—which is kinda funny, considering the things her dad has done.

"He's a gambling addict. *Possibly* a high functioning alcoholic. We were apparently like twenty thousand dollars in debt and he paid some of that off, but he never told Mom how."

"You didn't know?"

"No! I mean, Dad worked a lot when I was a kid. H-he travelled all the time. But holy shit, if all of this is true?" I sigh. "My *Mom*, dude. My freaking Mom."

She kept it all under wraps. Kept her shitty comments to a passive aggressive minimum. Never so much as hinted Dad had this secret life he was living when he wasn't with us. Did I ever really know my father? How much of his persona was just carefully crafted enough to hide his flaws? How long had Mom been forced to keep this all under wraps? And how could Dad lie to me for this long? How could he even be upset with Mom for doing what she did?

"I gotta call my dad."

Aspen shuffles uncomfortably where she sits. "Are you sure about that?"

I reach for my phone and she grabs my wrist and shakes her head. Her grip is firm but not aggressive. She gives me a squeeze.

"Look, Riley. You just learned a lot of heavy information. And you're exhausted. I want you to know that you don't have to feel like you need to say anything to him right now."

"I know, Aspen. But I have to."

As if on cue, Dad calls my phone, filling the tense room with urgent buzzing. I keep my eyes on Aspen.

"Hello?" I answer coldly.

He chuckles, in that kind of snide way he has when he's annoyed with you. "So, you are still going to be nasty to me when you were in the wrong?"

"Dad— "

"—Don't you *ever* hang up on me like that again. I can't believe you, Riley. Do you have any idea how scared I was?"

I grit my teeth. All my nerves feel like needles. He has no idea how terrified *I* have been. Me, one of the only survivors of an explosion. Me, who has lost almost everything. Me, who has almost died so many times. And he has the nerve to say that *I* scared him?

"Riley Anne Grishin, now would be an appropriate time to apologize." He scoffs. "'I'm sorry, Dad.' How hard is that?"

"Can you just chill out for a second?"

"*Chill out?*" He shouts back into the phone. "You're seriously telling me to chill out?"

"Twenty thousand dollars."

The sudden silence that follows is both chilling and satisfying. I wish I was there to see the look on his face when he realized the tables had turned. Several moments pass in silence. Aspen watches, her eyes wide and anxious. She strokes Tigger's back over and over again.

Finally, Dad speaks, his voice hoarse and soft. "What?"

"Twenty thousand dollars," I repeat, slowly. "I found out, Dad."

"What? What are you talking about?"

"Don't play dumb with me. You're not stupid and neither am I."

"I…"

"I found a journal that Mom apparently kept in the truck. And in it, she mentions that you gambled away twenty thousand dollars, and somehow paid off that debt, and didn't tell her how."

A pause.

"Does it matter how?" He sighs. "It's been taken care of; it's gone now. It's not something you'd ever have to worry about—"

"—*But how did you pay it off, Dad?*" I'm surprised at the sudden anger in my voice. The pure fury that stirs in my fiery stomach like a cauldron about to bubble over. If I could reach through the phone and smack him, I would. "You never explained why. And her parents don't have that kind of money and neither do yours."

He stays silent, and I pile it on.

"The past six months I have wondered, *desperately*, why my life is falling apart and why Mom made all these borderline insane decisions, and you knew the *whole* time! You knew that you ruined our lives, and you let her take the fall!"

"Let's get something straight here. I never said one *bad* word about your mother—"

"—You didn't have to! You acted like she was crazy! We both did, a-and she had valid reasons for doing what she did! Because she was *terrified*! And you have the nerve to sit here and tell me none of that matters?"

"I'm not saying it doesn't matter, I'm saying she overreacted." Dad's voice shakes. I can tell he's almost on the verge of tears. "She didn't have to do *everything*. She didn't have to take you away from me."

"Do you care, Dad?" I flip open the journal and fumble through the pages. I read glimpses of passages to him, about her pain, her heartbreak; the fact that he never supported her and always belittled her. "You drink! You g-gamble! And you had *affairs?*"

"That was a one-time thing! That wasn't even an affair, Riley!"

"Yeah? Well Jesus, Dad! Reading this now? Moving to Maine wasn't far enough!"

He sobs. It's heartbroken, strained, laced with regret. "Riley. I have had my share of fuckups. And maybe you're right. Maybe somewhere along the way, I fell out of love with your mother, or I didn't try hard enough with her. But one thing is for sure. I love *you*. You've always been a priority for me. Hell, that's why I'm driving across the entire country to get to you!"

I stiffen. "Go back."

"*What?*"

"Go. Back. I don't want to see you right now."

I'm sobbing, my tears blinding me. Every time I close my eyes I see my mom's face, with her ruby red lipstick and playful smile. Remember that I didn't reply to the last text she sent me. Remember how I spoke to her that morning, and every morning in Little Brook before that. Giving her shit, being angry, when she just wanted me to have a relationship with my father. To still see him through the rose-colored glasses I had always seen him through. Maybe it was wrong of her to keep me in the dark—honestly it probably was—but now I know she did it out of love. She loved me, even when I was at my worst.

And I couldn't even text her back on the day she died.

"Mom is dead now, and the last six months of her life, I treated her like shit because of *you*. You ruined my life. I don't even know if I ever want to see you again."

Before he can respond, I hang up. Aspen's arms immediately open for an embrace, and I cry for what feels like hours. She rubs my back, tracing circles against it.

"It's not your fault," she whispers. "It's not."

She rests her chin against my scalp, presses her lips into it. Her arms wrap around me and squeeze so tightly, I think my lungs are about to burst. I tap her leg and laugh.

"Hurts."

"Oh, sorry!" She holds me at arm's length, embarrassed. "The past few days I was…well, I knew to hold back a bit."

I laugh, but as soon as I do, another wave of sadness crashes over me and I'm sobbing again. She cups my face in her hands, forcing me to look at her. Her gaze is fierce, almost electrifying.

"I need you to know it's not your fault."

I shake my head. She leans in closer.

"Say it. 'It's not my fault.'"

My voice comes out in a hoarse whisper. "It's not my fault."

"I can't hear you."

"It's not my fault." I speak louder, but my voice is strangled by my own tears.

She beams with pride for the briefest of moments. Then serious again. "Now say, my mom loved me no matter what."

"My mom loved me," I whisper, "no matter what."

She smiles. "Good job."

"Can I have another hug?"

"You can have all the hugs in the world." She wraps her arms around me and pulls me in again. "I'm so sorry, Ri."

"What am I going to do?" I sob. "I was going to go to Seattle and *live* with him, Aspen."

"You have people. Your grandparents. Caia and Khalil. You have options." She squeezes me. "If there are two things I've learned about you Riley, it's that a lot of people love you."

"What's the other thing?"

"That you can really take a beating."

We laugh hysterically. Tigger whines and licks both of our faces, anxiously wriggling his way in between us. We both pet him and he rolls upside down, onto his belly, stretching his body across our laps. I grab his reindeer toy and for a while, the three of us play tug-of-war.

Tigger flops down in a state of exaggerated exhaustion. Aspen looks over at me. She has a curious expression on her face: biting her lip, holding back her vivacious smile.

"What?" I ask her, smiling back. "What do you want to do now?"

She grabs my phone, and flicks away what appears to be at least fifty notifications. She looks up at me.

"I'm just gonna block him for the night."

"Probably best."

She does this, and then opens Spotify. Cheesy eighties pop music pumps through the air. She bounces around a little bit, tousles her hair, and grabs my hands. We dance and we keep dancing, until we're both breathless from laughing. She doesn't take her eyes off mine.

Suddenly the music shifts. Slows. And so do we. She smiles shyly and gives a little curtsy. I bow. She places her hand on my hip and pulls me closer, till we almost touch, nose to nose. Her hand shifts to the small of my back, and she guides me in a tiny circle. We move so slowly but I feel so dizzy. My head weightless, my heart so light, as if everything that had happened has suddenly evaporated with her touch. That's her power. And I'm entranced by every part of her until I begin to focus and the sounds of the music filter through the haziness of this dream.

"Oh my God, I-I think I know this one," I say. "This is from *Shrek*."

"This is the Eels."

"No, this is from *Shrek*," I say, and from the nervous way she refuses to meet my eyes, I can tell something is up. "Aspen, have you never seen *Shrek*?"

"I have seen it. Just like, once though. When I was little." She laughs a little nervously. She still won't look at me. "When I watched it, I got uh…kinda depressed. Because like, I don't know. The whole concept of true love just seems so toxic to me."

"Really? You seem like a hopeless romantic type."

She wrinkles her nose and smiles. "Really?"

"No, I'm just giving you shit. But ok, why do you think true love is awful?"

"Because it's a fantasy. Because it could never happen to me, knowing what I am. And the idea of waiting however many years to meet my one true love is infinitely depressing."

"Damn."

"Not to mention, waiting that long just for *one* person to love me?"

"Fiona wasn't just loved by Shrek. There was Donkey too; they were friends."

"Ooh. Wow. *Donkey.*"

I laugh. "Okay, but did you ever see the sequels? They get so many friends! And kids!"

"And again, circling back to my first point…that's a fantasy." She shakes her head. "Could never be me."

"That's not true." I shake my head right back. "Just because it hasn't happened to you yet, doesn't mean it never will. If Caia and Khalil met you, I'm sure they'd love you. And my grandparents. You and Grandpa George could talk for hours about old music."

"If I ever wound up in Portland…"

I smile. "You'll just have to come with me."

"To Portland?"

"Yeah. I can't go to Seattle now…but I could go back to Portland. Live with my grandparents. You can live with us too."

"I…Riley, I couldn't thank you enough for that."

"You've saved my life like, twice. Least I could do."

"I mean, I'm kinda the reason your life was at risk in the first place."

"Don't ruin the moment."

She giggles. Her hand touches my cheek. "I'll bring it back. One more song."

We keep dancing. Somehow our bodies come even closer together, till not a breath of air could sneak between us. Her hands feel so warm it's almost like they could burn me. I'm so excited I could spontaneously combust. I try to drown out all of the self-doubt bubbling up in my head. *But look at you, you sad sack of shit. She could never.*

But when she smiles at me like that, it makes me wonder. Could she?

"So…I've been thinking about what you said earlier."

"Said a lot of things earlier. You'll have to refresh me." Her voice is deeper, yet softer. When she speaks, she almost presses her lips against my ear, and my knees quake.

"You mentioned you didn't like French kissing. But I don't have a good frame of reference…" I trail off, laughing nervously.

"No?"

"I had a girlfriend once for a little while, but we never French kissed. And like, I went on a really bad date with this Imagine Dragons fanboy who sorta mashed his teeth and tongue into me, it was—"

"—You want to try?"

"Yeah. Yeah, I do."

She cups my face in her hands steadily, but her body vibrates with excitement. I can feel my heart and stomach somersaulting over each other. The wild idea that she's just as eager to do this as I am. She leans in slowly, pausing just before our lips meet.

"Ri," she whispers. "You're supposed to close your eyes."

"O-oh."

She giggles as she presses her lips against mine, and I lean into the kiss. I open my mouth and I can taste her tongue, and faint traces of her strawberry lip gloss. She doesn't taste like anything, but she's warm, and eager, and *wants* me. The most beautiful girl I have ever met wants to kiss me until I can't breathe and run her fingers through my too-tangled hair. She's soft, and gentle, and when I kiss her, I finally understand why people love kissing. Because I love kissing her. And I never want to kiss anyone else.

I finally pull away for air. Aspen's satisfied smile grows big. She wiggles her eyebrows. What a dork. A stupidly hot dork.

"So…did I exceed your expectations?"

"Pretty great."

"Pretty great? I'm sorry, but your knees were shaking." She giggles. Kisses my cheek.

"Out of fear! I mean, you *did* say that you could only sometimes control your acid power."

My teasing won't diminish her triumphant smile. She's cocky and confident and for some reason looking at her face makes me feel as full and warm as kissing her.

She boops me on the nose with her finger. "I can't believe you acted like you weren't into me."

"Oh my God, Aspen, you *literally* said I wasn't your type."

"Yeah, because I didn't want you to freak out," she says, laughing. "And I wasn't into you until I got to know you better."

She wraps her arms around my waist and kisses my forehead. There's something so easy about how she does this. Intimate. Gentle. And I've never felt safer than I do in this moment. Like I'm right where I'm supposed to be.

Day 6 – Morning

"YEAH, I DON'T KNOW, ladies. I think this truck might be on its last legs."

It's the last thing you want to hear on a road trip, but at this point, Aspen and I just roll our eyes and exchange knowing looks. The bar was on the floor, and we just sank right under it. Will slides out from underneath the truck, wiping his face against the sleeve of his plaid shirt. Fern hovers anxiously in the background. Her fingernails have been in her mouth since we got here.

The inside of the shop is cavernous; I'm pretty sure it's the biggest building in the entire town. Steel beams run across the ceiling, and a massive skylight overhead lets in all the light the shop needs—which is actually unfortunate, because parts of this place are hella disgusting. On one wall, there's a pile of what I think are rolled up carpets that smell like Tigger when he rolls in goose shit. And they look vaguely wet, so that's also not a good sign. There're also numerous empty beer cans laying around the place, and an entire shelf dedicated to some fancy craft brews. Very much a man cave, despite it somehow being a place of business.

Will stands up, stretches, and migrates over to his workshop table. An open bag of sunflower seeds sits next to an assortment of wrenches, and despite his hands being covered in grime, he shakes out a few and pops them in his mouth. Fern shudders in disgust.

"Really, Will? Not even going to wipe them off?"

Will looks at her blankly and then wipes his hands on his (equally dirty) pants. "So yeah. I could probably fix up the engine, but I don't know if it's going to get you where you need to go. Minneapolis, right?"

"I mean…" I sigh heavily. "Yeah. I guess."

Fern tilts her head to the side. "What do you mean, you guess? That's what you said last night, right?"

"Uhh…" Aspen places a gentle hand on my shoulder. "Some stuff happened between her and her dad last night. But y'know, Minneapolis still works, because we could probably get a flight to Portland from there. Far easier than from Ohio."

"Honestly ladies, you're a hell of a lot closer to Cleveland or Columbus than Minneapolis." Will looks between the two of us.

I don't like the idea of flying out of Ohio, personally. We haven't put enough miles between us and Karine—although to do that, I think we'd have to fly to the surface of the sun. We'd probably be putting a ton of lives at risk just by stepping within fifteen miles of an airport.

Aspen shakes her head. I can tell from the look in her eyes that she's worried about the same things I am. "We can't. I mean, we did promise Riley's dad that we'd meet him in Minneapolis. Even if we're not going back to Seattle with him…we should probably meet him there."

"Yeah, so he doesn't declare us runaways."

I should probably unblock him from my phone. I make a mental note to do that.

Eventually.

Will looks between the two of us, completely bewildered. Fern notices this and rolls her eyes, as if she's seen that look so many times before.

"Will, you heard them. What do you need, and how long is it going to take to get this done?"

"Uhh…we're talking about five hundred dollars' worth of work here, Fern."

"Take it out of the alimony check."

Will shrugs his shoulders. "Okay. Done deal."

"We could put it on the credit card we have," I offer hoarsely, but part of me wonders if we even have that kind of credit. My mom didn't exactly have the best financial situation. There's probably some kind of limit, one that I'm sure we're only like, $200 away from.

Will shakes his head. "Sorry. I don't do credit." he wipes his hands on his pants once again. Why are they turning from black to green? "I'll get to work. Drive the car to you tomorrow morning."

"Works for us." Aspen looks at me and back at Will. She gives him an appreciative, beaming smile. "Thank you so much."

I can tell her charm worked. A smile finally cracks across his face, a pale blush. He ducks his head and tightens his baseball cap around his head, then looks at Fern. She smiles back at him, and between them, I can feel this indescribable energy. I don't know if it's love or nostalgia or history or what. Whatever it is, it's raw, and gives me this sad feeling. Like every time they see each other, they're reminded of everything they loved and lost.

"Ladies, I'm gonna talk to Will for a sec. Wanna go check on Tigger?"

We nod and exit the shop, into the near-blinding sunlight. When I glance over my shoulder, Fern is shyly approaching Will, a smile across her face. I turn my head back just before the door closes behind me and look in Tigger's direction. He's chilling in the back of the pickup, safely tied down, and with an already half-empty bowl of water.

"I'm sorry, boy. We were in there a while, weren't we," I murmur, scratching around his ears.

It's far too hot for me to be affectionate with him. He flicks his ears and lays his head down, exhausted. Aspen whistles.

"Damn. Rejected."

"He can set his own boundaries."

"He's a dog."

"He can still set his own boundaries. Dogs need them too."

Aspen cracks a smile. I watch as Fern walks out of the shop and jogs over to her car, fanning herself with her shirt. As she starts the engine, she rolls down her window.

"You ladies hungry for some lunch?"

BOTH ASPEN AND I are eager for the opportunity to eat a meal in a place that doesn't use bacon grease to cook everything. Fern opens the door to her house and lets us inside, and the first thing I notice are the pristine stacks of cardboard boxes. Labelled with her daughter's name, the cursive letters spelling *Hannah Jane,* followed by *School* or *Nursery* or *Clothes* or *Toys.* The inside of the house is cheerful, full of big windows with yellow sunlight sparkling through. It's a stark contrast to the darkness sitting in the space before us; the fact that Fern can fit her daughter's whole life into just fifteen boxes.

"I'm gonna donate those. Eventually. Will and I gotta come to an agreement." She jingles her keys nervously. "Can you kick off your shoes before coming into the kitchen?"

Aspen and I comply. It feels so nice to be in our socks for once; to feel the grainy texture of the oak hardwood floors beneath our feet. We walk down a hallway into an open concept kitchen and living room. A little half wall divides the kitchen from the circular red dining table. The fridge is still decorated with kindergarten arts and crafts; fingerpainted turkeys made from little hands and stick-figure family portraits in weak watercolors. Fern migrates over to the sink and pours us each a glass of tap water before plopping in a few ice cubes. We each grab our glass and murmur a respective thank you, but the heaviness of the space weighs on us. No wonder she didn't want us to sleep in her house last night. It feels like a never-ending funeral.

"I know." She acknowledges this fact, nodding slowly. "I'm planning on selling soon. Leaving town."

"Really?"

"It's hard to sit with the weight of everything," she says quietly. "Even three years later."

"Three years isn't a long time." Aspen says, and I resist the urge to shoot her a look.

"In the grand scheme of things, it isn't. But when…" she trails off, unable to say it. Just nods. "Trust me, it feels like a lifetime."

I elbow Aspen. "It's a beautiful house. This is the kind of place I've always wanted to live in. Natural wood and lots of sunlight."

"It's good if you're a painter or an artist. Will was. Is. Honestly, I don't know if he still draws in his spare time anymore. But he did when we were younger, before our daughter was born. Used to make these big, beautiful landscapes and portraits. It was unreal." Fern pokes her head inside her fridge, and glances over her shoulder at us. "So, y'all eat turkey meat?"

"Uh, yeah."

"Good. Because that's all I got. Also, they'll have to be half sandwiches because I forgot to go grocery shopping." She laughs and drags out the ingredients. Grabs a cutting board from a nearby drawer crammed with far too many utensils and sets to work. "Lettuce, tomato, mayo? Promise I'll remove the wilted parts."

"Sure."

"And what will your boy have? Turkey?"

I shake my head and laugh. "He only eats breakfast and dinner. No lunch. Gotta keep his weight down."

"Me and him both." She plates one sandwich and passes it to Aspen, then another to me. "I've been thinking about getting out on the trails lately."

"There are hiking trails?"

"Oh, plenty. Real pretty country out here, too. Flat. Probably not like the mountains and the big forests that you're used to." She smiles at me. "Riley, you didn't grow up in Maine, did you?"

"Me? No."

"I figured. Aspen has a different accent than you do."

Aspen blinks, surprised. "Really?"

She nods and taps her ears. "I can hear it just a little bit."

"I grew up in Portland, Oregon."

"Oregon sounds beautiful. Just the best of everything, all in one space. Mountains. Endless trees. Ocean waters. Been thinking that I might move there after I sell this place."

"It is beautiful." I take a nervous sip of water. "Did you grow up here, Fern?"

"Yeah. Well, a little further out. Will and I went to high school together. The rest was history."

"Is it kinda hard? Thinking about leaving a place where you've grown up?"

I can tell from the way she stares at me that I've asked the wrong question. I bite my sandwich and avert my eyes. She takes a deep breath, folds her arms, and contemplatively stares down at the table.

"Hard was burying my daughter," she says carefully. "But I feel like I owe it to her and to myself to keep moving forward. To live my life as best I can. It's taken me three years to realize it but spending all day crying over her is not gonna bring her back."

When she says this, I inhale sharply, almost like she's punched me in the gut. But Fern says this with a calmness and strength that I cannot fathom. I haven't gone a single day without crying since losing my mom. The world has felt like it was ending perpetually since that date. How Fern could wake up in the morning and not feel like the sun was gone is either a testament to her strength, or how time heals all wounds.

"Sorry, darling." She nods apologetically in my direction. "You guys are at the beginning of your grief journey. Don't think that you can't cry. Weeks, months, years, however long it takes. It's gonna take up almost all the space in your heart and that's okay. Anyone you loved and lost should take up that much space. It just means that time with them was worth it."

I nod, and for the first time in days, don't have the urge to blink away tears as I take a sip of water. Underneath the table, Aspen takes my hand in hers. Squeezes it once, then twice. Reminds me again that I'm not going through this alone. And in that moment, that's all I need.

Day 7 — Morning

"LADIES!" A FAMILIAR, BOOMING voice echoes behind me.

I turn around, but I'm surprised that it's not Will. It's Elvis, with a big ol' smile plastered across his face, puttering up the road in a janky old Subaru—the last kind of car I would expect this man to drive, but then again, he's quirky like that. Maybe it's exactly the kind of car he should be driving.

Before the car even rolls to a stop, he sticks a plastic bag out his window. "Cinnamon rolls," he yells, as if that somehow explains why he randomly showed up here at eight a.m. Actually, that's a perfectly reasonable explanation, but I just can't believe the dude is nice enough to bring food here for two strangers, *this* early in the morning.

It's cool and crisp outside, and the dew is still fresh on the grass. Tigger, tail wagging and tongue hanging out, stands in the yard, covered in grass stains. One of his favorite things to do is roll around in fresh grass. Unfortunately, that means he's going to stink to high heaven when he gets inside the truck. Aspen and I both shuffle around, already exhausted before the day's journey has even begun. The morning light is barely breaking through the trees, and it's casting a golden light on the changing leaves.

I look in Fern's direction. She's wearing plaid pajamas, and has a thin weathered pink robe tied loosely around her waist. She rolls her eyes and takes a sip from her steaming oversized mug of hazelnut-scented coffee.

"He texted me last night and I told him you guys were leaving."

Aspen appears thrilled to see him. "Elvis! Are you finally going to play for us on your harmonica?"

A disappointed look crosses his face. "Damn it. That's what I forgot." He engages the emergency brake and the car creaks loudly in protest, but he pays it no mind. He steps out of the car without turning it off and Aspen rushes to take the box from him. "I just wanted to send you off and thank you for playing such good music the other night. Prettiest version of Walk the Line I have heard in all my forty-two years of living."

"Aww, thank you."

"And well… given all that has happened to you, I wanted to see you off. Make sure you were okay." He shoves his hands in his pockets and grins at Fern. "Although I'm sure Fern has taken *lovely* care of you both."

"She has." I smile at Fern.

Aspen removes the box of cinnamon rolls from their plastic bag and ever-eager Elvis opens up the box to grab a roll from inside.

He takes a huge bite, smudging the icing all over his face. Aspen offers Fern and me the box, and we each take one. We stand around, our fingers sticky as we munch into our delicious breakfast. They're sugary, but not so sweet that it hurts my mouth or leaves me with a sickly feeling in my stomach. And the texture is heavenly, fluffy on the inside but crisp on the edges.

"The Parlor makes these in the mornings," Elvis explains as he licks some of the icing from his fingers.

"Elvis. Use a napkin!"

"Does it look like I have a napkin?"

Fern rolls her eyes and heads back inside. Aspen and I giggle a little, and she returns with some napkins and hand sanitizer, passing them out to each of us. I stare at the hand sanitizer in surprise. Fern smiles.

"I noticed yesterday that you don't really use your napkin, but you washed your hands afterward. Trust me, I get it. My daughter was the same way."

I squirt some hand sanitizer into my hands to rub away the stickiness. When Aspen finishes her roll, she licks her fingers and eagerly does the same. Elvis grabs a fistful of the napkins and sort of wads them up in between his hands.

"Thank you so much, Elvis," I murmur. It's been so great to be in a place where no one is trying to kill us, and better yet, actually cares about us. Who will wake up however early in the morning to get to his job and get two random teenage girl's breakfast. "We really appreciate this. They're delicious."

He taps the box. "Be sure to take the rest. Whenever you stop in a hotel for the night, you can reheat them, and they'll still be good."

We can hear the sound of tires grinding against gravel and turn to see my truck heading up the road. It looks…good. Freshly cleaned, its pristine looking red paint almost glittering in the sun. Did Will wax it or something? Gone is the grime from the windshield, and even the hubcaps are sparkling. When the truck pulls to a stop, I can almost smell the freshness of the rubber on the brand-new tires.

Will turns it off and hops out of the truck. He smiles and swaggers up to us, keys in hand.

"Here you go."

"Thank you. It…it looks amazing," I stammer, surprised. Is this really the same truck? I could have sworn we took it to a car wash once or twice, but I guess Will just really knows what he's doing. That's a gift. "And you're sure that we don't o-owe you anything?"

"Lucky for you, Fern's taking care of it."

Fern gives my shoulder a little affectionate squeeze, pressing her cheek against mine. "Don't you worry about it. Again, it's the least I can do."

"No, Fern. It's so much," I whisper, my throat hoarse. I shake my head and turn back to her, and she appears just as emotional as me. We laugh and embrace each other tightly. These past two days, I think her and I have shared some kind of connection; some kind of bond that I can't exactly describe. It's too special to have words for. "I can't believe you'd do this for us. Thank you so much."

"Oh, come on, Riley." She laughs breathlessly, and I can tell she's trying not to cry too. She pulls away and holds me at arm's length. Looks at me with that broad smile of hers. "We gotta load up your truck, and you gotta get on the road! You still have a long ways to go."

We load up, and everyone pitches in. I can't help but notice as I pack the car that Will is watching me out of the corner of his eye. Every time his steely blue gaze turns in my direction, I feel a shiver down my spine, but I choose to ignore it. When we finally finish loading up the car, Elvis runs inside to use the restroom—briefly exclaiming that he drank *way* too much coffee—and Fern heads back into the house to grab us some extra food for our trip.

As soon as we're alone, Will immediately pulls us off to the side. He crosses his arms and glares at the two of us. My heart sinks lower and lower into my stomach. We don't even bother to ask him what's going on. It's obvious from the look on his face he definitely knows something. He looks between the two of us, reaches into the pocket of his tattered jeans, and withdraws a familiar object. Another tracker. Like the one we pulled out of Aspen's neck, but bigger, and a little flatter.

"I don't know what the hell is going on or what you two are up to, nor do I give a shit. But Fern cannot afford to be caught up in any dangerous games," he speaks slowly, in a way that's so controlled it makes me uneasy. "You're going to say your goodbyes with a smile on your face, and you're going to drive away, and not look back."

Aspen and I look at each other, and we say nothing. We turn back to Will, and we nod slowly. By the time Fern and Elvis come out to say goodbye, we're all smiles. Will is probably the worst actor out of all of us—the man can barely be bothered to turn up the corners of his lips. By the time we get in the truck, he's full-on scowling. I turn the key in the ignition and the engine roars to life. The tank is full of gas, and we're ready to rock.

Fern and Elvis eagerly wave to us.

"Give us a call if you need anything!" Fern shouts. "Take care, girls!"

"And friend me on Facebook!" Elvis adds. "I need someone to teach me how to use it!"

Aspen and I laugh. I try to blink back the tears that are quickly rising in my eyes as I wave goodbye. We turn onto the road, and as we drive away, I can hear their voices calling out all kinds of goodbyes and well wishes. Aspen takes my hand and kisses it, then holds it as we drive along.

"You think he's going to tell her what happened?" I ask, glancing over my shoulder. The little house recedes further and further into the woods, until it's finally eclipsed by a pine tree. I feel a pang in my gut. "He was really upset."

"I think if he's really scared about getting her involved in it, he's not going to tell her." Aspen shakes her head. "Because honestly the less she knows about what happened, the better. In case someone comes sniffing around. He clearly still cares a lot about her."

"You think so too? I was wondering about that."

"Yeah. Pretty obvious from how they looked at each other."

My chest flutters with some indescribable sadness. A broken family, still bonded by love. Maybe that love has changed or evolved into something else—I guess that's what grief and trauma can do to a person—but still, it was there, nonetheless. They were good people. The kind of people that we needed to meet on this hellish journey. People who made me feel like we could trust others again. Like we don't have to shoulder the weight of everything alone.

"You think that they're still after us?"

"If there's a tracker on the truck? Yeah, Riley. I don't think we're too far away from Katrice catching up to us."

"Karine."

"Same diff." She yawns and stretches, leaning back in her seat. "Damn, I wish Elvis had brought us some coffee. That would've hit the spot."

"It was nice of him to bring the rolls, though."

As we head down the main road into town, I take one last look around at everything. The Pizza Parlor. The little shops and homes. "I almost wish we could've stayed here longer, y'know?"

Aspen nods slowly. "It's better though that we get going. Last thing I'd want is for us to lose *more* friends."

Her voice sounds oddly hollow as she speaks. She stares out the window for a few moments, then turns back to me and raises her eyebrows. That warm, familiar smile resurfaces on her face.

"Besides, it was a small town. Don't think we could do much of this there." She glances down at our hands, still woven tightly together. "They'd probably flip a lid. Now I get to kiss you more."

It hits me. We haven't kissed since we danced together in the shed. We haven't gotten to do much of anything; we've been so distracted by our conversations with Fern and Elvis and taking care of Tigger.

Aspen winks at me, like she's realizing what I've just realized. And she leans in and gives me a kiss on the cheek. I turn my head back to her; kiss her full on the lips, a warmth and satisfaction filling my body with joy. But just as I do, I jerk away from her and steer us back onto the road. Tigger whines with frustration in the backseat.

"Smooth moves, Ri."

"Thank you." I pause for a moment, carefully surveying the signs as we approach the highway. In the rearview mirror, the town gets smaller and smaller. I've had to say goodbye to so many things lately, and it's not getting any easier. "Do you think they'll be okay, Aspen?"

Her brow furrows in deep thought for a moment, then her expression softens. "I think so." She glances at me. "Oh, you're not talking about Titan Tech, are you?"

"Not…entirely."

She drums her fingertips against her knees. "Like Fern said, grief is a journey."

Grief is a journey. A longwinded, emotionally exhausting journey which I've only just begun. Grief is also a beast. It divides people and consumes them, as it did with Fern and Will, as it's doing with Dad and me.

And then I realize.

"Aspen, wait, I didn't unblock my dad from my phone."

"Oh. Oh shit." She grabs it from the cupholder, unlocks it, and moves to the contacts. "Let's see. Alright, I fixed it." She glances in my direction. "Uh…do you want to call him?"

A queasy feeling churns my stomach. I bite my lip.

"You want *me* to do it?" She squirms uncomfortably in her seat.

"I mean, I didn't say that, but…"

"I'll do it for another kiss."

"What if I promised *two* kisses?"

"It's a done deal."

TO MY SURPRISE, WHEN Aspen called my dad, he didn't ask to speak to me. He was quiet and solemn, like all the fury he had had suddenly deflated. He was glad to hear that we're okay but told Aspen that we would need to talk soon. He also bitterly ended the call with a snide reminder that he could have totally called the police and reported us as runaways after the stunt we pulled.

I feel like my relationship with my dad has been irrevocably ruined, and Aspen keeps reminding me that it's not my fault. If she weren't here, I think I would have had another breakdown. We've got miles to go, and maybe two days of travelling left, and we'll be lucky if this old truck doesn't die on us before then. Or get us killed.

We stop for lunch at a burger joint, and the two of us solemnly swear that we're done with greasy, fattening food. It's Subway sandwiches and Wendy's salads from here on out, less we wind up growing out of our clothes before we even make it to our final destination. Today I'm wearing shorts that I swore fit me just last week, and somehow, they're pulling tight around my thighs, threatening to chafe my too-dry skin.

I think one of the reasons I feel so awful is I'm used to exercising every day, biking and hiking and running around with Tigger. But to sit in a car for hours upon hours is just brutal—hurts your butt, and your legs feel like Jell-O every time you move. And maybe this is TMI, but all this fast food isn't helping my bowel movements. I go back and forth between feeling so constipated I might explode, or— *y'know*—actually exploding. Also, my skin looks the worst it's ever been. Sunken-in raccoon circles and festering zits along my cheeks and between my unkempt bushy brows. I'm surprised Aspen is even attracted to me right now. I look and feel disgusting. She still looks like a goddess even when she's tired. Not a blemish or a dark mark on her. Maybe it's the monster DNA. Or maybe it's eating human flesh.

We drive in the car for another few hours, inching closer to Illinois. We beam excitedly at each other, realizing how close we are. First, it's Illinois, then Wisconsin, and then finally, Minnesota. Minneapolis is still a long way to go, but it feels that much more obtainable. Tigger's polite woof stirs us out of our reverie, and we end up needing to pull over at the next rest stop.

Aspen takes Tigger out to go pee while I make a dash for the restroom. This rest stop bathroom sucks—the door locks on all the stalls are broken. I pick the restroom furthest from the entrance and try to pop a squat over the stained toilet seat. I manage to lasso up the last of the toilet paper, which feels vaguely damp between my hands. Damp from previous piss-stained hands, or from the inescapable stench of mold and mildew, I don't know. I don't want to know.

I figure out there's no soap in the sink dispenser, and I'm overwhelmed by a sudden desire to bathe my body in bleach. I turn on the water and it's scalding—I grit my teeth and attempt to run them under. Why buy a gallon of bleach when I can burn my hands for free? But it's too hot to bear. I cry out in pain and smack the stupid faucet off. Bad decisions all around today. Should've just bitten the bullet and driven to the next gas station.

When I exit the building, I can't hide the look of disgust on my face. Aspen immediately approaches me with a knowing, teasing smile. She reaches into the pocket of her pants and pulls out a small bottle of sanitizer. I eagerly squirt it all over my hands.

"You're better off shitting by the side of the road. I feel gross. Do I smell?"

"Like what?"

"Poop? Piss?"

"Something you should know about me is I have a despicably good sense of smell. I can tell what someone last ate, where they've been, and when they…"

I blink. "So, you're saying I smell like shit? Like, really strongly of shit?"

She winces. "It doesn't smell as bad as other people smell. The dude with the Volvo at the last gas station we stopped at? Reeked."

"I can't believe you're attracted to me. Like, how are you attracted to me?"

She smiles. Blushes. Looks down at her feet. "Because. You're cute."

"You're sure about that?"

She pokes my nose. "One hundred percent, dork. Now take your dog. I'm going in."

"Are you nuts?"

"Are you? I'm not pooping by the side of the road, Riley. We have no toilet paper." She rolls her eyes.

"Having no toilet paper is better than the toilet paper that's in there. Also, can't you just transform into a monster?"

She props open the door with her foot and turns over her shoulder to look at me. "So, my shits can be like, three times as big?"

"Three times?"

"Yeah, Riley. Bigger colon. Bigger poops."

"I feel like we need to keep a sense of mystery in this relationship, and us talking about our bowel movements isn't helping."

"Okay, but you had a question, so I answered—y'know, never mind, I'll be out in just a minute."

She closes the door behind her. I wring my hands around Tigger's leash and walk around the rest stop some more. It's a pathetic little scrap of concrete on the side of the road, tucked near the edges of a scrappy forest. Withering trees, barely leafy branches. Looks like whoever is supposed to maintain this place hasn't been by in ages.

There're a couple of people sitting around already. A toddler naps in his mother's lap while she lunches with her husband. A group of tatted-up college kids sit on a picnic blanket in the shade, half-asleep. Everyone's feeling that mid-afternoon sluggishness. What I wouldn't give for coffee right about now. Wish I had drunk some at Fern's house this morning.

As I take another step forward, I don't know why, but a chill courses down my back. I listen. Road noise. People talking. Wind rustling the trees. A perfectly sunny sky overhead. There's nothing to worry about. But then my senses grow keener. And I can hear a faint *shk-shk-shk;* a bizarre scraping sound.

I look behind me, and I see a woman. Brunette. Waifish. She leans against the hood of a black SUV, filing her nails. I know from the way she dresses—elegant, in a long A-line skirt and a black button up blouse—and the way she's casually filing her nails at this dirty-ass rest stop, this is not an ordinary traveler. And when she looks up and her golden-flecked eyes meet mine, my worst suspicions are confirmed.

It's Karine.

Karine has found us.

I inhale sharply, almost a little too loudly, but no one looks in my direction. Tigger starts to growl at her, the hairs on the back of his neck bristling. But Karine smiles smugly and returns to filing her nails. *Shk-shk-shk. Shk-shk-shk.* They're painted a glittering ruby-red to match her skirt. She didn't have them the last time we saw her, and the thought makes me want to laugh out loud. After everything that happened, she *still* doesn't think of us as a threat? She's willing to in fact get her nails done and her hair curled and show up like we're just a mid-afternoon lunch date?

Either this lady is straight up stupid or she's one scary ass bitch. And judging by how she coldly left her coworkers to be torn apart by a monster, *and* lit a house on fire, I'm guessing that the latter would be a more accurate assessment.

She sets down her nail file. Her lips curl back in a Cheshire cat-like smile. "Are you just going to stand there?"

I anxiously look in the direction of the bathroom. To my surprise, Aspen exits right away. She smiles when she sees me, but it vanishes when she notices the panic on my face. She looks in the direction of Karine, and her eyes start to glow. I grab her arm and shake her head.

"You can't transform," I whisper. "There's people around."

She grits her teeth. Tigger won't stop growling, and judging from how loud his voice is getting, he's going to start barking really soon. The picnickers are looking our way now, wondering what the hell is going on.. Karine rolls her eyes and approaches us.

At this point, Tigger barks, snarling in that ferocious way he did when he first met Aspen. But she looks at him with those sharp eyes of hers and doesn't even need to say a word. He silences immediately, cowering behind me with his tail tucked between his legs. The glow in Aspen's eyes intensifies. I can see her pupils thinning; that familiar cold reptilian stare overtaking her humanoid features.

"Happy to see you girls made it out." Karine slides the nail file into her alligator patterned purse and zips it shut. She smiles thinly.

"Really?" Aspen stares. "Are you?"

"Sure."

"That doesn't sound too convincing."

"Well forgive me for not being so enthusiastic." She tightens her grip on her purse, her freshly manicured nails scratching the surface. "I mean, you did eat my coworkers after all—or did you just gore them?"

"I ate them. And I can arrange the same for you." Aspen smiles, but her eyes keep flickering. It's like she's desperately fighting back the urge to transform.

"I'm sure you can, dear." She pouts, her lips pressed together tightly. "You can't even help yourself, can you? It's like watching a recovering meth addict tweak out on Claritin. You look like you're about to have a seizure."

"Shut up," she responds through gritted teeth, and now I notice her body's shaking. She's not doing well. The others are still staring at us, a little uncertain. The whispers intensify.

I nudge her gently. "Aspen. We can't do this here."

"See, this is the problem, Aspen. Now I disagree with my employer's methods, but…," she shakes her head, perturbed. Holds up a finger. "Let me back up a minute."

"If you're not going to do anything, then we're leaving." Aspen brushes past me and heads for the truck.

She's twitching and agitated, and as she breathes, I can hear a heavy growl in her voice. Like that part of her is so close to breaking out. I swallow back a lump of fear rising in my throat. If she transforms here, no one is safe—not even me. All these people are going to be monster-food.

Karine looks at her. She raises her voice slightly, though it's not laced with malice. "You girls should meet me elsewhere. Why don't you follow my car?"

"Why?"

Karine's gaze snaps back to me. "I think you'll be interested in hearing what I have to say, especially when it comes to Healey. And despite what our previous encounter may have led you to believe, as good as I am at hunting you, I don't want to hurt you."

My throat feels so dry I can't find the words to say anything. Healey. If she was working with him before, she *would* know about his plans, wouldn't she? Although the events of the night we met are a scrambled mess inside my head, I can remember that Emile and Enzo were suspicious of her actions. Maybe there's more to this woman than meets the eye. Or maybe not. But she's right when she says that we don't really have a choice in this situation.

I stare at her as she wanders back over to her car and gets inside. Aspen shakes her head ferociously, her nostrils flaring. She looks in my direction.

"Riley, let's go," she almost-snarls, throwing open the creaky door of the truck and climbing inside.

I put Tigger in the backseat and hop behind the wheel. Aspen pulls her legs up onto the seat and curls up in a tight ball, holding her head in her hands. Her breathing is labored and shallow. She inhales sharply through her nostrils and then exhales slowly.

"She wants to meet us somewhere."

"And I guess we have to follow her?"

"Unless you want to fight her?"

Aspen shakes her head. "Not now. Not with all these people around."

I sit there dumbly for a few moments, not knowing what to do. She braces herself against the floor of the truck and releases a strangled noise—like a growl crossed with her scream. Tigger whines and whimpers in the back seat. She glances over at me, her eyes flashing.

"Riley. *Drive.*"

I shift the truck into gear and swiftly back out of our parking space, aiming in the direction of the black SUV. She pulls out onto the entrance ramp to the freeway, and we follow close behind her. I glance over at Aspen. Beads of sweat have broken out on her skin, but she's stopped twitching. Her pale skin somehow looks even more flushed than before. She wipes at the droplets of sweat on her forehead with the sleeve of her shirt.

"You good?"

She holds up a finger and reaches into the backseat, fishing for a water bottle. She cracks it open with a satisfied sigh and takes a deep sip.

"I don't know how we're going to get out of this now." She shakes her head and looks over at me. "Give me a minute. I gotta think."

I give her a minute. I give her fifteen, in fact, as we follow Karine down the highway and onto the third exit. We pass a blue metal sign, stained by years of rainwater, which reads "NO SERVICES." Shit. No place to go for help if we end up needing it—and we probably will. She pulls over to the side and I follow. We stop there, on the gravel dirt road, watching as the dust settles around the cars. She steps out, purse in hand, and unloads a few of…lawn chairs…from the back of the vehicle. Then sets the three of them up, two across from one. She promptly takes a seat and withdraws her nail file. Aspen and I stare at each other in confusion, but her sharp gaze commands us to exit.

We shuffle out, and I leave the window rolled down for Tigger. He sticks his head out and whines, and I place a finger to my lips, muttering for him to be quiet. I take a seat next to Aspen, who is still sweaty. Karine smiles at both of us.

"I have to hand it to the two of you for making it out of that situation. Pretty levelheaded for such stupid girls." She rolls her eyes. "I can't believe you actually followed us back to that house. I told Enzo it wouldn't work; kids these days know all the tricks…what with their

TikTok." She stops. "Guess you girls don't use TikTok? Or you were never taught common sense?"

"To be fair, I assumed you were a human trafficker."

"And to be fair, I was the stupid one." Aspen crosses her arms against her chest. She doesn't smile. "But then again, I figured I could handle myself. Given who I am. *What* I am."

"See, therein lies the problem." She opens her purse, and retrieves a vial filled with liquid—and I immediately recognize it. It's the fluid they withdrew from Aspen the night they kidnapped us. Still viscous and glowing, but somehow bluer than I remember.

"What happened to it?"

"This here? Is Aspen's cerebral spinal fluid. But it's undergone a bit of a modification since we took it from her. My lab partners were able to experiment with it a bit more, and I think we've isolated the particular hormone that triggers your transformation. This is what your fluids look like when…that particular element's been removed."

"Wow. Cool science experiment. I really like the part when you strapped me down to a table and stole that from my body."

She holds up a hand. "I can understand your anger."

"No, you can't."

"I can." Karine takes a deep breath as she puts the vial back inside her purse. She holds out her hands, and I watch as her long, spindly nails recede into the flesh of her fingers. Small scales, soft and sinewy like butterfly wings, form on the surface; so light and delicate, you could probably scrape them off. And I notice now how her amber eyes seem to glow.

She's just like Aspen.

I hold my breath as I look at her. Aspen is astounded. Her green eyes alarmed and unable to look away from Karine's scale covered fingertips. Her mouth drops open, and I can see in her eyes, she's wondering if she's met the person who'll give her the answers to every question she's been asking her whole life.

"You're like me?" Aspen asks, her voice escaping her chest in a whisper, soft and childlike, alive with wonder. "You…what are you? What are we?"

Karine chuckles softly. A sad expression surfaces in her eyes. The scales recede and the glow dissipates. "Unfortunately, I don't have that answer."

Aspen squeezes her eyes shut. I can tell that response immediately felt like a punch to the gut. Karine clears her throat and crosses her legs.

"I can tell you that…I, for one, am human. Or at least pretty close to it. A few years ago, I was working as a Russian intelligence agent, and during a recon mission at the Pentagon, I was captured by the CIA." She notably winces as she says this; her pride is clearly still wounded. "During my interrogation—which, as you can imagine, was grueling—I was introduced to a man who, along with the investigating agent, offered me a plea bargain of sorts."

"And?" Aspen asks. "Who was the man?"

"Your father."

The breath catches in Aspen's throat. I can feel my heart pulsing in my echo-chamber of a chest. How deep does this whole thing go?

"So," Karine continues, "having very few options left, I agreed. And I was inducted into Titan Tech's A-Genome project."

"But wait," Aspen says. "Why you? Why would they want you?"

"Russian intelligence. Besides that, what does the American government prioritize more than its own people? Weapons. They're interested in building human bioweapons, and a bioweapon that can heal itself with exponential speed is the best kind."

Bioweapons. That's why her dad did what he did. He wasn't interested in her healing properties so much as he was her ability to kill and destroy. It makes sense why he was collecting so many samples from her body; why he forced her through so many tests that provoked the beast within. He had to figure out how far he could go.

"Over the course of the nine months or so that I was a patient within the program, they would splice my DNA with yours. They referred to you as the true originator. Patient Zero. It wasn't until after I'd won Healey's good graces that I learned your true identity."

Aspen shuffles in her seat uncomfortably. "You worked for them, even knowing the DNA came from a human girl?"

"Certainly not ethical. But don't we all do unethical things in pursuit of our freedoms?" She stops, takes a breath. "Not that I don't feel regret. At least sometimes. But I have a greater purpose at this point."

"And what?" I shake my head. I'm tired. It's hot. And we're sitting at the side of a gravel road in lawn chairs, for no reason. "Cut to the chase. What do you want?"

"No patience, this one, huh?" She wags a finger dismissively at me. "After the trouble you two have caused, you think that you'd be eager for someone to help you out."

"What? Help?" Aspen interrupts, just as confused as I am. "You want to help us?"

"Yes."

Now it's my turn to be angry. My pulse quickens and I can feel the blood pounding in my ears. I go to rise out of my seat, but Aspen clings to my wrist, keeping me grounded. "You tried to kill us, and now you're saying you want to help us?"

"I did not. We were performing a scientific experiment. Your friend transformed and attacked *them* first. She showed the first signs of aggression. Just as she did back in…what was it? Little Brook?"

"She did not," I snap. "Some stupid boy cornered her and started harassing her. He wouldn't let her go."

"Harassed her? Please. What is a little harassment when you can bite a man's head off, or in this case, topple an entire town?" She smirks. "You children cry about everything all the time. Everything is harassment. A man looks at you the wrong way one time and you accuse him of violence beyond your comprehension. It's pathetic. You would've never lasted growing up when I did, when they were *much, much* worse."

I glare ferociously back at her. I have nothing to say. I have no words. There's no helping someone like this—and there's no way someone who says something so vile is capable of empathizing with our struggles. I stand up and wrench my wrist out of Aspen's grasp.

"We're done here."

"Sit down," she replies calmly. "I decide when we're done."

"And I decide when I get to shove my foot up your ass."

I kick the chair out of the way and stomp back over to the truck. My entire body feels like it's on fire, and I want nothing more than to take a swing at her and her stupid alligator purse. What kind of self-important priss brings a purse worth *thousands* of dollars on a road trip? An asshole, that's who.

I climb into the truck, but I'm surprised to see that Aspen isn't following me. She looks back pleadingly in my direction, biting her lip. She wants to call me back over, but she's resisting the urge. Karine says something to her, and I watch as the two of them begin to converse again. I pull up a game on my phone and start playing, pretending not to pay attention to the rest of the conversation.

"I know that you seek answers. And I seek solutions. As Patient Zero, my team and I believe that your DNA holds the key to helping the others."

"Others?"

"As I said, there are more of us. More people like me, I should say." She takes a deep breath. "No living being deserves to be imprisoned and experimented on; completely absolved of their free will. I've lived through it, and I would not wish it on anyone. My mission's changed. It changed the moment they put the first syringe in my body." A softness surfaces in her expression, haunted by what she has experienced. For the first time, I believe she's being genuine.

"Since I started with them, I've been aiming to take them down. Titan Tech doesn't want to help people like us. They want to keep us enslaved. Medicalize us and profit off of our bodies."

Aspen shuffles uncomfortably in her seat. "I agree with that. But...I don't know if I can trust you."

"So, don't. Let me earn that trust. I think we can work together to find a way for you to harness your powers for yourself, instead of other people. And through that, I can hope to do the same for all the victims of Titan Tech."

Aspen sighs. "So, what do you want?"

"I want you to come with me," she says gently. "Come stay with me, at my research facility. I'll show you what I've been working on."

"I don't...I don't know." Aspen swallows. I can hear the trepidation in her voice as well as a soft yearning.

"You want answers, and if you come with me, my team and I can help you figure them out." Karine says. "I would say it's worth a shot at this point. Wouldn't you?""

Aspen glances back at the car. I can't help but lock eyes with her. I know from her sheepish expression she's going to agree to this. And she does. Karine shakes her hand and flashes that domineering smile before loading up the chairs in her trunk and hopping into the driver's seat of her vehicle. Aspen sluggishly makes her way back to the car, not saying anything to me.

I stare at her in disbelief. "You want us to follow her?"

"I don't...Riley, I just..." She squeezes her eyes shut. "Maybe she has a point. If she's like me, then maybe she can help me. Maybe I misunderstood her."

"You've literally exchanged twenty sentences with this woman. And I can assure you, she's an asshole, through and through."

"Maybe, but she knows more about me than I do. She *knows,* Riley. She says that she's got a whole team of people working with her, and if she says she can help me, then I think…I think I need to hear her out." Aspen blinks rapidly, as if she's holding back tears. "I think I owe it to everyone's life that I destroyed. Including yours."

I open my mouth to protest, but she shakes her head and dismisses me. She nods in the direction of the SUV.

"Can you just follow her? If we don't like it, we can always leave. I promise. I won't let anything bad happen this time."

I stare at her. "You can't make promises like that."

She sighs and turns to look out the window. And regrettably, I put the car into gear. I know she's right. I know Aspen needs help and needs some way to either suppress or control her powers—for both her safety and mine.

But everything's comes with a cost, and I don't know what kind of price we'll have to pay.

Day 7 - Evening

WE DRIVE FOR ANOTHER hour, and I realize that dusk is starting to settle. The sky turns a purplish pink hue. I ask Aspen to call my dad to let him know we'll be stopping somewhere for the night, and he's egregiously upset, as I predicted him to be. He demands to talk to me, and I begrudgingly accept.

"I wasn't kidding when I said I would report you as runaways. Riley, this is a drive that's supposed to take you twenty-four hours. Why is it taking so long?"

"I don't know. We overslept a couple days, I guess. And traffic has been terrible." These things are true, but I also can't exactly tell him about all the detours we took when we were running for our lives. Almost certainly can't tell him about how we're following our previous captor to her lair, which is probably in a bat cave or something equally ridiculous.

"You don't know? Riley, I'm already in Minneapolis. Waiting for you."

"I didn't know that."

"You would've known that the other day when I called you." His voice grows thick with emotion. I can hear a tired sigh. "Should I drive to Chicago and meet you guys there instead? I just don't understand."

"I told you to go home, and that I didn't want to see you."

"I'm your father, Riley. I'm not about to just leave you stranded in the middle of the Midwest. If you would get here, then we could talk more—"

"—Dad, there's *nothing* to talk about," I snap. "You lied. You lied about some really *awful* things."

He barks right back at me. "Riley! You should already be in Minnesota by now! The fact that you're not here is *deeply* concerning! What happened?"

I can feel panic setting into my body. I want to tell him everything, but I know that I can't. I grip the steering wheel so tightly my knuckles turn white. I look over at Aspen.

"The truck," she mouths.

"T-the truck. The truck broke down and we couldn't drive for a couple of days. We're in Illinois now. But we're tired, and we were told b-by the mechanic to take it slow," I say, resisting the urge to gulp down more air. "So, we haven't been able to go over the speed limit."

"Why didn't your little friend tell me about the breakdown?"

"I don't know, Dad," I snap back. "Jesus, can you just stop? I'm *trying*. Acting like this isn't going to make it better."

"Pot, kettle, black."

What an ass. I hang up and toss the phone haphazardly back to Aspen, who scrambles to catch it before it hits the floor. I shake my head.

"We have to get to Minnesota. He's freaking out. Apparently, he's been there for a few days?"

She flinches. "Oh. Right. I forgot to tell you that."

"It's not your fault. He needs to calm down. We're in a truck that is probably being held together by luck and a lil' bit of duct tape, driving through places that are literally on fire, *and* we're being chased by mad scientists. Not to mention Tigger needs to stop and pee every once in a while. In my opinion, we're making good time."

"We're really not."

"No, we're not." I sigh and drum my fingertips against the steering wheel. "I think we can only stay with her one night."

She flinches again, and this time I look at her directly. She bites her lip and nervously squirms in her seat, then nods.

"If…if she *really* has what it takes to help me, then I'll stay."

"What?" I shake my head, and when I turn my attention back to the road, I realize Karine has stopped.

I slam on my brakes, nearly flinging us through the windshield. Karine steps out of her SUV and stares at us, as if perplexed as to why I wasn't paying attention. I look out at a path winding up a lopsided hill, which leads to a massive house resting between a velvety forest of deciduous trees. It's a haunting and gorgeous multi-storied Victorian home, with a weathered dusty-blue exterior. A six-foot-tall iron fence surrounds the property, and a shed with peeling roof tiles rests on the outskirts. This looks more like a vacation home or a haunted house than it does a scientific headquarters. Then again, I don't know what to expect anymore.

There is a small outpost stationed on the outskirts of the house. Karine approaches the security guard, and he presses a button, causing the gates to whir open. She gets back inside her car and drives further into the compound, and we trail slowly after her. We come to a complete stop outside the porch.

Aspen and I climb out of the car, and I retrieve Tigger. Karine leads us up the porch and holds open the door for us to enter. Inside, the house is nothing like what I was expecting. The outside is elegant and gives off *Jane Eyre* vibes, the inside is more *Rocky Horror*. Laminated tiles desaturated and strange. Wood paneling all over the walls, but smooth and untextured, like a fancy cabin-of-the-future you'd find on an episode of HGTV. I'm not one to care about original architecture or anything, but this place 100% has to look uglier than it was before.

Crates and book carts clutter the floors. People in white lab coats sit and chat by a steaming oversized coffee maker. They're as disheveled as we are, looking tired, but still talking and joking with one another in an easygoing manner. They seem to have known each other for a long time.

We're led to the back of the house, which is surprisingly more domestic than the front. Rugs cover the floors. Long velvety sheets are draped over paintings that are propped up against the hallway walls. Karine guides us up a circling staircase, onto a floor that has none of the ugly tiles or wood paneling. Just plush, albeit gross with age, carpet, and wallpaper decorated with overgrown flowers. Even with the massive floor-to-ceiling windows behind us, there's very little light up here. A few lamps decorate the space.

Karine opens a door and gestures for us to enter. We shuffle past her, into the room. It's big, and so pink, it almost makes my eyes bleed. Baby-pink pillows, baby-pink bed, baby-pink light fixture.

Everything in here smells a little dusty, and I fight back the urge to sneeze. A door on the wall opposite the bed leads to a bathroom with a claw footed bathtub. Ooh. Fancy.

"Rest," she says to us. "In the morning, I'll show you what we have."

She shuts the door without saying anything else. I lay our bags on the of the bed and invite Tigger up on top. I sit down beside him, and I'm surprised at the plushness of the mattress. Damn. Little weird to say that I'm excited to sleep in this bed tonight.

Aspen's inspecting the various knickknacks on the bookshelf—a collection of porcelain figures with rosy cheeks and small wooden toys.

"So," I say. "Who do you think she had to kill to get this house?"

Aspen doesn't say anything. She simply shakes her head. I trace my fingers over the woven throw blanket and watch her a little more. She still doesn't say anything.

"Are we going to talk about what you said in the car?"

"I should stay here. If this works out…I should stay here," she reiterates slowly. "It only makes sense. You and Tigger can go to Minnesota, and I could stay here with Karine and figure out how to harness my powers."

"You're getting ahead of yourself. Let me just say that I'm not super impressed with how she waltzed us in here and shut the door, without showing us any of her supposed 'secrets.'" I cross my arms. "You and I both know that this is a trap, okay? We just couldn't run, because we were at that rest stop. I say we run now, or we take her out. We've got her right where we want her, and—"

"—Riley, be quiet. What if she hears you?"

"So what? I'm done with people bossing us around. When they're not hunting us down, they're chasing us out of town, or yelling at us for not driving fast enough. So, let's end this with her. At least she'll be one less thing to worry about."

A ferocious look of anger surfaces in Aspen's eyes. She sets her jaw. "I know you're frustrated, but you can't possibly be suggesting I just *murder* innocent people?"

"She's not innocent."

"The rest of them are."

"You don't know that."

"And you don't know they're evil! Riley! I don't want to keep killing people! So just stop!"

Shame washes over me, but I still can't shake the nagging feeling that something here is going to go horribly wrong. "I just don't want you to be naive about this. I get it. She can relate to you in some way, and—"

"—You don't get it, so don't say that."

I exhale slowly. "I don't get it, but I accept that I don't get it. And I accept that *you* feel like she can help you in some way. But I also don't want you to be taken advantage of."

She immediately deflates. Plops down on the bed beside me and bounces her leg, too jittery to contain herself. "I know. You're right. I know."

"So, don't worry about us separating just yet, okay? We can talk about it *when* she proves she can help you."

"We really can't. You have to get to Minnesota." She shakes her head. "Your dad *knows* something's up, Riley. And I don't want to drag him into this, o-or for us to be chased down by cops or the military or something. And the longer you stay out on the road with me, the more chaotic your life becomes."

"What about yours?"

"I'm used to the chaos." She smiles, but her eyes are tired.

I want to tell her that she doesn't have to be a martyr, but I don't know how to get that through to her. And I don't know if I can. I'm not the one who destroyed our hometown. I'm so tied up in my own grief, that I don't know if I can begin to comprehend the guilt— the absolute *agony*—that's been weighing on her since we've been out here together. Looking at Aspen's face, I don't think she understands it either. We've been treading water this whole time, just trying to keep breathing. Would one more death on her conscience break her completely?

She kisses my shoulder and gently squeezes my hand. "I'm going to get changed, okay? And then maybe I'll see if someone can bring us some food."

When she enters the bathroom, I curl up on my side and pull Tigger close against my body. His chest rises and falls with each breath he takes. In the midst of all this chaos, I'm glad he's here. If he's sleeping soundly, I know for sure the monsters won't come tonight.

Day 8 - Morning

I AWAKE TO THE sound of rain droplets softly hitting the window. My head is buried in the crook of Aspen's shoulder and, to my surprise, she's already awake. She smiles at me and brushes back a strand of my hair and I feel like melting. Embarrassed, I bury my face against her shoulder. She giggles quietly, trying to keep her voice down.

"What? I didn't say anything."

"You're too bright and sunshiny. Isn't it like five in the morning?"

"6:15."

I groan. "Aspen, why are you awake?"

"Because someone wouldn't stop cuddling me."

"Aren't you the one cuddling me?" I yawn and try to curl up against her. She kisses my forehead and my nose, and I laugh. "Aspen...," her lips meet mine, and I can't help but lean into the kiss. I kiss her until all the breath from my body leaves my chest. She slides her hand along my waist, down my thigh, and I shiver. Something about how she touches me just...electrifies me.

Tigger whines a little bit, and we both freeze. I push down some of the blankets so that I can see him. He lays curled up on the end of the bed, an anxious expression on his face. I guess it's hard for dogs to tell the difference between making out and getting mauled. And with Aspen, I mean, either could honestly happen to me at any given moment. In a deeply messed up way, that's also what makes it...exciting?

Ugh. I need so much therapy.

Aspen smiles and looks at me. "Do you want me to lock him in the bathroom?"

I stare blankly back at her. "Why?"

"So, he doesn't bother us." She kisses my neck and—*oh my God.* I don't think I've ever felt anything better.

"But...wait...I..." It feels like every single one of my hormones is screaming at me to go for it. But screaming even louder is my common sense, telling me that we've only been together for a few days. "I...I don't know if I can."

"If you can what?"

"Uh…" God, I feel so stupid. That stupid smile of hers isn't helping me feel any less stupid, either. "Have sex?"

She stares at me in shock for a moment, and then bursts out laughing. An embarrassed blush rises on my face, and I elbow her. She deflects the blow, still laughing, and grabs my frustrated hands. She pulls me on top of her, and she's so strong that I can't wriggle away.

"I just wanted to make out with you. I wasn't trying to do anything else," Aspen says, laughing. "My game is just that good, huh?"

"N-no! You said you were going to put Tigger in the bathroom, and I just…I *thought* that's what you were implying."

"I know it's a stereotype that queer women move too fast, but I promise that not even I will move that fast." She wraps her arms around my waist and presses my body against hers. Presses the tip of her nose against mine. "You know what I've been through. I don't think I'm ready."

"I don't think I'm ready, either."

I've never so much as made it to second base. At least, I don't think I have. What is second base, exactly? I don't really know. Every time I Google it a different answer comes up. It's either a hand on the boob or fingering. Neither of which have happened to me. And while Mom and I had plenty of conversations about sex—about consent, about birth control, about knowing when you're ready—we never talked about sex between women. That wasn't Mom's area of expertise, and while she was definitely supportive of me when I came out of the closet, I could tell my attraction to women still made her somewhat squeamish. She never knew how to navigate that part of me, and good luck trying to have those kinds of conversations with Dad. The first time I told him I had a boyfriend it was like a little light switched off inside his head, like he couldn't process the information. He just nodded like it was interesting and went back to reading his paper.

"Then we won't." She shrugs. "But I'd still like to keep kissing you. And maybe a few other things?" She places her hands gently underneath my shirt, just above my waist, and I shudder at the touch of her warm hands against my cool bare skin. I nod and lean into her kiss once more.

But just as she pulls me in again, I hear the bedroom doorknob turn. Tigger barks and scrambles off the bed. He growls at the door, and Karine swings it open unceremoniously. We stare at her in confusion. She takes one look at us—at me, basically straddling Aspen—and doesn't even blink.

"If you're awake, why don't we get to it?" She gestures for us to follow her out the door but doesn't wait for us. She simply leaves the door hanging open.

I groan in frustration. Aspen smiles.

"Something, something, patience is a virtue?"

"She doesn't even have the patience to knock."

WE TAKE TIGGER OUT to pee before following Karine downstairs into the basement. Apparently, each floor of the house is drastically different from the other—the basement is lined with a monochrome, silvery material that reflects the bright white fluorescent lights overhead. We brush past one of the scientists and proceed into a hallway lined floor to ceiling with white subway tiles. Damn. You'd think a woman who dresses the way she does would have better taste in decor, but I guess not.

We head down the hallway, leisurely wandering past observation windows reinforced with steel bars. As we make our way further down, we pass by people sitting on examination tables inside, talking with other people in white lab coats. Each of these "patients" looks a little different from the others. People of different races and genders, but also…different features. One person I swear to God has gills. Another has webbed fingers and toes. One girl T-poses in an examination room. When we walk by, she turns to face me, and her glowing reptilian eyes meet mine. They're like Aspen's, but yellower. Then the realization hits me: these are other people like Karine. People who've had their DNA spliced with Aspen's.

"These are some of the specimens we've recovered from the facilities on the coasts. Well, the ones that aren't in the burn ward, at least."

"Wait, what?" I ask. The girl on the other side of the glass stares back at me unnervingly. "You were able to save the others?"

"Yeah, wait a second," Aspen says, turning to face Karine. "How? How did you know to rescue them?"

"Not everyone who works with Titan Tech wants to be a part of Titan Tech," Karine replies. "When you want to tear down a conglomerate, you have to break it apart from the inside. Not difficult to rally people together either when they're being asked to commit crimes against humanity."

"But that's just the thing. Why? Why were all the facilities blown up?"

Her brow furrows in confusion. "Because of what happened in Little Brook. I thought that that was obvious."

"Context," I tell her heatedly. "*Who* decided to blow up the facilities? Was it you guys? Were you trying to break them out?"

"Wrong. Oh my." She sighs, as if frustrated. "I understand why Riley is clueless, but I would've thought you knew the answer already, Aspen." She fixates her intense golden gaze on her. "You *do* know the answer, don't you?"

Aspen stares. "My father?"

Karine doesn't say anything. She nods, and stares at her feet, an unusually humble gesture for her; like she's suddenly too nervous to face us. Shock floods Aspen's face. She had long suspected this, but now it's finally confirmed.

Aspen's father ordered the destruction of the Titan Tech laboratories. And consequently, the destruction of everything we once held dear in our lives.

"When you had your…little tantrum…" Karine winces. I can tell for once that she doesn't mean to be callous, but that it's difficult for her to find the words. "You grew rapidly, within a short amount of time, to the largest size you've ever been. Healey had said there was nothing left to do but go full scorched earth."

"So, my father… is he still alive?"

Karine bites her lip and folds her hands in front of her. "The last I heard he was making his way to one of the underground escape routes before the self-destruction finished its countdown. But they've lost contact with him since."

What? "How can they just 'lose' contact with him? Wasn't he with Healey?"

"Healey was in D.C., so no, he wasn't in Little Brook at that time. I don't want to speak authoritatively about his whereabouts," she replies calmly, diplomatically. "We do not know where Dr. Montehugh—sorry, Aspen's father—is. My intel has been unable to obtain that information, and frankly, that hasn't been a priority so much as tracking down any surviving test subjects. For that, I am sorry."

"Well, he was always good at covering his tracks," Aspen says, her voice faint yet intensely bitter.

Karine swallows. "Indeed."

The girl on the other side of the window moves her arm in a strange way. It takes a minute to register that she's trying to wave at us. Aspen waves back at her. Her mouth flickers, as if she's struggling to make a smile, but the muscles in her jaw seem far too damaged to maintain it for long.

"So, what's going on with these people?" Aspen asks, her voice hoarse. She's trying to change the subject so that she doesn't have a total breakdown.

Karine seems confused by her sudden change of tone, but she answers her question. "We're currently running some tests on them. Trying to see how they respond to the formula. The one I showed you yesterday?" Karine glances over her shoulder at us. "Out of six participants, four of them have shown considerable improvements so far."

"Four participants aren't much of a sample size," Aspen replies grimly.

"We have more people who we could be testing, but for whatever reasons they aren't ready. When it comes to working with those mentally and physically healthy enough to endure the trials? Four out of six is a very, very good number."

"What about her?" I say, pointing to the girl with the lizard eyes.

Karine shakes her head. "She's one of the other two."

"Ahh."

"The two individuals that did not respond to the trial well are nonverbal. They cannot communicate with human language. I have reason to suspect they are not spliced specimens, such as myself, but instead embryos."

Aspen stops dead in her tracks. "What did you say?"

"My apologies. Genetically modified embryos."

"Like…m-made with my…"

Karine tilts her head to the side, confused. But then she realizes. "No. No such thing exists. At least, not to my knowledge. These were human embryos obtained secondhand through clinics and other contractors. They were spliced in utero."

"Oh," Aspen stammers, and I rub her shoulder reassuringly. Each of these patients are clearly deeply messed up—I can't begin to grasp how many human rights are actually being violated here. Or *were*, considering these people were experimented on at different Titan Tech facilities in the past. Then again, I'm not sure if lizard-girl would have consented to being taken here, so while Karine may be trying to help, she's not exactly off my shit list.

Karine takes us to an open room. It's sterile and coated in stainless steel. A man, probably in his thirties, lays in a chair that kind of looks like the ones they use when you go to the dentist. But it's a little more metallic than that, and he's been held down with restraints. A couple of gloved scientists carefully extract blood from him.

"How are you doing?" Karine asks the man, stopping near his feet.

A few drops of perspiration drip down his face. "Not bad. How about yourself?"

It takes me a minute to realize, but I notice what's causing him discomfort. From the gap between the seat and the top of the chair, there's a smooth-ended tail protruding from his back. It appears to be pushing his hips forward, out of alignment. His legs are somewhat twisted, like he's been run over by a truck. He's got fairly muscular arms and shoulders, but his bottom half looks weaker and withered.

Karine looks at me. "It's impolite to stare."

"Sorry." My body fills with shame.

"This is Martin. He was a Special Ops member who was crushed under a vehicle, after an IED blew up his squadron." She shifts her gaze to Aspen. "Your father promised he could help him. But the procedure backfired. That *thing* is growing from his spine."

"And no cool powers either," Martin says, wincing as yet another vial of blood is drained from his system. "Not even healing ones."

"Wait, so…"

"He has an open wound in his back from the tail, which needs to be covered and treated with dressings and bandages daily. He's been wheelchair bound for almost two years." Karine's expression softens for a moment. From off the table, she picks up a bottle of nearby serum, and passes it to Aspen. "This is why you're so important. You can help him. The more access we have to you, the more tests we can conduct. The better quality of life we can ensure. And the more specimens we find, the more we can help. The more damage we can undo."

Interesting that she's talking about quality of life when all these patients, except for her, seem to be trapped within this basement. Even more interesting that she propositions herself as some kind of Mother Theresa when just days ago, she had no problem kidnapping and drugging Aspen instead of explaining things like a normal human being. Unless Karine absolutely had to be that way to avoid blowing her cover, but I'm still unsure. I watch with wary eyes as one of the scientists prepares a vial of the blue serum. He looks at Martin, who nods affirmatively, before looking at Karine. Karine's gaze fixates on us.

"Watch this."

The scientist injects the serum into Martin, and almost immediately, his body seizes. Even his feet, which I had thought were paralyzed, are clenched up, curling in reaction to the medicine. His skin turns red, and becomes wet, like every droplet of sweat is trying to escape. He groans in pain, and his head rolls from side to side. I can catch glimpses of his eyes, with now razor thin pupils. This isn't going well.

A heart monitor's beeping accelerates. He wrestles back and forth in his chair, his teeth bared, tugging at the restraints around his body. The scientists stand back, their arms defensively raised. His panicked groans of pain have descended into feral snarls. Aspen takes my hand and squeezes it tightly, and I can feel how fast her heart is beating. It's in time with mine.

For the briefest moment, I notice Karine flinch, as if in fear. Her voice is stern. "Be strong, Martin. Work through this."

He thrashes his head against the side of the chair. He clenches his teeth, and when he opens his mouth again, a fountain of blood spurts out, coating one of the scientists, who shrieks in terror. For a moment, I can't figure out what's going on, but then I see the blood is burning acidic holes in her lab coat.

The other scientist scrambles over to a doorway and pounds on an emergency button. Martin continues spitting up acidic blood, burning fiery holes in everything it touches—including his own flesh. We all back up slowly, until we're tightly pressed against the walls. Karine keeps shouting to him, her voice faint over the din of his screams. And soon they subside. There's a ringing in my ears, and then I realize that it's not a ringing, it's the sound of the heart monitor flatlining. What's left on the table is a shriveled corpse, decaying under the droplets of its own blood.

This man is dead.

Yet another man just died in front of us.

A strangled sob leaves someone's throat, and to my surprise, it's Karine. She presses her face into her hands as other scientists rush into the room. They wear white hazmat suits; their faces are fully masked. They splash some sort of solution on the ground, which stops the acid from eating at the surfaces. Everyone huddles around his body, unsure of what to do.

Aspen's eyes burn with tears. She shoves the vial of blue serum into my hands and clenches her fists. She hangs her head. And I can't take my eyes off Martin.

"This didn't happen yesterday." Karine booms at the scientists, her voice hoarse through her tears. "I need tests done. *Now!* And cease any further serum injections!"

"Patient eight is in Room 2A," one of the scientists says.

"Then *stop* them!" she screeches through clenched teeth. "Let's go! Move!"

A few of them scramble out of the room, and the others carefully approach Martin's body. His corpse is still warm as they wheel him out of the room. Aspen looks accusingly at Karine.

"You said you were *helping* people."

"We are. We're *trying*," Karine hisses, her eyes wet. "I didn't say this was going to be easy."

"He just died! Y-you killed him!"

"Sooner or later his affliction would have." The familiar, elegant monotone returns to her voice. Her eyes suddenly seem far away. She wipes away her remaining tears. "He responded favorably to the treatment the other day. It's possible this dosage was simply too much. The autopsy report will explain what went wrong."

Aspen shakes her head, over and over again. Karine notices this, and grabs her shoulders, looking her square in the eyes.

"Don't behave like this. This is bigger than you."

"It's always been bigger than me," Aspen responds flatly.

"Listen to me. These people need your help. People like me need your help. And we are only going to get it if you agree to work with us." She shakes her head, and her voice sounds almost desperate. "Y-you are the strongest specimen. You're the original. Patient Zero. You would survive any trial we put you through. I have that confidence. I wouldn't have asked you for your help if I didn't."

"I'm not going to do it," Aspen says, her voice firm. "I'm not taking the serum, and I'm not doing any kind of treatment. You're just doing what my father was claiming to do. 'Save people.'" She gestures to the rest of the room, full of acidic holes and blood. "This is *not* how you save people!"

"It is when you're working with *very* limited resources," she snaps. "And remember we aren't the only ones who need saving. You do too."

"I'd rather figure it out on my own, thanks." She shakes her head and buries her face in her hands.

"Aspen," Karine says, shaking her shoulder. "Aspen. Listen to me. I know you don't trust me, but you have to understand there are people *worse* than me who are—"

A thunderous crack splits the air, and everyone in the room freezes. It reverberates and echoes down the hallway, and for a moment, I wonder if we're experiencing some kind of earthquake. But then I see smoke filling the hallway behind us. People screaming, shouting, racing past the observation windows. Karine's eyes widen and she stumbles away from the windows.

"No," she whispers, her voice hoarse. "*No.*"

I watch as more people race past the glass: armed men dressed in black. They fire at fleeing scientists in the hallways. Everyone in the room screams and races for the door at the opposite end of the lab. Karine howls with fury, and I watch as her nails form claws once again. Aspen grabs my hand and we sprint for the exit. We burst through the other side into the hallway, and just as we do, a round is fired off. *BANG!* A bullet splits the head of the scientist in front of us. He flops to the ground and convulses in a puddle of murky red blood. Two mercs stop to reload their rifles.

"Riley, behind me!" Aspen throws me behind her and holds up her arm, and within seconds, the girl I know is gone. The monster is back, speaking with guttural growls and nasty hisses. Her skin — her scales? — radiate heat and are damp to the touch. She hasn't nearly reached her full size. I hear the pop-pop of the rifles again, but Aspen barely budges. She hisses, and charges forward, her massive jaws open. In moments, their upper torsos are missing, and all that's left are a pile of legs.

"FIRE!"

A ricochet of bullets sprays the air. I immediately fall to the ground. I don't know if I've been hit or not. I lay with my head pressed to the ground, staring into the open-white eyes of the scientist beside me. Feel his still-warm blood against my fingertips as it spills out from the open holes in his body. *Breathe, Riley, breathe.* Aspen pummels through the barrage of bullets and uses her massive tail to swipe at their feet, sending a few men flying against the walls and banging into the ceiling. More men keep coming, and she keeps fighting. Behind them, stands one man—someone I've never seen before. He's dressed in a long black jacket, and while he has a rifle strapped to his back, he's making no move to shoot. He surveys the scene with a quiet intensity that makes me sick in ways I don't understand. A couple of men run up behind him, with bigger guns—but they fire out nets instead of bullets. Aspen thrashes underneath the weight of the nets, furiously roaring and wiggling; struggling to break free. A loud *VVVT! VVVT!* echoes out, and purple crackles of electricity spark in the air. Her body convulses and she howls in pain.

The man fixes his steely blue gaze on me. He doesn't smile. Doesn't show any kind of emotion. I hear stomping from behind, and Karine approaches, unscathed.

"Healey, you bastard," she snarls. "Haven't you done enough?"

The weight of the name hits me like a freight train. *Healey.* Healey is with Titan Tech. He's her boss. He's the man who sent those assassins after us at that diner. He's the one who tortured Aspen, robbed her of her body, and orchestrated all this chaos. To finally see him in the flesh is beyond distressing. Half of me wants to scream and run away in terror, and the other wants to kill him.

"I could ask you the same thing." A faint tug at the corner of his full lips. "Didn't realize after that little fiasco in Ohio you'd tuck your tail between your legs and run here."

Karine crouches down and digs her nails into my shoulder, pulling me to my feet. Her grip is rough, but oddly...protective? She glares at him.

"This is all going down one way or another. You can choose to drag it out. Or you can choose to end it here." She squeezes my shoulder. "These girls have been through enough."

He sputters into laughter. It's deep, rich, and bone-chilling. His eyes don't move when he laughs—it's like watching a ventriloquist dummy. "Are you kidding me? Now you want to play Mother Hen? Isn't that the same girl you slapped the hell out of in that basement?"

I can feel Karine fidgeting. And then I notice her hand slipping into the pocket of her pants. I look up at her. She swallows, but her mouth remains set in that line of determination. She's planning something. What is she going to do to me?

"I saw the footage, Karine. Cute of you to think you could raze the entire place and we wouldn't be able to figure out what you did. You've definitely lost it. Your mind, and your touch." He shakes his head, stepping closer to us.

Aspen lunges for him, but she can't get her jaws through the rope. He doesn't even flinch. Just stands right beside her. He looks at her with a bored expression on his face.

"Keep pissing that girl off, and you're going to have a lot more problems on your hands than just some rogue employees," Karine hisses. "T-that isn't even her full form. You know that."

"Don't lecture me. I know what I'm doing. You don't." he raises his hand, and everyone raises their rifles in unison.

Oh shit.

He's going to kill us.

"Take me," she says. "Take Aspen, even. We're who you want. But my workers and this girl have nothing to do with this. They're completely innocent."

"I'll take who and what I want," he replies, and I hear the sickening clicks of barrels circling in unison. "So do me a favor and stop prolonging the inevitable."

She shrugs her shoulders. "I will stop. Once you're dead."

Karine pulls out a syringe from her pocket, one filled with the blue serum. She injects it directly into her gut, and shouts in pain. The effects are almost immediate. Her skin crackles, and her body transforms rapidly. Healey and the other mercs stare in pure shock. He turns to one of his bodyguards.

"Fire another one!" he points to the large-barreled net-shooter.

He shakes his head. "S-sir, I can't! The gun has to recharge first!"

Katrine's neck elongates, and grayish-green scales emerge from her skin. Her fancy clothes hang about her body in tattered shreds. But the most horrific thing about her is her smile—her lips have been peeled back halfway around her face, and overgrown teeth jut out from between her lips. Pulsating bubbles form underneath her skin, threatening to burst. She groans and staggers forward. Her form is somewhere halfway between human and monster. Healey lifts his arm and drops it, and the onslaught of bullets starts once more.

As each one hits Karine's skin, something odd happens—the bubbles on her skin burst open, but they seal just as quickly as they tear apart. The bullets just seem to vanish. Karine swipes at some of the men with her massive claws. This time they don't fly back against the walls; they're simply torn open. Intestines and blood gush from their bodies and onto the floor. Segmented body parts and torsos slide off autonomously standing legs, before crumpling all together. Karine turns her back to the rest of the bullets and her claws tear through the electric net, even as Healey's assistants desperately try to shock her with it. Although it's difficult to see through the chaos, I can catch glimpses of Aspen as she wriggles out of the hole and turns her attention back to the men. She picks them off one by one, and Karine barrels down the hallway after Healey and his assistants. I stand there frozen, covering my ears. Panicked thoughts race through my mind, and this time, I make no attempt to quell them.

When Aspen kills the last mercenary, I hear Karine shrieking in the distance. I scramble over to Aspen, placing my hands on her head. She hisses and recoils, jaws open, as if ready to strike. Gristly pieces of innards and flesh glisten in between her sharp teeth. Her small pupils struggle to focus on me. I hold up my hands defensively.

"Aspen, it's me!"

She makes a weird sound, like a cross between a dog bark and a growl. She inches toward me, and although I'm talking to her, she doesn't seem to recognize me. Karine screams again.

I have no other choice left.

I sprint for it.

Aspen scrambles, lunging after me, the sharp meaty clamp of her jaws at my back, and I just narrowly dodge out of her reach. Flashing lights and sirens guide me toward the exits. Other wounded scientists attempt to exit the building, and I flail my hands in the air wildly.

"Move, move!" I screech, tearing around a corner.

They cry out in horror as Aspen's massive body drags into view. Is she bigger than before, or is she just more terrifying when she wants to play with her food? Blood and sweat drip down my face and I run harder, till my heart is thrashing against my rib cage and my lungs feel like they're about to burst. Every time Karine screams, I feel like I'm so much closer but still farther away.

I turn another corner and I find her, laying in the center of what appears to be some sort of underground entrance. One car is overturned and leaks brown oil onto the dirty cement floor. Another car is already on fire, black smoke rising from the heaps of dented metal wreckage. A reinforced steel arch leads the way into a dark tunnel with no end in sight. In the center of the room, Karine, thrashes about. Half of her torso is trapped underneath another electric net. Healey's assistants take turns firing shots into her body. She cries out with pain each time, and I realize something: the bullets aren't disappearing. She's *absorbing* them. When the bubbles open up, the bullets dissolve into the open wound...like acid.

Acidic.

She's acidic.

She's a giant acidic monster and we're trapped in an underground garage filled with gasoline and flames.

"Hey!" I yell at Healey. "Asshole! Let her go!"

Karine looks in my direction. Her face looks like its melting; half of it droops to one side, dripping dangerously close to the ground. The serum is making destabilizing her. She's not going to last much longer. Her eyes flit about the room, completely devoid of any kind of light or recognition, but full of pain.

I cough and pull my shirt over my mouth, trying to create a barrier between my lungs and the smoke that's quickly filling the space. "If you keep shooting at her, she's going to blow—"

The sound of Aspen's frustrated roar cuts through the air and she skids into the room, toppling over a couple more cars. The bodyguards turn their attention away from Karine and raise their rifles. Aspen snarls, her claws digging into the cement like it's nothing more than tissue paper. She's *definitely* bigger than before, and she's growing larger. She's hunched over her front legs, and her back almost touches the ceiling. Either she collapses this thing, or Karine explodes us. She lunges forward and attacks the bodyguards. She swallows the first whole and bites the head off the second. But Healey is undisturbed by all of this, content to leave his men to try to fight her off.

He turns his attention back to me. "You've had your hands full, haven't you?" He walks toward me, and I raise my fists, ready to strike. He comes in close and I throw a roundhouse kick into his face. Predictably, my yellow belt karate knowledge can't save me here. He swings his elbow out to block the blow, grabs my ankle, and throws me to the ground. Karine watches us. She pushes her drooping eye back into what was formerly her eye socket. Her mouth opens, and she whispers in a hoarse, distorted voice.

"Let them go, Healey. Look at her. She's transforming." She smiles, her sharp teeth glistening with blood. "You're losing."

"Really?" He lifts his foot, and threatens to stomp me, but I roll out of his way. "Losing?"

I scramble to my feet, and dive behind a scrap of metal. Healey approaches from one side, and I circle to the other. He smirks, scoffs, and stops in his tracks. Looks over his shoulder at Karine, who is struggling through each shallow breath she takes.

"I honestly don't care if I bring Patient Zero home or not. Toppling your secret empire? That's enough success for me for one day."

"Even if it costs you your life?"

A limp, lifeless corpse drips from Aspen's mouth, and she stares at Healey with a violent intensity. Any semblance of human emotion is gone from her eyes, but there's one thing that remains: contempt. She *recognizes* this man.

Healey points to her. "If you think she's defending you, you're wrong. Everyone is prey to her."

I stare at him. He laughs a little.

"You seem confused." He exhales slowly and tosses his head, frustrated. He finally reaches for the rifle that's strapped to his back. "That thing back there? Is not human. Not even when it looks human."

The way that he calls her "a thing" makes my skin crawl. I shake my head and back further away. My eyes dart around the space and I try to look for a weapon—any kind of weapon. A pipe. A flaming piece of metal. Shards of glass. But the flames are spreading quickly, and the hazy heat is making it harder to see the world around me.

"You see what Karine made—half-baked scientist that she is—is only going to make her more unstable. But what I've got?" he reaches into the pocket of his sport coat and withdraws another vial. This time, it's orange. It looks almost like soda. He shakes it around a little. "This is what's going to fix her."

"What do you mean?"

"You're just going to have to trust me on this one, kid."

Karine hisses through gritted teeth. "Do *not* trust him, Riley."

I lock eyes with Karine. The outline of her body has dissolved; she's starting to sink into a puddle on the ground. The holes in her body ooze blood and pus, like oil paint dripping down a canvas. Her cracked, pleading lips purse together as she utters her last words:

"Use your head."

The explosion is sudden, and she doesn't scream. Her body balloons upward before finally bursting, spraying acid across the space. The oil catches fire and the flames form a crisscrossed web on the floor, preventing any escape. Black smoke curls around the ceiling. I duck behind the metal scrap and brace for impact, squeezing my eyes shut. Healey shouts, but his voice is overtaken by Aspen's roars.

The heat intensifies, and I can feel my hands blistering against the cement floor. Sweat pours down my forehead, and even when I try to open my eyes, I can't see. Pain explodes inside my head, and the world around me

ceases

to

exist.

Day 9 – Afternoon

FOR A LONG TIME, I find myself floating in nothingness, and the whole time, I'm aware of how hot it is. It's like I'm on fire while in a state of sleep paralysis. I wonder if my skin is melting off my body; if when I wake up, I'm going to be a pile of goo, just like Karine.

Time passes, and I finally feel some sort of coolness. Almost damp. It feels delicious and refreshing, and I no longer feel the urge to wake up. When the white sunlight peels through my eyelids, I think that this is it—that maybe I died in the fire and went to heaven. But then my vision focuses, and I realize I'm lying face-up in a clearing in the forest. From the placement of the sun in the sky, it has to be about mid-afternoon. I try to sit up, but a wave of dizziness hits me, forcing me to lay back down. My ears are ringing. *Loudly.* It feels like the sounds are circling around in my ear drums like a drill, sending pain shooting through my forehead. What is this? I know what this is called. Tinny-something. *Tinnitus?* Shit.

I cup my hands over my ears and grit my teeth, shaking my head from side to side. I stare straight into the undergrowth, willing my eyes to focus. Eventually, the ringing subsides, but my head still throbs. I sit up and plant my hands firmly on the ground to stay upright. The woods are dark, deep, and endless. A mess of jagged branches and wilting autumn leaves. I look over my shoulder and see a pathway behind me cutting through the trees. In the distance, I can see a smoldering shell. *The house.*

Tigger.

I stumble to my feet, and my body screams in agony, but I grit my teeth and fight through the pain. There's something wrong with my leg—it's sort of twisting to the side when I walk, and all the nerve endings seem to frizz when I step forward. It's connected to a sharp left pain in my hip. But I don't stop moving. I keep pushing through, up the pathway, dragging my other leg behind me.

I try to shout, but I can't. My throat feels like ash. All around me the sounds of the forest seem to amplify—or is that the ringing in my head? Birds, birds, birds. Each step I take toward the house, I feel so much further away. I hear thrashings in the trees and whip my head in every direction to see what's there. But I see nothing. Is it Aspen?

Tigger? Woodland creatures? Or am I hallucinating? Is any of this real? Or is this some special sort of purgatory?

THUMP! I go tumbling head over heels, onto the ground. My body goes limp. My leg throbs and spasms, the pain shooting up my spine. Flakes of ash fly into my mouth and I desperately try to spit them out. Saliva mixed with blood stains the forest floor a muddy maroon. I fumble for my phone in my pocket, but it's gone.

I swallow back a lump of tears and press my forehead into the ground. *Get up, Riley.* Lifting my head only to fall back down under the weight of it all. Arms shaking. *Ring-ring-ring.* Oh God. I'm losing control of my body. *Ring-ring-ring.* I'm losing control of my mind. I feel my heart in my throat; feel something coming up and it's all ash.

No, wait.

That's puke.

I turn to the side and belch, then vomit onto the ground. It's black and grimy. Is that from my lungs? It smells of smoke and bile. I roll over to the side, away from it, and lay on my back, staring up at the sky. I feel like I have lived a thousand lifetimes. A thousand different lives. One day a daughter. The next day not. One day in love with a girl. The next the keeper of a monster. A thousand different lifetimes but I can't die here. I'm not ready to meet my mom again.

Then I hear it.

A bark. Surprised, then urgent.

And Tigger descends on me, whimpering and crying in contorted yowls, covering me with kisses and reviving me. I bury my face against his body and look into his beautiful eyes. A small cut on his forehead, a few concerning patches of scorched fur. My eyes fill with tears, and I wrap my arms around him. My beautiful boy. My sweet boy. My loyal boy. I'll never leave you again. I don't know how he made it through the fire and collapse of an entire house, but I'm whispering my thank-you prayers to whatever Gods ensured it.

I finally find the strength to stand again. Tigger stands beside me, trying to steady me, and sure enough, I stumble onto my knees again. He barks urgently, and I dismissively wave him away. He stands, frigid, his eyes wide. I slip my fingers underneath his collar, using one hand to pull myself forward. I keep my arm resting across his back, and he gently pulls me up the hill, out of the darkness, and into the sunlight.

The house is a smoking shell of what it was before. It sits on a patch of downtrodden mud, overturned cars and upchucked patches of sod scattered across the yard. The house is brittle and black, like a candle burned down to the wick. I try to stand again, and when I place my hand against the siding to support myself, it crumbles. I look around the space. A few dead bodies. A few missing heads. White eyes. Blood mixed in with mud, shining so bright in the light of the afternoon sun. Looks like raspberry filling for a chocolate cake. Just the thought makes me hurl again.

Tigger anxiously circles the space, his tail stiff and alert. I wipe my mouth with the back of my hand.

"Tig," I call out hoarsely. "Where's Aspen?"

Tigger looks at me blankly. I shake my head from side to side, trying to get rid of the ringing in my ears. I end up plugging one of my ears with my finger—it seems to help at least a little bit. I make my way through the carnage, following Tigger. He keeps his nose pressed low to the ground, snuffling. He sniffs the faces of dead men and whines, then continues on.

"Aspen!" I call out, but my voice breaks, and I start coughing uncontrollably. I sound like a strangled cat. "Aspen!"

I hear the sound of tires grinding against the ground. Over my shoulder, I see a truck. An armored black truck, with the Titan Tech logo emblazoned on the side. A couple men hop out, their eyes wide with horror. They look at the burnt house, their mouths agape. One man drags a hand over his face. They are armed, but only with small pistols on their holsters. They don't wear a lot of armor; maybe just a bullet proof vest underneath, making their chests appear bulky and square.

Tigger barks and runs toward them. They hold up their hands defensively and he sniffs them. One man gently touches his head, and Tigger snaps at him.

"Easy, easy," he says. He crouches and extends a hand for Tigger to sniff. At first, he growls, but then he starts circling the men. The man looks at his coworker and shakes his head. "Donnie, call someone."

The man grabs a radio on his utility belt and lifts it into the air. He walks around for a few moments, shaking it a little. "I'm not getting any service, Cole."

"We gotta call someone. What the hell happened here?" the man scans the area, his face ghost white. "Jesus. I think I'm gonna be sick." His eyes land on me, and he points in my direction. "Hey! You!"

I stand there dumbly, not knowing what to do. Cole and Donnie jog over to me, Tigger hot on their heels. Donnie yelps in surprise at the sight of a man with his face ripped off, and a string of curse words follow soon after. I try to focus on Cole's face. He's not as young as I thought he was. Crow's feet, kind eyes, strong jawline. He grabs my shoulders to steady me. I hadn't even realized I was swaying from side to side. Snaps his fingers in front of my face.

"Ay!" he says. "Miss? Can you tell me your name?"

I want to say it. "Ri…" But I'm too exhausted. Nothing comes out of my mouth. Cole holds me steady and looks to Donnie.

"Get the water from the truck."

Donnie retrieves a water bottle and races back over. Cole cracks it open and lifts it to my lips for me to sip. I take one sip, then two deep gulps, and have to push it back into his hands. A wave of nausea overcomes me, and I struggle to choke back the bile. Oh shit. No. I want to keep this down. Cole offers some of the water to Tigger, who eagerly gulps it down.

"Miss, you're really fucked up, pardon my French. We gotta get you to a hospital."

I shake my head. Aspen. I need to find Aspen. But the words only come out as "…pen." The men exchange stares of confusion. Donnie places a finger against his chin and glances back in the direction of the truck.

"I don't think we have any paper she can write on."

Cole shakes his head and looks back at me. "You're gonna have to try. Use your words as best you can."

"As…pen," I say, my tongue feeling like mush in my mouth. I grab the water bottle, and after a few more sips, can finally feel its moisture coating my throat. "Aspen."

"You had a friend?" he sucks in air through his teeth, his eyes wide and looks at Donnie, who shakes his head pitifully. "Honey. We gotta get you out of here. Come on, let's go." He grabs my arm and tries to lead me away, but I wrench away from him.

"No. Aspen," I say. I'm aware of the fact I'm not making any sense, but I can still barely talk. I'm not leaving her behind. I have to know what happened to her.

"We should call someone."

"We can't just leave her here."

"You can't force her into the truck, either."

"Donnie, would you quit being useless and help me? I mean, grab her arm or something so we can haul her back to the car. It's not like we can just leave a civilian here for dead."

"Corporate would probably prefer she be dead." He eyes me warily, then casts his eyes away, as if ashamed. "Wouldn't have to deal with the liability."

171

"Corporate's not here." Cole snorts and tosses his head. "Mr. Bigshot probably got eaten up by that monster. From the look of it, that's what happened to everyone. Christ Almighty, this is worse than the time in Kuwait."

He looks at me once more and grabs my arm. Donnie grabs the other, and they start to drag me back to the car. I'm much too tired to protest, but too awake to not cry. The tears stream down my cheeks and drip onto the ground. The mud sinks in between the toes of my ripped shoes.

"Jesus. She's just a kid," Donnie says, his voice thin and quiet.

They open the door of the truck, and Cole lifts me into the passenger seat. Tigger wriggles past him and onto the truck as Cole buckles me in.

"That your dog?" he asks, and I nod slowly. "Beautiful dog."

I wipe at the tears on my face, and when I look at my hands, I see nothing but soot and blood. Cole notices me staring at them, and he smiles almost apologetically.

"We'll take you to the hospital and get you cleaned up. Donnie, let's you and I check the perimeter for any other survivors, and we'll head on out."

"Aspen," I repeat again, urgently. "*Aspen.*"

Donnie narrows his eyes. "Why does she keep saying that?"

"She's obviously in shock, Donnie, cut her a goddamn break—" and then he stops and frowns. Looks up at me and Donnie. "Wait a minute. What's the name of that girl?"

"I think her name was…" Donnie trails off. His eyes widen. "Oh shit. *Aspen.* That's the name of the girl."

"The girl?"

"Patient Zero."

I nod slowly, still too disoriented to elaborate further. Donnie fumbles through his utility belt and withdraws a vial. It's the same orange stuff that Healey showed me last night.

"I don't need you to talk, just answer yes or no," Cole says. "Did you see her transform?"

I nod.

"And have you seen her since?"

I shake my head. They exchange looks with each other again and reach for their weapons. My eyes widen. Donnie waves a hand dismissively. He inserts the vial into his gun. *Oh.* It's not a normal pistol. It's a tranquilizer. Or at least, that's what Donnie has. The sharp clicks coming from Cole's weapon let me know there's bullets in there.

"Hang tight," Cole says with a reassuring smile. "Let's see if we can round her up. Donnie, let's move out."

I watch as he and Donnie walk back toward the smoldering house, their weapons pointed up and out. Cole leads the way, with Donnie close behind him. I run my hands through Tigger's fur, slowly stroking his head. I don't want to keep watching them, but I'm too anxious to look away.

Then I see something round the corner of the house. Limping. Frizzy blond hair, singed with soot and dirt and blood. A smoldering green-eyed gaze that is somehow murderous and vapid. It's Aspen, but it isn't her. As she gets closer, I can see the thin crooked line wrapping its way across her face, the layers of armored black scales underneath her tattered clothes. She hasn't transformed back into human form yet. I breathe in deeply; my lungs suddenly feel shallow, like I'm underwater.

I don't know if she heard me breathing, but she looks at me directly. Locks eyes with me. Burning, burning, burning. She stands against the side of the house, her feet planted firmly on the ground; not moving forward. Then she hears their voices. Donnie and Cole, creeping back around the corner, debating whether or not they want to split up. Aspen tilts her head to the side. She hears them. The pupils of her eyes dart in their direction.

I shake my head violently. A little growl tickles the back of Tigger's throat. I tighten my grip on his collar and wrap my arms around his body. I keep my eyes on Aspen. She wouldn't. Would she?

Aspen's gaze locks on mine once again.

"No!" I shout.

Donnie and Cole look in my direction, alarmed, their eyes wide and white. I point ferociously back at Aspen, my body trembling with fear. Aspen runs out from her hiding spot, and I watch as her skin recedes into her scales, as her mouth grows wide, and her teeth grow sharp. The men scream, racing back toward the truck. Aspen releases a guttural roar, and I cover my eyes with my hands, watching from behind my crooked fingers. Tigger yowls and barks and wrenches around in my hands but I don't let him go. I lift him as tightly into my arms as I can; I can't let him go. Whoever that monster is out there, it isn't Aspen. It's *not*. It can't be.

Cole twists over his shoulder and fires a round. It manages to lodge just above her upper lip, looking like a swollen, overgrown blackhead ready to burst open. Aspen shrieks, stops, and removes it from her jaw before popping it into her mouth. Her face still bleeding, she charges forward, and leaps onto Donnie's back. Her claws sink into the side of his neck and shoulders, severing his carotid artery, and his knees buckle beneath him. He tries to scream but can't, only choking. He drops the tranquilizer and holds up his hands defensively, but she bends down and presses her mouth against his gushing wounds, tearing out chunks of flesh and strings of muscle. Cole shouts Donnie's name over and over again, trembling in shock.

When Aspen gulps down her bite, she licks her lips, her long pointed tongue seamlessly swiping away all the drops of blood. She blinks a few times, her reptilian gaze focusing on Cole. He fires another round directly at her head, and her scales move to deflect them. I think a bullet backfires, because he howls in pain and clutches his knee, collapsing to the ground. I'm screaming; Tigger's yowling. Aspen slowly approaches Cole, her body growing and assuming its full monster shape. He's curled up on the ground in a fetal position. He raises his shaking hands, and I can hear his soft, kind voice.

"Please," he begs her. "Please."

This time, she doesn't bite. She raises her massive foot and brings it down on top of his head. I hear him screaming, hear bone crunching and something squishing-oozing, and by God, he's *not* dead. She raises her foot again and slams it down. Still screaming. I can't tell if it's Cole or me. *WHAM!* Ringing. Ringing in my ears. I can't tell what I'm hearing and what I'm not hearing anymore, but I know my mouth is open, and my lungs feel like they're going to burst.

Aspen bends down and takes a bite from the smashed-up corpse. Blood dribbles down her face. She stares at me. And I lose consciousness.

Day 9 - Night

BY THE TIME I wake up, it's night. Tigger is nowhere to be found. I hear the sounds of someone snoring softly, and I look over my shoulder. Aspen is curled up like an animal at the back of the truck. Still covered in blood.

I rub my eyes and look outside. A full moon, glistening white, illuminates the space. Somehow the blood looks darker than the night sky itself. I slowly grip the armrests of my seat and rise to my feet. It creaks underneath me. I flinch and whip my head around to see if Aspen has moved. Nope. Still sleeping.

I drag a hand over my face. Why would she do that? Did she think she was protecting me? Didn't she hear me screaming no? Did I *actually* scream no? Those men weren't going to hurt us—at least, I don't think they were. If they wanted to kill her, wouldn't Cole have just gone after her with the pistol, and abandoned the tranq altogether?

My mind is reeling. She can't control her powers. Not even a little bit. Not even when she's mostly in a human state, which is what I thought she had told me. She's never been in control of her powers, not once. And what happens when she gets hungry again, and I'm the only one around? How am I supposed to protect myself, or Tigger?

I take a deep breath and slowly, quietly, make my way off the truck. Tigger runs up to me. Even though he's wagging his tail, his eyes look up at me mournfully. He's so scared. And I am too.

Dread creeps in. I cast a look in the direction of where I last saw Donnie and Cole. And even though I don't want to, I stumble over. I can't explain why. I feel compelled to. Tigger whines nervously and hangs back by the truck. One heavy foot after the other accompanied by the sounds of flies buzzing even in the dead of night. I see them— or what used to be them. Cole is a crumpled pile of bones and sloppy rotting organs spilling out of what appears to be his chest cavity. I struggle to keep back the bile that's forcefully climbing its way up my throat. I look over at Donnie, half eaten, his head mostly gone, and his hands outstretched and stiff. My eyes water. They seemed like *good* people. Nice men. People who were just going to get us out of here as quickly as possible. No one deserves to die like this.

Sniffling, I wipe at the tears forming in the corners of my eyes. And then I see it. The damaged end of the tranq gun. I crouch down and pick it up, turning the weapon over and over in my hands. It's heavier than I expected and looks cartoonishly large in my small hands. The front end is damaged—looks like it's been smashed by Aspen when she was in her monster form. A small panel rests atop the barrel of the gun. I crack it open and find the vial underneath. The vial, almost completely intact, glittering and orange in the moonlight. I slowly peel it out and grip it between two fingers.

Healey said that this could help her. That it would fix her. Fix. Not kill. It can stop her powers, can't it? Maybe not completely rid her of them but subdue them. Reduce them. I can't forget the damage she's caused. I know I can't. But it's not her fault. Even now I know it's not her fault. And I know I can still save her. I can still save us. Enough is enough. How many more lives must be lost or overturned by the violence that we leave in our wake? Maybe the vial is what they want. To remove everything that makes Aspen special.

But maybe by removing what makes her special, we could finally be free.

And then bad men won't have to chase us anymore, and we won't have to cry anymore, and we could drive back to Portland, and we could just be teenage girls in love. And I could slow dance with her in my grandparents' living room and take her to boba with Caia and Khalil after school and spend every Friday night curled up on the couch with Tigger watching all the artsy award winning movies I know I'm too dumb to understand.

This is our only hope.

This is the only way we can be free.

Grimacing, I glance back over my shoulder at Donnie's corpse. I creep closer to it, the stench searing my nostrils, and the sight so gruesome, it makes my knees shake. I crouch down, and my knees immediately feel damp. I know without looking that it's blood.

"I'm so sorry." I whisper, and my shaking hands stretch forward. I unclip the utility belt from around his body and drag it out from underneath him. Tigger whines, and I look over in his direction. He's still parked right by the truck, but he's definitely upset with me. "Keep quiet, boy."

I drag the utility belt over to me and start fumbling through the different packs. Small plastic packages of rations. Medication. Bullets. *Damn it.* I need a syringe. *I just raided a dead man's corpse for nothing. No Riley, stop feeling guilty.* I stop, and think for a moment, and I almost want to smack myself when I realize it. *The truck.* They came here in the truck I was just sleeping in. If they had a syringe, it would be in there.

I slowly make my way back over, taking extra care to be as quiet as possible. Tigger waits for me, his tail tucked between his legs. I wave a hand at him dismissively and climb up the truck's steps, pop open the dash. Among an arsenal of tools and discarded fast food wrappers, I find them. Syringes. I unscrew the cap from the vial, insert the needle into the liquid, and pull up the plunger. It slurps it up hungrily, ticking up each little line until finally, I can't withdraw anymore.

Anxiously, I set the empty vial and syringe on the dash. It glistens and glows in the faint light, and in the darkness, it reminds me of a little beacon floating on a lake. It could guide us to safety. It could guide us both home. But in the midst of my hopeful reverie, I hear something behind me. A soft yawn. The gentle rustling of clothing as a body turns over. I glance in Aspen's direction. She's yawning and stretching in the faint light.

Instinctively, I freeze. My eyes dart around the darkness of the truck. I see it. An unloaded rifle, leaning up against the side. Looks like either Donnie or Cole was in the middle of cleaning it before they got here, because there's a greasy rag on the floor beside it and an open box of ammunition. It's hard, but it won't be hard enough to kill her. Just a hit to the head with the barrel, and she should be out cold. But only if I can catch her by surprise.

I sidestep closer to it in the shadows and place my hands on it. Metal creaks under my feet. Aspen looks in my direction. Her mouth moves to say my name and before the words escape her lips, I bring the barrel down on her head.

She falls to the floor limply, and I set it back to the side. Her breathing is shallow, but she isn't bleeding. I crouch by her body and using all my strength, lift her into my arms. Tigger barks as I stagger out of the truck—he even has the nerve to growl at me. But I shake my head and keep moving. When we first got here, I saw a shed. Blue like the house. Right on the outskirts of the property. I stumble around in the darkness, trudging through the sloppy mud, my eyes scanning the area for any sign of it. Past the crumbling edge of the house's porch, I spot it. Half of it is scorched, but the other half is still intact. I kick open the door and set Aspen in a chair. Then I sprint back to the truck and retrieve the vial.

Tigger snarls at me. I shake my head and push him back. "Stop it!" But he keeps coming after me, growling, his ears pushed back and his eyes wide. He's staring at the syringe. "Bad dog!" I throw open the door of the shed and just before he enters, I slam it shut. I twist the ancient rusty lock into place and ignore his frantic barks.

I look back at Aspen. Look at the syringe. And for the second time this week, I'm suddenly confronted by one of the most dreadful choices I've ever had to make in my life.

Day 10 - Early Morning

AND NOW HERE WE are. Quarantined in a wooden shed on the edge of ruin, Tigger ferociously barking outside. Aspen, her torso and wrists chained to a splintery wooden chair. Me, my shin throbbing, desperately trying to withstand her bodychecks as we writhe around on the floor, screaming at each other, desperate to reach that little orange vial. Beneath her weight and struggling, the chair breaks, splinters of wood splitting away and crumbling to the floor.

Aspen's face is red and burns with anguish and fury. Her voice is hoarse and almost alien-sounding, as her animalistic growls splice in her human-girl cries. Tears stream down her cheeks. She's so weak she can't tear apart these metal chains, which clink like chattering teeth. But that might not be the case for long: the beast within flickers in those reptilian pupils of hers, fighting to break free. For as hard as she's trying, she can't control it. We're mere minutes away from her losing herself once more, and I won't survive that.

"Riley, I'm begging you," she cries out. "I don't want to hurt you!"

"You won't have to, anymore. I'm going to make sure of that." As the words leave my mouth, I feel a chill course down my spine. These words felt so different inside my head. A *good* person does whatever it takes to save her girlfriend, and that's what I'm doing. But she doesn't want this. She's afraid. *You're scaring her, Riley.* Taking away another choice that should be hers. But what choices do I have? How can I save us both from the nightmare we're living in?

"They didn't deserve to *die*, Aspen. You're wrong. You weren't doing what you had to do. I am." Mustering all my strength, I kick her away from me and she cries out in pain. I wriggle like a caterpillar against the floor, and as my hand reaches to pull myself forward, it scrapes against the grooves in the wood. Splinters puncture my fingers like thousands of little bee stings. I grit my teeth and wrap my fingers around the end of the syringe.

Whipping around to face her, adrenaline rippling through my body, I know I can fix this. I can still fix her. It's okay that she's afraid. We can both be afraid together, just as we've been this whole time. But at least after we endure this final scary thing, it should be over. Healey promised. He's the head of R&D. He had to know what he was talking about—had to know better than Karine, right?

She cowers now, her eyes wide with fear. Tears dripping down her cheeks and snot bubbling in her nose. She whimpers as I grab her wrist and yelps in pain as I insert the needle. Oh shit. *Shit.* Am I even doing this right? I can feel a little bit of resistance, like I'm poking into muscle. Syringes *go* in muscle, don't they? Oh God. I convinced myself that this was the right thing—that I was doing what I *should* do—but I never stopped to think if I *could* do it. Still, I'm overcome by my desperate urge to try, try anything. I push down on the plunger ever so slightly. A little bit of the liquid trickles in, and she screams, like she's being lit on fire. She cries, begs for me to withdraw it, and I watch as her face contorts turning red.

Panic sears through my body, fresh and hot like a wildfire, as I see the agony on her face. I don't see Aspen any longer. I see a little girl; a little girl whose father should have been taking her to the beach or to the movies and instead introduced her to a hell unlike any other. A little girl who desperately tried in vain to find her mother so she could stop the men from controlling her and her body. A little girl who gave her heart to a boy who only thought he owned her, just as they had.

I'm no better than any of them.

I'm the monster.

Not her.

"Riley," she pleads. Heartbreak. Exhaustion. Hope, inching closer to its death with each second I pump the poison into her veins.

I pull out the syringe and throw it to the side.

Then wrap my arms around her shaking, little shoulders.

And we both sob, intertwined in a mass of grief and guilt.

Golden sunlight bleeds through the cracks in the shed. Through blurry eyes, I hold her at arm's length and stare at her. She smiles warmly at me.

"Minneapolis?" she asks, her voice hoarse.

I squeeze her hands. "Minneapolis."

Then suddenly she twists away from me and wretches onto the floor. Blood is mixed in with the carnage from yesterday. Her face turns from red to ashy, and more bile bubbles up at the mouth. She coughs and chokes. My wild eyes stare back at the syringe. Not all of the liquid made its way into her body; I wouldn't even say a quarter of it did. And the reaction is *this* bad? Oh shit. Oh shit, I've made a horrible mistake. She convulses and rolls onto her side, her body shuddering, acting like she can't breathe. The vomit stops, but she can't stop wheezing.

"Aspen?"

She stares at me with wide, terrified eyes. I shake my head over and over. I lift her off the ground and into my arms, and although my legs are screaming in pain, I ignore it. I unlock the door and kick it open. Tigger barks excitedly, but there's no time for a happy reunion. With Aspen curled up in my arms, I trudge through the wreckage, and then I finally see it. My truck, the passenger side window completely shattered, but otherwise intact. With one hand, I reach inside, ignoring the glass that prickles my skin, and wrench open the door using the handle. I slide her into the passenger's seat and buckle her up, then throw Tigger into the backseat. Thankful the key is still in my pant pocket, I turn the key in the ignition, and the engine roars to life. I look over at Aspen, whose breathing is still shallow. I squeeze her hand.

"Hang on."

The truck jerks forward unsteadily, then budges. I curse and smack my hand against the steering wheel, then press down harder on the gas. The gears grind and the tires make a high-pitched screaming sound, then finally, break forward. I whip the truck around toward the entrance, and head for the driveway. Down the road, past the flurry of haunted trees and scraggly green growth, for what seems like forever, until we finally reach the highway once again.

For a moment, as we burn rubber on the hot asphalt stretch ahead of us, everything feels surreal and hopeful. I roll down the windows and let the air whip through our hair. Feel the sunlight once again, washing away the guilt and the grossness.

But then I see them, this thin black line on the horizon, and as we edge nearer, they become clearer. Fifteen, twenty, maybe thirty? Armored vehicles, a couple with giant artillery mechanisms mounted on top. All with the Titan Tech logo emblazoned on the sides. A few highway patrol cars flanking the fleet. I slam on the brakes, the tires skidding and squealing against the asphalt, then reach for Aspen's hand. About thirty armed members of the Titan Tech guard are forming a human wall, and at the forefront…

… Dad! His face is red, eyes filled with tears, looking distraught.

And Healey. A few scars and scratches, but otherwise perfectly intact.

This bastard. He escaped, but still left his men to die. Just so he could turn and run for help like a coward?

Aspen refuses to meet my gaze. She just shakes her head over and over again. Healey lifts the megaphone in his hands and presses down on the button. His voice echoes out in electric crackles, but it's loud and clear.

"Aspen Montehugh, you are holding Riley Grishin hostage. We're here to negotiate for her release." My dad elbows him and whispers something. Healey passes the megaphone to him.

"Please let go of my daughter," Dad cries breathlessly. "Please! I just want Riley back!"

Shrill feedback echoes from the megaphone and my grief-stricken father collapses to his knees, sobbing. Healey wrenches the device out from underneath him. He holds up the megaphone again.

I grit my teeth and throw open the car door. Aspen cries out my name, but I hold up my hand. I'm sick of this shit. I plant my feet on the ground and spread my arms wide. A few members of the guard advance forward, but Healey holds up a hand, urging them to wait.

"Hey, Healey! Nice to see you! Glad to see you made it out of the fire you left me to *burn* in!"

Healey doesn't flinch, but a few members of the guard look at each other, deeply confused. I don't bother looking at him. I stare at my father. My father, who I both love and hate. Who's been manipulated and done his fair share of manipulating. I cup my hands over my mouth and bellow as loudly as I can. He stops crying, and his hands drop from his face. He looks at me sternly, but earnestly.

"Dad, these assholes have been *hunting* us down across the entire country!"

My dad does a double take. His eyebrows narrow. Healey finally rolls his eyes, cracks his neck from side to side, and speaks into the megaphone once more, with an air so casual and callous, it makes my blood boil.

"The girl sitting in this car is responsible for burning down Little Brook. She must be taken into protective custody. Do not listen to a single word she says. Stand your ground."

I shake my head again. "*You* should be taken into custody! You're the one who said they should burn down Little Brook!"

I can tell from the stiffness of their body language I'm losing them. I redirect the conversation.

"Dad, he's been trying to kill us! Aspen has been protecting me!" Hot tears burn at the corner of my eyes and my body shakes. "Please believe me!"

Anxious murmurs amongst the crowd.

"I tried that cure you bragged about, Healey, and guess what? She's sick! We need to get her to a hospital!"

"If Aspen needs medical attention, we can arrange that for her." Healey coaxes in a condescending tone of voice. "Riley, I understand you're deeply confused. But I can assure you we're here to help. Not harm you."

I've been confused about the people we've met along our journey. We trusted people that we shouldn't have. Mistrusted others who only wanted to help us no matter the cost. Hell, Aspen and I, we've lacked trust in each other. But looking into this man's cold, beady eyes? There's no way in hell he cares for either one of us. That he even sees us as humans. No well-tailored suit or army of men or ungodly amount of money is going to convince me otherwise. Aspen's sitting in this car right now, fighting for her life.

And it's up to me to save it, come hell or high water.

I throw open the driver's seat and reach into the back. I stare pitifully at Tigger and drag him out by the collar and set him gently on the ground. "Dad, call Tigger!"

Confused, Dad calls for him, but to my surprise, Tigger stands there reluctantly. I ruffle his ears and kiss his nose, staring at him gently.

"Please, boy. Go to Dad."

Tigger whines. Dad calls his name again and Tigger finally races over to him. Dad grabs him by the collar and stares back at me, wildly confused. The soldiers look amongst each other, uncertain. Healey's poker face doesn't flinch for a second.

I climb back in the driver's seat. I turn the key in the ignition despite my dad's screams of protest. And I throw the truck in reverse. Spin the wheel around and around until we're pointed in the opposite direction, and then I accelerate. The truck revs to life, and I hear the shouts of the Titan Tech army behind us. Aspen groans, her head rolling from side to side. I keep one hand on her and the other on the steering wheel, my foot pressed down hard on the gas pedal.

I hear the thunderous roars of armored vehicles behind me. The *rat-tat-tat-tat* of guns, first spraying the road ahead of me, then hitting the back windshield. I duck my head low and keep going. I can hear the ferocious shouts of men behind me but can't make out what they're saying. The gunfire ceases. The thunderous roar of the engines, coupled with the raucous road noise as we push eighty, is near deafening. The vehicles inch so close they nearly hit my bumper, but again, shouts—and they fall back. Perplexed, I watch in the rearview as they drift further and further away. Some of them peel off the main road, but a few linger ominously behind us. Then I see it. Signs for a hospital. Not even these assholes would dare shoot up a hospital, right?

I make a beeline for the exit and then I hear it: a loud, ominous *pop!* And a wham from the side, toward the rear of the car, and suddenly, I'm spinning, tumbling through the air, as the truck rolls over and over down the side of the exit. Through the windows and blur of chaos, I can see one of the armored vehicles pulling to a stop behind us. With a thunderous crash, the car flips upside-down and pain radiates through my body with a lightning-fast intensity. I hang in the cab, held in place only by my seatbelt. I shove down the airbags as best I can, till they're out of the way. I look toward Aspen

Wriggling in my seat, I tug on the seat belt until finally, it loosens. Guess this truck being an old piece of shit worked out in my favor for once. I drop from my seat, coughing, my muscles shaking from exhaustion, and push through the window. I hover on the outside of the truck, reach inside, unbuckle Aspen, and pull her through.

Her face is so pale. Her green eyes, bleary and barely open, are so small and thin. She's desperately clinging to consciousness. I press my fingers against her wrist and check her pulse. Not good. Weak. Fluttery. I grit my teeth and wipe the blood from my eyes again.

"I'm going to get us out of here even if it fucking kills me."

I lift her up into my arms, and onto my back, and my body threatens to crumple beneath me, but I fight through it. I hook my arms underneath her legs, and she limply wraps her arms around my neck. I haul ass up the freeway ramp. But of course, I'm not nearly fast enough. The armored trucks skid out in front of me, blocking the path. Armed soldiers climb out and lift their weapons once more.

"Get the fuck out of my way!"

My screams are strangled by my sobs, but I'm not afraid of them, and I'm no longer afraid of dying. A few of the soldiers are unnerved by my cries. I manage to push past one of them but run right into the barrel of another. Wait. Not another. Healey. A gun pressed between my eyes, staring at me like I was the scum of the earth, and he can't wait to put me out of my misery. I glare ferociously at him and take another step forward, and he pulls back on the trigger. It clicks loudly as a bullet enters the barrel. Gasps erupt around me.

"Sir!" a soldier cries out in protest. "She's just a kid!"

"If she's just a kid, then why the hell haven't you taken care of her yet?" Healey snaps, rolling his eyes. He speaks through clenched teeth, seething with rage. "You take another step, and it's the last one you'll ever take, little girl."

"You're a monster," I snarl, my grip on Aspen tightening. I press my forehead against the barrel and to my surprise, Healey raises the pistol and smacks me with it.

It sends me tumbling head over heels. I fall backward on top of Aspen, and we tumble down the ramp, back toward the smoldering wreckage of the car. Every bump my body rolls over sends agony searing through me. Cries of protest rise from the militia, but even so, as I come to a stop and lay face down in the dirt, I feel blows landing against me. A foot against my ribcage, another to my spine. Screaming,

I bring my arms up in front of my face, and I manage to sit upright. Healey grabs my hair and tugs my head around to face him. Aspen lays on the ground several feet away from me. Her eyes closed. Her body crumpled in an odd way, like a wounded animal.

"I've had just about enough of you, you little shit. I played nice with you. You had chance after chance to walk away. And you didn't do it."

I swish my tongue around my teeth and spit blood into his face. He stares back at me murderously. Wipes the blood with his sleeve. Turns back and looks toward the militia, who have lowered their weapons, and are aggressively yelling at him. A highway patrol officer appears deeply confused and furious.

"Mr. Healey!" he shouts. "That's enough! These girls need medical attention!"

"And I've told you, officer, we'll handle it." He motions for the soldiers to grab Aspen, and I shriek in protest. My scream rips out my throat, reverberating through the air with a fierceness I didn't know was within me.

"Don't touch her!" I screech. "Officer, if you let them take her, they will *kill* her!"

The soldiers stare at me in confusion. I shake my head and plead with them.

"Please, look at her! She's not a monster! She's a girl! A girl who is dying because of something *he* created!"

"And yet, you were the one who gave it to her." Healey smiles smugly, revealing white teeth.

Tears burn my eyes. "I wanted to help her."

"No, you didn't. I was right. You're terrified of her." He stares straight at me, his hot breath clouding up my vision.

"Because you manipulated me."

"I only stated the truth. She's dangerous, and responsible for the deaths of hundreds of people."

"If she is, then so are you."

I try to twist my head away from him, but he holds fast. I slam my forehead forward, connecting with the bridge of his nose. Healey roars in pain and recoils, and I sprint for Aspen. The patrol officer walks up to him, shouting at him about protocol. I hear none of it. Only the blood pounding in my ears, and a faint *ring-ring-ring*. The soldiers back away, and I roll Aspen onto her back. Press my ear against her chest. And I can't hear anything anymore. A sob escapes my throat.

Why won't anyone help us? What can I even do now? How am I supposed to fix this?

I fumble in the pockets of my sweatshirt and jeans, desperately hoping to find the answer. And my fingers find something. Smooth. *Glass?* I reach into my pocket and withdraw it. A small vial of blue serum, spiderwebs of cracks circling the glass. It's the one Aspen gave to me yesterday, after we watched Martin die. Somehow still intact. I don't even know if it would work, but this is the only option I have. If they both came from her body, then maybe they can counteract each other? It may not completely bring her back to normal, but hopefully, it could stabilize her.

I pull down on Aspen's jaw. Crack open the vial of serum and pour it into her mouth. I tilt her head forward to help her swallow. Wait. And wait. My eyes are so blurry with tears, I can't even tell if her chest is moving. The world, which had been loud and chaotic only minutes ago, is now so silent it's like freefalling into an abyss. And when another moment passes without her so much as twitching, I think I'm never going to crawl out. This is it. This is how it all ends. The wildest, funniest, most intelligent, and beautiful girl I've ever known, and ever will know, dying in my arms from my actions. Risking life and limb to save me when all I did was betray her. Just like everyone else did.

"Aspen, baby," I whisper, my thumb rubbing away the dirt on her cheek. "Please. Hold on just a little longer; just a little longer."

But her body remains still. And I collapse on top of her, sobbing endlessly. My mind floats back to the day I found out about her monster powers. How she had cried, and clung to me, and told me that she would have died in that fire if it meant that Mom would've lived. But right now, I would die a thousand times over if it meant she would live.

Then slowly, a twitch of her fingers. A sharp, sudden inhale. And those beautiful green eyes open once again. A shocked sob escapes my throat, and I throw my arms around her. I shower her with kisses on her forehead, on her cheeks.

"Riley," she mutters, her voice hoarse. "I can't breathe."

I tear away from her. She notices the fear on my face and smirks. Runs a hand through my beachy, beachy hair.

"No more experimenting with weird-ass laboratory potions for you."

I place a hand over my heart. "For the rest of my life. However short it may be."

She coughs as I help her sit up. Healey turns away from the patrol officer and beams, clearly trying—but obviously failing—to restrain his anger.

"See? She's fine, now we'll be on our way."

The officer blocks Healey's path. "You just assaulted a minor. You ain't going anywhere."

"Assaulted a minor?"

"This isn't the goddamn Wild West. You can't just perform a PIT maneuver and assault a minor and expect to walk away."

"It's of *utmost* importance that I take that girl in by any means necessary."

The patrol officer stares coolly back. "So far, the only dangerous person I've seen this morning is you."

Healey has the audacity to push him, sending the officer stumbling back. "It's a matter of national security that we bring this girl back under our control."

"While that's true, Mr. Healey, you most certainly don't have the approval of national security to take her in."

Aspen and I look in the direction of the new voice. A black car sits behind the wreckage of our truck. Two men dressed in ink-black suits flank either side of the vehicle. One has slicked back, stark white hair, whereas the other's is dark and shaved close to his skull. He reaches into the pocket of his jacket and withdraws a badge, which he flashes to the crowd. Victor Moreno. FBI. Aspen and I glance at each other, and we smirk wickedly. Now Healey looks scared, his skin growing even paler.

"I-I thought that I made it clear to Director Marshall that I had this under control!" he sputters, his pupils so wide, he almost appears childlike.

Victor arches a brow dryly. "Well, let's just say a little birdie assisting in our investigation of the explosions told us you don't."

"A little…" Healey trails off, and his eyes widen with realization just as my heart skips a beat.

Karine. Saving us from beyond the grave.

"You think you'd know better than to trust a double agent," Victor scoffs, laughs a little.

Both agents square their shoulders and approach Healey slowly, like hyenas circling a wounded antelope. He scrambles backward, finally spooked. Victor's smile remains plastered across his face, like he's savoring every moment of this.

"She made it quite clear that if she went AWOL, we should come looking for you first. And guess who we lost contact with last night?"

Healey swallows, unable to say anything.

"So yeah, you're not taking these girls anywhere. In fact," Victor says, "you're under arrest."

The officers swiftly apprehend Healey, and he screeches in disbelief, wrestling with them even as they lift him into the back of one of the squad cars. An ambulance, its lights on but its siren off, slowly approaches. Victor motions to them with a wave of his hand. Before I can comprehend what's happening, EMTs are lifting Aspen and I off the ground and carrying us to stretchers in the vehicle. Even though I should feel safe, I am frightened—they're strong, and their hands are rough, and I don't understand anything of what they're saying to each other.

"Riley!"

My dad catches the door of the ambulance just before it closes. Tears run down his cheeks like water from a faucet. The paramedic shouts for him to leave but my dad yells back in protest.

"She's a minor, and she's my daughter, and you will *not* be taking her anywhere without me there!" he snaps, jabbing his finger into the man's chest.

"Then you can drive behind us and follow us there," the medic says, clapping my father on the back. "She's going to be okay."

"You hear that, sweet pea?" Dad says, backing away from the door. "Y-you're going to be okay. I'm going to be right behind you!"

The doors close, and the paramedic turns his attention back to me. My eyelids flutter, and I suddenly feel incredibly sleepy. The paramedic shakes his head and squeezes my hand.

"Hold on, kid. Just a little longer."

Day 12 — Evening

EIGHT BRUISED RIBS, HEAD trauma, several sprains and possible microfractures— not to mention severe dehydration. That's what the doc tells me when we're finally taken to the hospital. They run a handful of tests on us and throw us in a hospital room together. A nurse sticks me with an IV but can't manage to stick one in Aspen because the scales won't recede from her arms. Dad comes to visit, but I insist to the nurses I don't want to see him right now.

Later, one of the nurses manages to find us a deck of cards, and Aspen and I sit on our beds and she teaches me how to play blackjack until we both fell asleep around nine thirty. I don't think I've had a night's rest this deep and good since I was a baby.

Day 13 - Evening

TODAY IS BETTER FOR me, at least physically. They disconnect the IV and I spend some time stretching and trying to regain mobility in my sore limbs. They serve us obviously fake scrambled eggs and toast for breakfast, and to my surprise, I immediately miss the hot n' ready stuff we got at all the motels along the way here.

In the afternoon, one of the FBI agents comes by to have a conversation with Aspen—not Victor, but the one with the white hair; I think his name is Trip or something. I want to stay, but the nurse tells me I have to speak with my doctor about my recovery plan. Dad sits in the room, and I'll never forget the way he looks at me. Horrified, but also deeply offended. Like not letting him see me the day before was the greatest betrayal I could've ever bestowed upon him. But I can't find it in myself to care. I just stare right through him and ask how Tigger is doing. Part of me feels guilty. My poor dog's been traumatized beyond belief, and now he's staying with my dad, who's practically a stranger to him. But even if I could bring him to the hospital, it wouldn't be good for him. Too many people. I think Tigger's had enough of people.

Doc says one more night of rest would be good for me, and after I get home, I immediately have to start physical therapy. I mentioned my tinnitus, but doc says that it's common after events like this, and that it's too early to tell if it's going to be a chronic problem. It's in and out, so I don't really know for sure either. But it sucks when it happens, and I'm tired of the headaches.

I'm escorted back to my room by one of the nurses and I can tell from the look on Aspen's face that whatever happened while I was gone wasn't exactly great. We play another round of cards and then we sit in silence and stare out the window, watching as cars enter and exit the parking lot. A mother in a wheelchair is loaded into a van by her husband, her baby in her arms. A little girl with a bald head joyously toddles toward her grandparents. Kids exit with their arms in slings.

At night, Aspen and I stare out the window, hand in hand. I've asked her a few times about what the FBI agent said, but she hasn't said anything. A nurse delivered dinner about forty-five minutes ago, but neither one of us wanted to touch it. It looks like Velveeta mac and cheese, which is both repulsive and depressing, but not nearly as bad as the wilted iceberg lettuce they tried to pass as a "house salad." I'm not exactly going to "recover" from my traumas if I'm subjected to more of this food.

"What're you thinking about?" I ask, shuffling through the deck of cards. "Want to teach me another game?"

"What other game?"

"I don't know. Is gin rummy any fun?"

"There are only three fun card games. Blackjack, Go Fish, and Uno." Aspen smirks a little. Shakes her head and sighs. Her eyes focus on the floor.

"What happened? What did the FBI ask you about?"

"They just wanted a recounting of what Healey did. Not that I think it's going to help."

"No?"

"No. Like…this man has money on top of money. Richer than God." She rubs her eyes. "I think even if they charged him, he'd find some way to weasel his way out of it. That's just kinda how things shake out for people like him. They absolve themselves of any kind of responsibility and run from one place to the next. It's what money buys you."

"But he killed people." I think of the scientists that were helplessly slaughtered. Karine's oozing face as she slowly died trying to protect us. Cole and Donnie, who were sent to search for any survivors, but ended up being torn apart. The fact that he—along with Aspen's father—is responsible for blowing up several facilities on the east coast, leading to the deaths of thousands. There's no way he could get away with something like that. The thought is simply too dark. But maybe I'm just stupid for having a little bit of hope.

Aspen seems far, far away. Like she has something to say, but she doesn't want to say it. I try to think of what it could be. And when I realize what it is, I reach across and squeeze her hand.

"You can't run away now."

"What?" For a moment she plays dumb, but from the way my voice shakes, it's like she knows she can't be that cruel. She turns her body to face me completely.

I look over my shoulder toward the hospital room door, which is still closed. I try to keep my voice low, but I can't help crying. We face each other completely. The cards fall off my lap and onto the floor, and the sound they make when they hit the cold tile feels amplified, like glass shattering. For several painstaking moments, we wait for the other to speak. And somehow, I feel closer to death at this moment than I did in my overturned car.

"I love you," she whispers quietly. "You know that, right? I know it's too soon. I know it's fast. But I *know* I love you. And that's why I can't…"

She trails off, and my sobs fill the spaces between her sentences. I have to take a minute to catch my breath before I speak.

"It's over. It's over for now."

"It's never going to be over, Ri. Healey's not the last of them, and with my dad possibly still out there, more people are going to crawl out from whatever slimy rock they've been hiding under. And I keep thinking about what Karine said, and…"

"No." I shake my head firmly. "No. Not now. Come back with me to Portland. I-if you hate it, then I promise you, you can leave."

"Your grandparents aren't going to be eager to take in another teenager they're not even related to. Especially not after the death of their daughter."

"I can't…I could convince them." I squeeze her hands. "It wouldn't take much. Besides, y-you'd love it there if you gave it a chance. And you could meet Caia and Khalil. And I could finally watch all those movies you said you wanted me to watch."

"Riley." She smiles softly, and I hate the way she can smile at me when she's so sad. The ginger way she tries to push her heartbreak underneath her skin and never let it show on her face. "Riley, babe. Don't do this to me. You know it can't happen. I'm not the type of person who gets a home."

"You could have one. You just don't want it, and you don't want me," I say, and it's an awful lie, the worst I've ever told, but everything she's saying is tearing me to shreds. How the hell can she break my heart and still hold my hand? Still look at me like that?

"No, Riley. They're going to chase me to the ends of the earth. And what good is that? A life on the run? Ruining your other friendships? Your relationships? You just lost your mother."

"You've lost everything!" I cry out. "When does the hurt stop for *you*, Aspen? When do *you* stop making sacrifices?"

She flinches, and I know I've struck a nerve. Finally, she can't hold her facade anymore. The tears bubble up in her eyes. She cups my face in her hands and shakes her head, then kisses my forehead.

"That's not fair. You know I can't let anything else happen to you. You deserve time to heal. That time has come for you." She wipes the tears dripping from my eyes, her voice as soft and crooning as the night we had our first dance. "But it hasn't come for me, babe. I still have a lot left to do. You remember what Fern said?"

I shake my head, sobbing; inconsolable. She can't leave me. She can't tell me she loves me and in the same breath leave me. I have to believe she and I deserve better. That girls like us deserve love and to be in love, and to live in happiness, and to not spend every waking minute of our lives running from ourselves or people trying to kill us. There has to be an end to the suffering. But even though it hurts, I know as well as she knows that it's not going to end here. Not right now. She's right—if there's a Healey, there's another one right behind him. Her father, potentially still alive and orchestrating all this from the shadows. I would so much rather Aspen be in control of her next steps than for me or anyone else to be in control of her. She's more than earned it at this point.

"Fern said that everyone's got a grief journey. And i-it's different for each of us, babe. I can't hold you back from that, I won't. I gotta protect you."

"But who's going to protect you?" I sob.

I bury my face against her chest. She wraps her arms tightly around me. This little woman; my beautiful monster, my whole heart and soul. I want to lay here forever in her too-strong embrace.

"You know I can protect myself." She says this with a little laugh. "I'm more than capable of it. And I gotta save everyone else. There're more out there like me. Maybe siblings? Or cousins? Clones? I don't know. But…if I don't get to them before the others do, they're going to end up dead. Or y'know, flattening entire towns."

"If you're going to do this, then don't expect me to be okay with it. That's all I'm gonna say." I pull away and wipe my face.

She smiles sadly. "That's okay."

"Okay." I nod slowly, look back toward the door. The nurses haven't come in yet. "What do you need me to do?"

"Nothing." She lowers her voice to a whisper. "Turns out security at this place is shittier than I thought it'd be." She stands up and pulls open the window a little bit, giving me a perplexed expression. "And I guess they missed the memo where I'm a monster and can scale walls and shit."

"You can scale walls?"

"Well. Not scale, per say. But I can jump from this height without breaking a leg." She shuts the window again. "So…it'll be easy."

"When?"

She takes a deep breath. "Tonight."

I nod. She takes a seat again and stares out the window. I climb into her lap and lock my arms around her neck, burying my face against the crook of her shoulder. If she's going to leave in a few hours, I'm going to take in everything. Every little part of her that was mine for the past two weeks. Smell her shampoo one more time and count the number of freckles on her cheeks and feel how her body radiates heat.

"Kind of a bummer that we didn't bone when we had the chance."

She sputters into laughter and slaps my arm playfully. And I see the tears in her eyes. I crack a smile and it's my turn to wipe them away.

"We still could. I mean, the nurses would just be listening."

"Hmm. I don't think having an audience is my thing."

"Nah," she laughs. "Not my thing either."

We sit like that, wrapped up in one another, until the lights go off in the room and the nurses tell us to go to bed. Neither one of us sleeps. We stare at each other from across the room. Around three in the morning, she slips out of her bed, and kisses the top of my head. I hear the window open, and I don't hear anything else.

Everything After

ALTHOUGH I'M CLEARED FOR release the morning after Aspen leaves, the FBI still has to have a word with me, of course. I tell them one truth and one lie—the lie being I didn't know she was planning on leaving, and the truth, that I don't have any idea where she's going. Part of me thinks it's gonna be wherever she last heard from her mother, which I think was Arizona, but I'm not quite sure. It's not like it's going to help them anyways, and honestly, now that I think about it, they don't need the help. Just look for the monster. *Duh.* Dad and I sign some forms, basically saying we won't publicly talk about what happened. There was a fire. I ran away. I got into a car accident in Illinois. No mentioning of Aspen. Or Karine. Or Healey. Or giant monsters.

The morning of my release, we get into Dad's rented SUV, and I reunite with Tigger, who cries because he's so happy to see me. Big, urgent yowls, and I know what he's saying. *How could you leave me?* I let him shower me with kisses and love and I feel slightly less sad.

But just for a minute.

We drive to Chicago, and board a flight to Portland. Unfortunately for Tigger, he has to ride in a kennel. Dad and I don't speak the entire time. I don't think it's just because of the obvious resentment we have toward one another. We're both exhausted. I still have bruised ribs, after all. That shit ain't going away for a few weeks…maybe months. I'm not looking forward to all the physical therapy visits they said I'll have to suffer through. Absolute pain in the ass.

Grandpa George, Grandma Lucy, and Aunt Cheryl find us at the luggage claim. My grandparents both seem so much smaller than when I last saw them. They still have outrageously tan skin from working in their garden for so long. Aunt Cheryl has dyed her hair blue again, but the brown roots are clearly showing through. Even though they smile when they see me, they're obviously tired. And the moment they hold me in their arms, the grief comes flooding back, and we all cry.

It's been a few days now since we arrived at my grandparents' house and began planning Mom's funeral, but most of my time has been spent holed up in the guest bedroom, cuddling with Tigger. I got a new phone since my other one was destroyed during the battle at Karine's. I've called Caia and Khalil to let them know I'm back in town, but also let them know I can't really do anything right now. It's not just that I have no energy to hang out, it's also about how everyone in my family is planning the funeral. Wait, is it a funeral, or is it a wake? Can you have a funeral when there's no body to bury?

Jesus. That's dark.

Last night, Dad came by my room, wanting to talk with me. He sat down on the edge of the bed and the two of us stared at each other for a few minutes. He kept opening and closing his mouth, almost like a fish in water.

"I don't know what to say," he said finally. "I know that you're dealing with a lot right now. A lot more than I can understand, but…I feel like if we don't talk, you and I aren't going to get through this. And we're going to need each other."

I crossed my arms and looked up at the ceiling. "I need space right now."

"I know you think that, Riley, but—"

"—I'm tired, and I need space. I don't want to have this conversation with you right now." My eyes burned. "You lost your ex-wife. I lost my mother. And to be completely honest, Dad, I keep thinking if you hadn't done what you did? We wouldn't have been in Little Brook."

Dad's eyes widened with shock. He was slack jawed. "You're not *honestly* saying I'm responsible for your mother's death, are you, Riley?" his voice grew harder, angrier. "That is such a sick and twisted thing to say. Who *are* you?" He shook his head as he slowly rose to his feet. "Not my daughter."

"What do you expect me to say, Dad? I'm so sorry I read her journal? I'm so sorry I learned the truth? If you and Mom hadn't lied to me about what was really going on, maybe I would've—"

"You would've been upset either way, Riley. Nothing would have changed, okay? Nothing about this situation would have changed."

"Nothing would have *changed?*" Anger burns in my throat. I'm not going to cry, but I'm trying not to scream. "I learned about what you did *days* after my mother died. I treated her like shit for months, because I thought she was ruining my life thanks to some random midlife crisis. Do you know what that's like? Do you have any idea how *guilty* I feel?"

"What about how *I* feel?"

"You're not the one who didn't text her back the day she died." I swallow. "So quite frankly, Dad? I don't want to hear about how bad it's been for you, when you don't even want to acknowledge how bad this has been for me."

Knock-knock. We're snapped out of our tension. I look to see Aunt Cheryl hovering in the doorway, anxiously looking back and forth between me and Dad. She looks at him.

"Hey, Ivan? I think it's best to let her rest." She smiles, tight-lipped. Like there's more she wants to say but knows not to say it in front of me. I wonder how much she knows.

Dad doesn't say anything. His mouth sets in a firm line, the way he does when he really wants to yell but thinks you're too stupid to understand what he's angry about. He brushes past Aunt Cheryl and heads down the hall. She wraps her little fish-patterned robe tighter around her body and sits down on the bed. Reaches out and gently places her hand on my knee.

"Be gentle with yourself," she says quietly. "I don't know what happened, and I don't need to know. But you're right; you deserve space."

I nod. She leans over and kisses my forehead; cups my face in her hands. It's hard to look her in the eyes when she looks so much like Mom. And I think she knows that.

"Night, honey." she leaves the room, but not before shutting the door.

Around five the next day, they call me down for dinner. And I know that even though they don't say it, they're gearing up for a big family discussion. Dad and Grandpa set the table while Grandma finishes preparing the food. Looks like take-and-bake mostaccioli from Dino's—not my favorite, but definitely not the worst. Grandma knows to add extra cheese to it, too, so there's that. We sit down at the table, and Grandma and Grandpa say grace while Dad and I just stare at our water glasses. Aunt Cheryl helps herself to what I think might be her third glass of wine that evening.

Grandpa takes a sip of water and stares straight ahead, not bothering to make eye contact with anyone. "Lorraine's wake will be held this Saturday."

"Cool." I push around the food on my plate. Suddenly the noodles don't look remotely scrumptious. And the cheese looks like glue between the twines of my fork. Gross. "I'll think of what I want to say."

"Do you want to help me pick out pictures of you and your mom, Riley?" Aunt Cheryl asks gently. She takes a sip from her wine glass and offers me a sad little smile. "I was going to put together the slideshow, and if you're up for it, you can help."

I shrug my shoulders. It's weird, but I don't know if I can stand to look at pictures of before. The first few days after my mother's passing, I wanted nothing more than to be close to her; to take every remaining thing about her and hold it as close as possible. To read her diary even though it might kill me. But now, something about picking out pictures for the slideshow holds a sense of permanence—and that's too uncomfortable for me to even think about.

Aunt Cheryl's smile doesn't fade. "That's okay."

Not for Grandma. A troubled expression crosses her face, as her wary eyes roll from Aunt Cheryl over to me. She clears her throat and dabs at her mouth with a napkin although no food is there. She tends to do that when she's nervous or frustrated about something— find something to do with her hands just to have that distraction. We're kind of alike in that way.

"Riley, this is your mother's funeral," Grandma says quietly as she sets down her napkin. "You need to help plan. At least a little bit."

"And I will. I'll have something to say at the funeral. I just don't know if I want to look at pictures of my dead mother right now, Grandma."

I try to take another bite of pasta but almost immediately have to spit it out into my napkin. My stomach gurgles in protest, and a wave of nausea hits my body. Oh God. Don't tell me I'm so anxious I'm going to throw up right here in front of all my relatives. Don't I deserve a little bit of dignity, universe?

Grandma makes a big, dismissive sigh and Aunt Cheryl shakes her head. "Mom. Come on. Let it go."

Grandma doesn't say anything, but I can tell from the look in her eyes that she's not about to let it go. She's opting to harbor resentment instead, which as I've now realized, is something we do a lot of in this family. No one talks. We all keep secrets.

"We also have to talk about what happens after." Grandpa says quietly.

"Dad," Aunt Cheryl says. "We don't need to do this right now."

"We should."

Dad looks up from his plate of pasta, which is already halfway gone. He wipes at his face with a napkin and doesn't bother to look at me. "Riley's coming with me to Seattle."

"What? No!" I cry out, pushing back from the table. Some of my silverware falls onto the floor. "I'm not going back with Dad!"

My grandparents take a deep breath, and the aura seems heavier than ever. My dad, wounded, stares directly at me. He sets his fork down on his plate and folds his hands together, calmly surveying me. But Aunt Cheryl looks incredibly confused; almost disturbed by what's happening. Her eyes keep darting around the table, like she's looking for answers, but no one is giving them to her.

And then I realize what they're all trying to say: Grandma and Grandpa don't want me.

They don't *want* me?

"I don't want to go with Dad to Seattle. Not after what he's done."

Grandpa sighs. "Riley, I know that you're angry, but—"

"—Angry doesn't even *begin* to cover what I'm feeling right now, Grandpa." I swallow back a lump of tears in my throat. "I want to stay in Portland. I-I want to go back to school and be closer with my friends; I need them right now. Why can't I stay with you and Grandma?"

"Riley," Grandma says gently, and I resent the pity in her eyes. "You know that Grandpa and I were planning on selling this house this fall. I-it's just not practical for us to keep this place when we can barely make it up the stairs anymore. And I love your sweet little dog, but honey, my allergies have been bad since he's gotten here."

I feel like I have tunnel vision. Like suddenly everyone sitting here is a stranger. Wow. Holy shit. Aspen was right. There wasn't going to be a happy ending for us. We would've been separated regardless. Not that that makes me feel any better, or less angry at this moment.

"So, you would let me go live with *him*?" I ask, pointing at Dad directly. "Knowing what he did to my mother? Knowing that it might be unsafe for me?"

Grandpa's brow furrows in frustration, a look he usually reserves for the evening news. "Riley, you need to calm down."

"Easy," Dad warns, grinding his jaw. It's obvious from his body language that he wants them to back off, but knowing him, he's still trying to be polite.

But even with my dad defending me, I can't sit there any longer. All I see are angry faces. Anger, anger, anger. I have so much of it that I can't stew in it. Holding back tears, I push back from the table and head for the door, Tigger trailing nervously after me. I grab his leash and clip it onto his collar, then we're gone. At first, I walk briskly, but then I break into a sprint, the streetlights illuminating our path through the misty evening fog, once so familiar, now suffocating. The raindrops from above mix with the tears now freely coursing down my face. Every breath I take feels like a punch to the chest, but it feels like a punch I deserve.

"Riley!"

I turn, and through teary eyes, look over my shoulder. My father, holding onto his knees, trying desperately to catch his breath. Equally breathless is my Aunt Cheryl behind him. Dad winces as he tries to stand again, placing one firm hand on his hip. Tigger whines urgently, pulling at the leash.

"You're right," he says so softly I can barely hear him above the pattering of the rain against the sidewalk. He approaches slowly. "*I'm* the reason everything fell apart. *I'm* what drove your mother away. And now, I'm driving you away, too. So, you know what? No more. I hurt Lorraine enough. I'm not going to do the same to my daughter."

My shoulders tremble. There's a fluttering at the back of my throat, another scalding lump of tears that threatens to break me completely. His eyes are equally wet as mine, his expression so earnest and kind. This is the father I remember. The father I thought I had.

Maybe I still have him.

"I know that I can't ask you to come with me to Seattle," he says. "So I won't."

"What do you mean?"

Aunt Cheryl bites her lip. "The other night, your father and I talked, and… well, we both know how important it is for you to be in Portland. To be with your friends and be close to family, and hopefully have some stability. So, for a little while, the two of you can stay with me, until you find a new place to live."

"W-What?" I stammer, completely blindsided by this. "But— Dad, what about your job?"

He ever so slightly grins. "Perks of software development, kiddo. I get to be anywhere. And now I have a reason to be here again. You." His smile falters. "So, Ri? What do you say? Can we give this one more shot?"

He holds his arms open. And I step into them. Let him hold me and we cry together for everything that we lost.

And everything that we're about to gain.

MOM'S WAKE COMES AND goes in a blur. Dad held my hand in the pews the entire time. In the end, I never worked up the courage to say anything, but I did pick out the photo of her that I loved the most: a shot of her standing at the edge of the ocean in Seaside, a pleasant smile on her face, her eyes closed as she felt the warmth of the sun against her skin. The photo itself is a memento from one of the family vacations we had when I was little. Mom was at her happiest when life was at its simplest; when she was surrounded by nature and the people she loved.

That's how I want to remember her.

After the funeral, Dad and I flew to Seattle to move his things back to Portland. Boxing up item after item, we slowly reconnected. Each night we spent there, we made bougie grilled cheese sandwiches, and watched horrible monster movies, and talked about Mom. When we got back to Portland, Aunt Cheryl welcomed us with open arms. While I'm surprised that she chose to give up some of her wild child lifestyle, I was immediately grateful for her company. Dad's back in my life on a regular basis now, but his job still keeps him busy—and aside from grilled cheese sandwiches, he's not that great of a cook. But Aunt Cheryl is a hardcore foodie, so she'll make things like paellas or try (and fail miserably) at making homemade sushi and sashimi. And I got to reconnect with Caia and Khalil, who were all too thrilled to catch me up on the gossip at school—and hold me whenever I felt like I was going to fall apart. Which at first, was often. But now less so.

Three months later, and I've eased into my new normal: school, then therapy downtown, and back home to see what new concoction Aunt Cheryl is whipping up in the kitchen. Little by little, things are getting better, but I'm not without my scars. Dad's debts float at the back of my mind, a little reminder of more trouble to come. At night I'm welcomed by various nightmares, each as vivid as the last. And in every spare moment, my thoughts are filled with Aspen.

Aspen, Aspen, Aspen. I wished I knew where she was. Wished there was some sign she was okay. Oddly enough, there's been absolutely no news coverage. You would think a giant monster would be difficult to hide, but I guess Aspen's been good about laying low.

Or something really bad happened to her, and I just don't know about it. But I try my best not to think about that. Whenever those negative thoughts float into my mind, I remember the best of her. The way that the wind ripped through her hair as we drove down the road, her voice raucous and proud as she sung her favorite songs.

The soft, smug little smirk on her face after she kissed me for the first time and left me absolutely breathless. The protective squeeze of her hand as we faced the onslaught of obstacles before us.

God, how I miss her. And some days that longing hits harder. Like today, when I went to this indie bookstore to pick up a book for class, and I saw a Johnny Cash vinyl, placed at the front of a display. Sure enough, it was one that had Walk the Line on it. It felt a little bizarre, almost serendipitous, that on a day I'm thinking more about her than others that I'd see this. But that sounds crazy, right? I feel tempted to pick it up, but I don't have a record player at home, so instead, I leave it. After browsing the towering bookshelves, I locate a copy of *A Separate Peace* and make my way to the checkout.

The girl at the counter looks me up and down curiously. Rude. I know I'm wearing my most slovenly pair of sweatpants today, but you don't have to call attention to it.

"Is there a problem?"

She squints at a crinkled pink post-it note on the counter. There's a message scrawled on it that I can't decipher.

After a moment, she looks back at me. "Are you...Riley, by chance?"

"Uh...yeah?" Who is she, someone from school?

"Oh, cool." Her face brightens, and she turns to grab something off the counter behind her. "Your girlfriend came by a little while ago. Asked me to give it to you once you got to the checkout counter."

"Uh. That wouldn't be me," I stammer, perplexed. "I don't...have a girlfriend."

She turns back to me with a confused expression, holding a crisp white paper bag. "Really? Weird. You're wearing exactly what she said you'd be wearing." A teasing smile crosses her glossy pink lips. "If you had a fight with her, I really hope that this cheers you up. She was really excited about it. It's already paid for and everything."

"Uh..."

My heart throbs in my chest, and with shaking hands, I place the money that I owe for the book on the counter, then take the bag from her. It's heavy, and a few tufts of tissue paper stick out the top; the efforts of a haphazard, hasty wrapping job. My head swivels every which way, trying to see if there's someone watching me. But no. Everyone is acting normal, going about their business. With reddened cheeks, I mumble a hasty thank you to the cashier and exit.

Out in the open, I take a deep breath. Then another. My body trembles, but whether it's from fear or excitement, I'm not entirely sure. It's far too crowded on the city sidewalk to look inside the bag, so I make my way to the nearest MAX light rail station and hop aboard a car just before it departs. It's one of those rare afternoons where hardly any people are aboard the train. An elderly man snores softly in the back, and a couple of girls dressed in Catholic school uniforms giggle at some gossipy text messages on their phones. I creep to an open seat by the window and watch the city breeze by me in a kaleidoscope of colors. Take a few more breaths. Then finally, I open the bag and remove the mass of tissue paper.

Wait a minute, there's something *on* the tissue paper. Writing? It's… it's handwriting. Familiar loops and curls and carefully crossed *t*s. *"REQUIRED VIEWING FOR THE NEXT TIME WE MEET."* Below, a list of films, starting with *But I'm A Cheerleader*, moving to *The Half of It, The Handmaiden,* continuing down to the edge of the sheet.

Wrapped inside the paper are a few things: a Sony Walkman portable disc player, a janky pair of earbuds, and a copy of Hootie & the Blowfish's Cracked Rear View. A wave of emotions flood my body as images flash through my mind. Her fingers intertwining with mine across the center console. Her head thrown back, laughing as she sings. Those green, green eyes, effervescent and full of hope; the ones I fell so recklessly in love with. The ones I still love even now. All these memories, suddenly sitting with me in the palm of my hands. Tears flood my eyes, and I choke back a sob. I don't know when she was at the store that day. But she *was* there. She was there, she's alive, and she wanted me to know that she was okay.

I crack open the case, put the disc in the Walkman, and press play.

ACKNOWLEDGEMENTS

MONSTERSONA STARTED AS A novel that allowed me to explore grief, trauma, love, and the messy ways that all of those things intertwined. It's been an arduous two years, starting in October of 2020 before finishing the first draft in June of 2021, and then querying tirelessly for a year afterward. It took a long time to cross this finish line, and I have so many people to thank for that.

First off, I want to give a very sincere thank you to Josh and the staff and other authors of Tiny Ghost Press who have been so supportive and kind throughout this entire process. I am so unbelievably proud to be a Tiny Ghost Press author. Thank you for believing in me, and for believing that this story needed to be told. Also, an extra big thank you to Alex Moore, who made the cover for this book better than I could've ever imagined; you are so ridiculously talented.

My friends Cody, Aurora, and Rachel have supported and cheered me on for every single creative project I've ever done, and *Monstersona* is no exception to this. Thank you all for being there for me through everything, every day, even though we're separated by hundreds of thousands of miles.

I would also like to thank J. Scott Coatsworth and others within the Queer Sci-Fi Community for lending me your expertise and helping me with the querying process. Scott, you have always been so kind and supportive to me since the earliest stages of my writing career. Words cannot express how much I appreciate that.

My writing skill would not be where it is today without the tireless help I've received from countless teachers at Woodbury High School, the University of Oregon, and the Savannah College of Art and Design Atlanta. Your wisdom, support, and valuable life lessons carry with me each day. I am so lucky to have had all of you.

And finally, thank you to Mom, Dad, Mike and Joe, for all your love and support.

ABOUT THE AUTHOR

Minnesota native Chloe Spencer is an award-winning writer,
indie game developer, and filmmaker. She enjoys writing sci-
fi/fantasy, horror, and romance. In her spare time, she enjoys
playing video games, trying her best at Pilates, and cuddling
with her cats. She holds a BA in Journalism from the University
of Oregon and an MFA in Film and Television from SCAD
Atlanta.

CPSIA information can be obtained
at www.ICGtesting.com
Printed in the USA
JSHW082141081222
34565JS00010B/530